"TERRIFYINGLY FUN! Max Brallier's *The Last Kids on Earth* delivers big thrills and even bigger laughs." —JEFF KINNEY, author of the #1 *New York Times* bestseller *Diary of a Wimpy Kid*

★ "A GROSS-OUT GOOD TIME with surprisingly nuanced character development."
—*School Library Journal*, starred review

★ "Classic ACTION-PACKED, monster-fighting fun." —*Kirkus Reviews*, starred review

★ "SNARKY END-OF-THE-WORLD FUN."
—*Publishers Weekly*, starred review

"The likable cast, lots of adventure, and GOOFY, OOZY MONSTER SLIME GALORE keep the pages turning." —*Booklist*

"HILARIOUS and FULL OF HEART." —*Boys' Life*

"This clever mix of black-and-white drawings and vivid prose brings NEW LIFE TO THE LIVING DEAD." —Common Sense Media

Winner of the Texas Bluebonnet Award

THE MONSTER-BATTLING FUN DOESN'T STOP HERE!

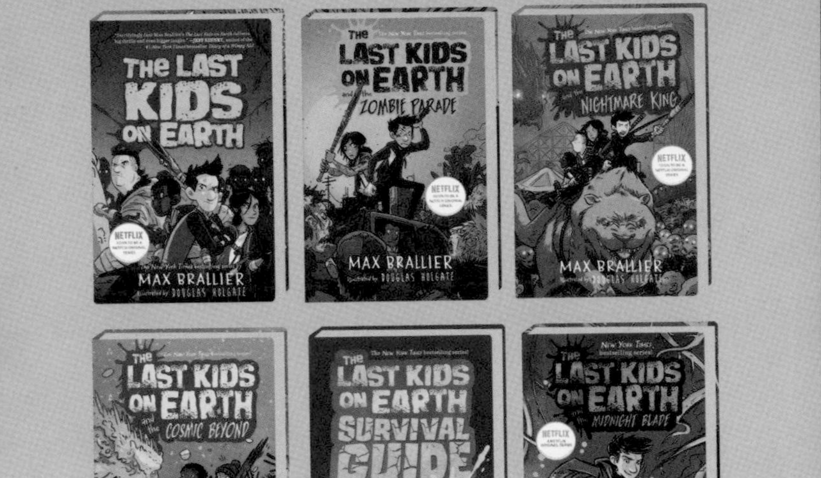
THE LAST KIDS ON EARTH
MAX BRALLIER
THE LAST KIDS ON EARTH and the ZOMBIE PARADE
MAX BRALLIER
THE LAST KIDS ON EARTH and the NIGHTMARE KING
MAX BRALLIER
THE LAST KIDS ON EARTH and the COSMIC BEYOND
MAX BRALLIER
THE LAST KIDS ON EARTH SURVIVAL GUIDE
MAX BRALLIER
THE LAST KIDS ON EARTH and the MIDNIGHT BLADE
MAX BRALLIER
THE LAST KIDS ON EARTH JUNE'S WILD FLIGHT
MAX BRALLIER
THE LAST KIDS ON EARTH and the SKELETON ROAD
MAX BRALLIER
THE LAST KIDS ON EARTH THRILLING TALES FROM THE TREE HOUSE
MAX BRALLIER
THE LAST KIDS ON EARTH and the DOOMSDAY RACE
MAX BRALLIER

TheLastKidsOnEarth.com

Check out more books in the bestselling

THE LAST KIDS ON EARTH SERIES

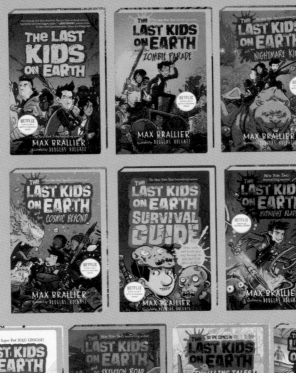

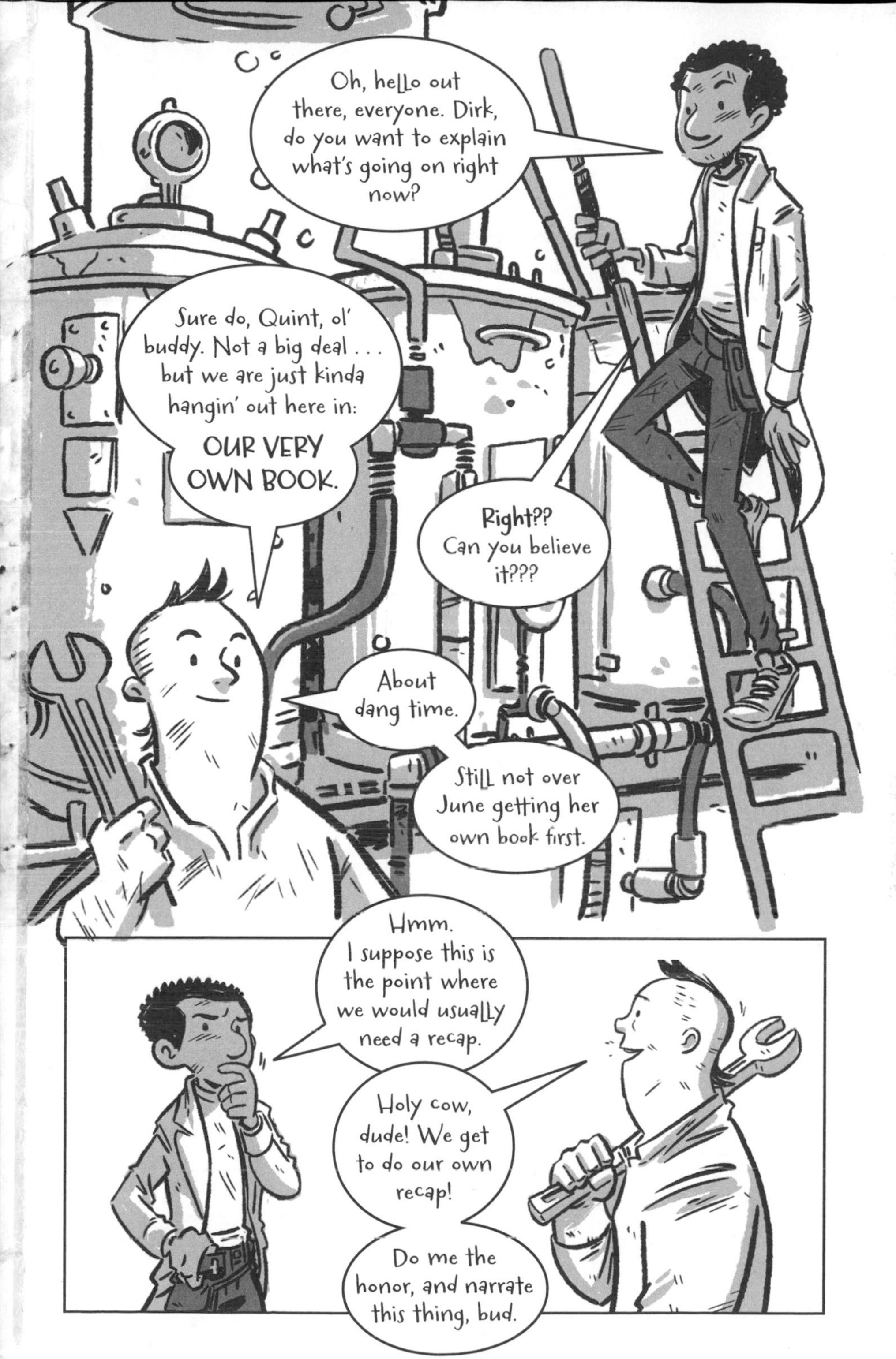
Oh, hello out there, everyone. Dirk, do you want to explain what's going on right now?
Sure do, Quint, ol' buddy. Not a big deal . . . but we are just kinda hangin' out here in:
OUR VERY OWN BOOK.
Right?? Can you believe it???
About dang time.
Still not over June getting her own book first.
Hmm. I suppose this is the point where we would usually need a recap.
Holy cow, dude! We get to do our own recap!
Do me the honor, and narrate this thing, bud.

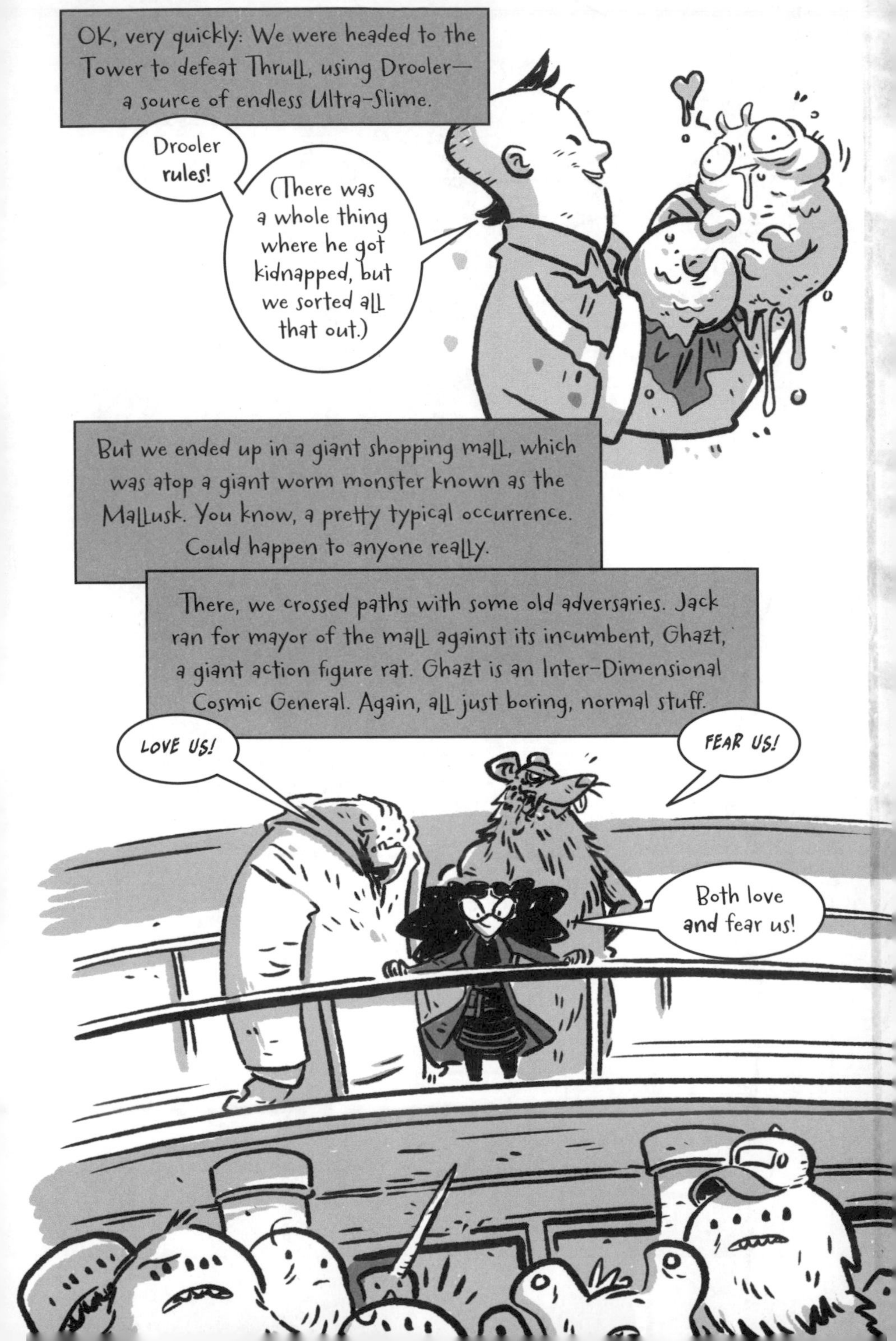
OK, very quickly: We were headed to the Tower to defeat Thrull, using Drooler—a source of endless Ultra-Slime.
Drooler rules!
(There was a whole thing where he got kidnapped, but we sorted all that out.)
But we ended up in a giant shopping mall, which was atop a giant worm monster known as the Mallusk. You know, a pretty typical occurrence. Could happen to anyone really.
There, we crossed paths with some old adversaries. Jack ran for mayor of the mall against its incumbent, Ghazt, a giant action figure rat. Ghazt is an Inter-Dimensional Cosmic General. Again, all just boring, normal stuff.
LOVE US!
FEAR US!
Both love and fear us!

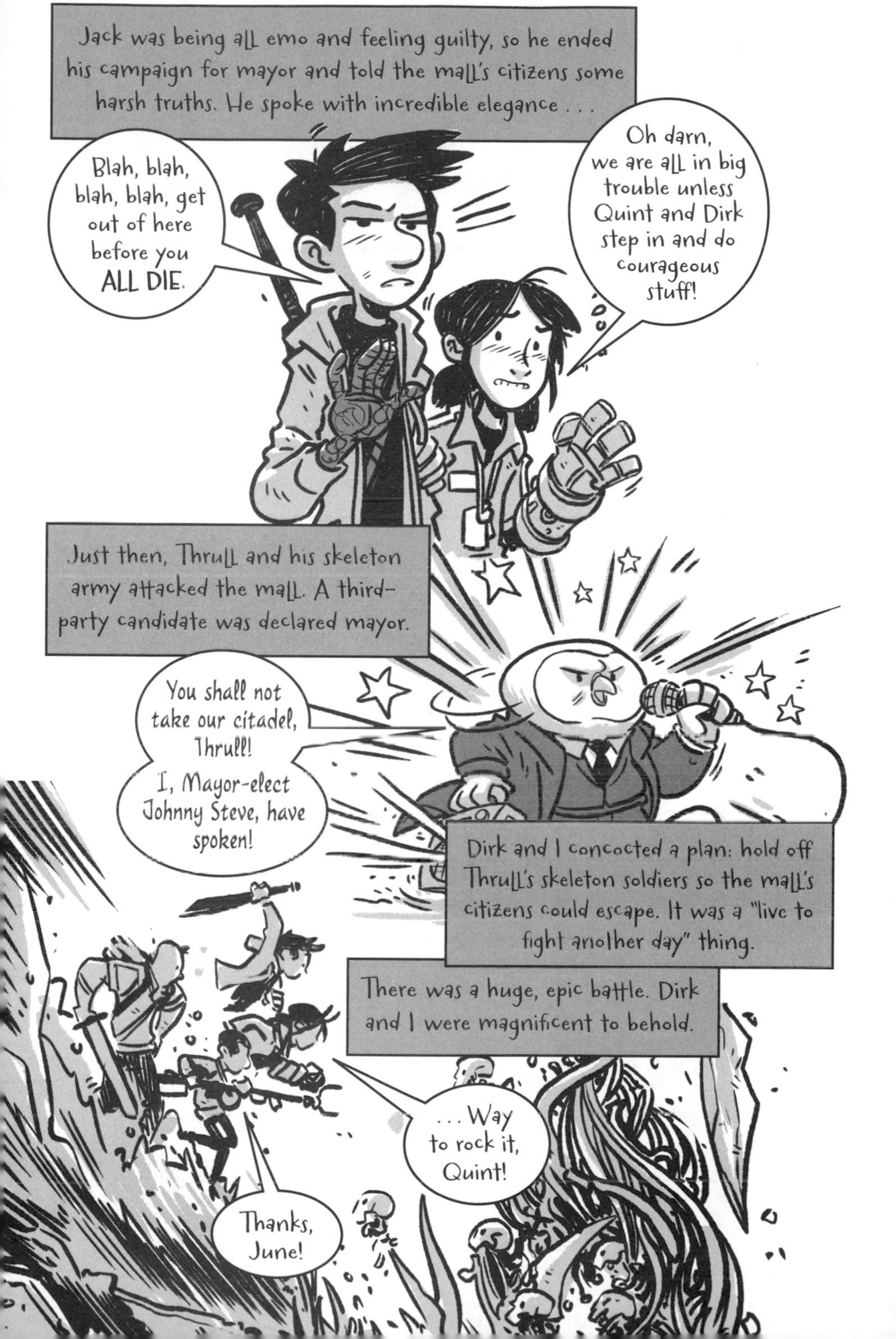
Jack was being all emo and feeling guilty, so he ended his campaign for mayor and told the mall's citizens some harsh truths. He spoke with incredible elegance . . .
Blah, blah, blah, blah, get out of here before you ALL DIE.
Oh darn, we are all in big trouble unless Quint and Dirk step in and do courageous stuff!
Just then, Thrull and his skeleton army attacked the mall. A third-party candidate was declared mayor.
You shall not take our citadel, Thrull!
I, Mayor-elect Johnny Steve, have spoken!
Dirk and I concocted a plan: hold off Thrull's skeleton soldiers so the mall's citizens could escape. It was a "live to fight another day" thing.
There was a huge, epic battle. Dirk and I were magnificent to behold.
. . . Way to rock it, Quint!
Thanks, June!

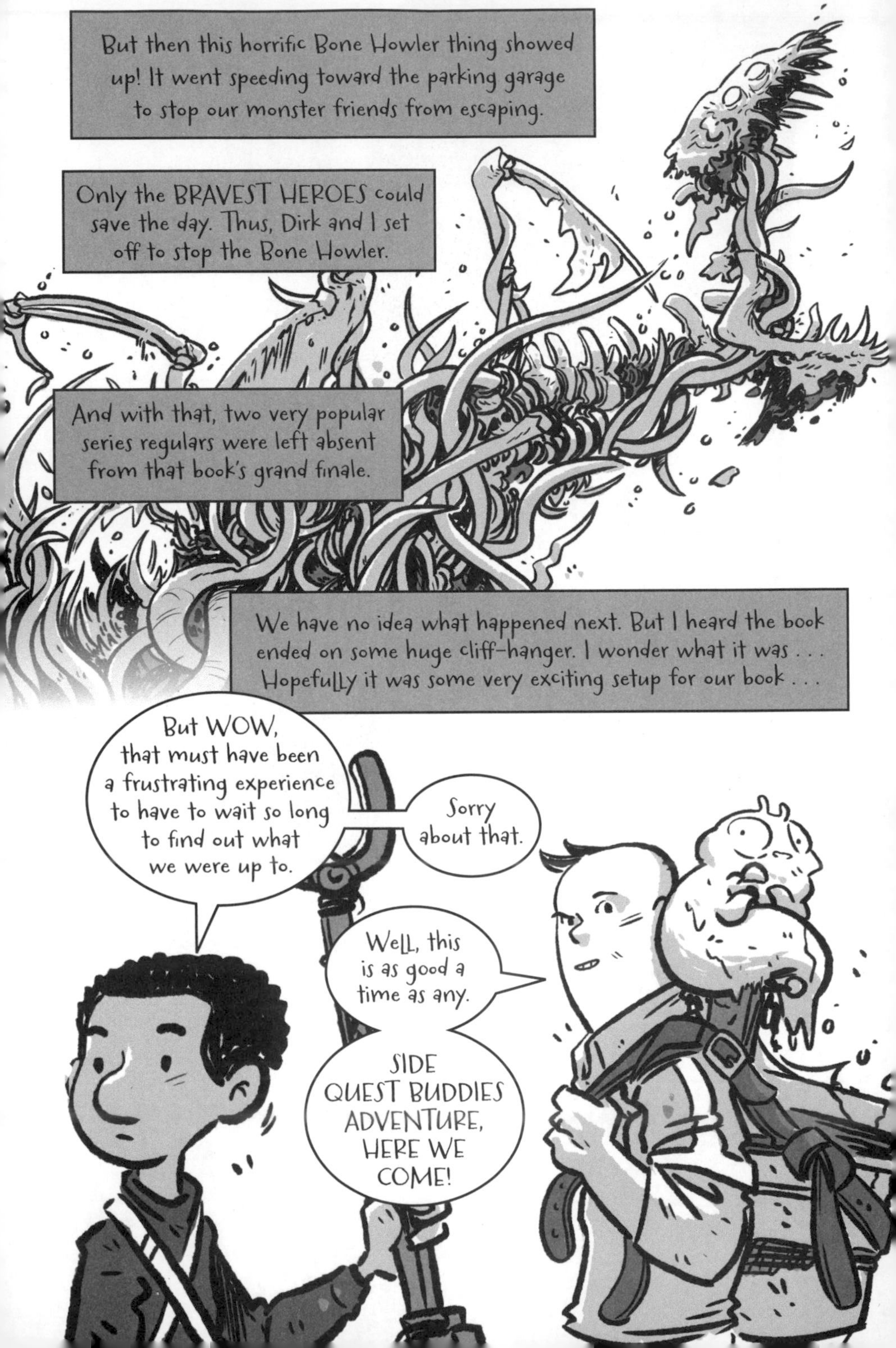
But then this horrific Bone Howler thing showed up! It went speeding toward the parking garage to stop our monster friends from escaping.
Only the BRAVEST HEROES could save the day. Thus, Dirk and I set off to stop the Bone Howler.
And with that, two very popular series regulars were left absent from that book's grand finale.
We have no idea what happened next. But I heard the book ended on some huge cliff-hanger. I wonder what it was . . . Hopefully it was some very exciting setup for our book . . .
But WOW, that must have been a frustrating experience to have to wait so long to find out what we were up to.
Sorry about that.
Well, this is as good a time as any.
SIDE QUEST BUDDIES ADVENTURE, HERE WE COME!

THE LAST KIDS ON EARTH

QUINT AND DIRK'S HERO QUEST

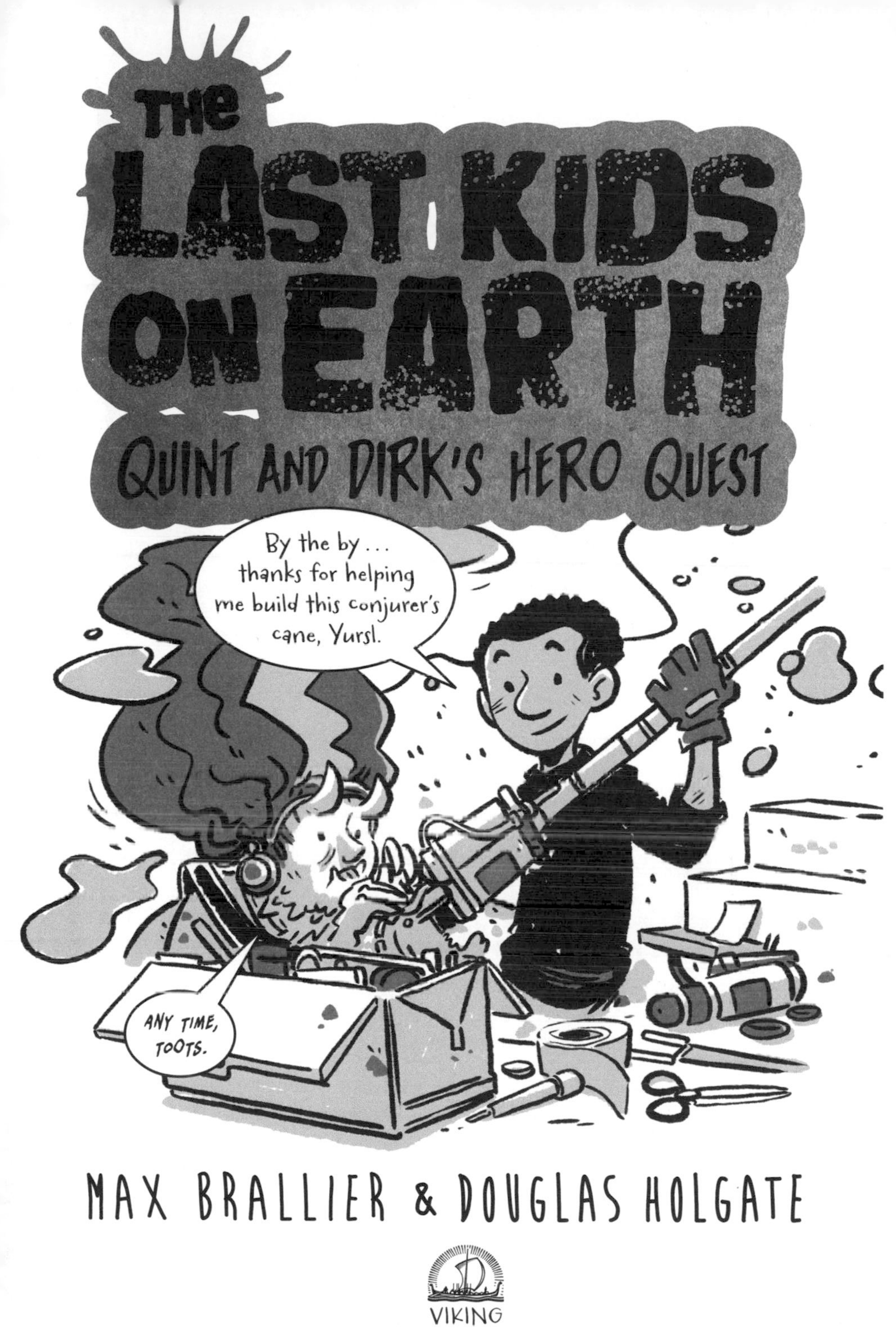
By the by . . . thanks for helping me build this conjurer's cane, Yursl.
ANY TIME, TOOTS.

MAX BRALLIER & DOUGLAS HOLGATE

VIKING

VIKING
An imprint of Penguin Random House LLC, New York

First published in the United States of America by Viking,
an imprint of Penguin Random House LLC, 2022

Visit us online at penguinrandomhouse.com.

Library of Congress Cataloging-in-Publication Data is available.

Printed in the United States of America

ISBN 9780593405352 (Hardcover)

10   9   8   7   6   5   4   3   2   1

ISBN 9780593527238 (International Edition)

10   9   8   7   6   5   4   3   2   1

CJKB

Book design by Jim Hoover
Set in Cosmiqua Com and Carrotflower

For buddies everywhere.

—M. B.

For Michael
(a pretty good brother . . .),
Danni, Maggie, and Tartan.

—D. H.

chapter one

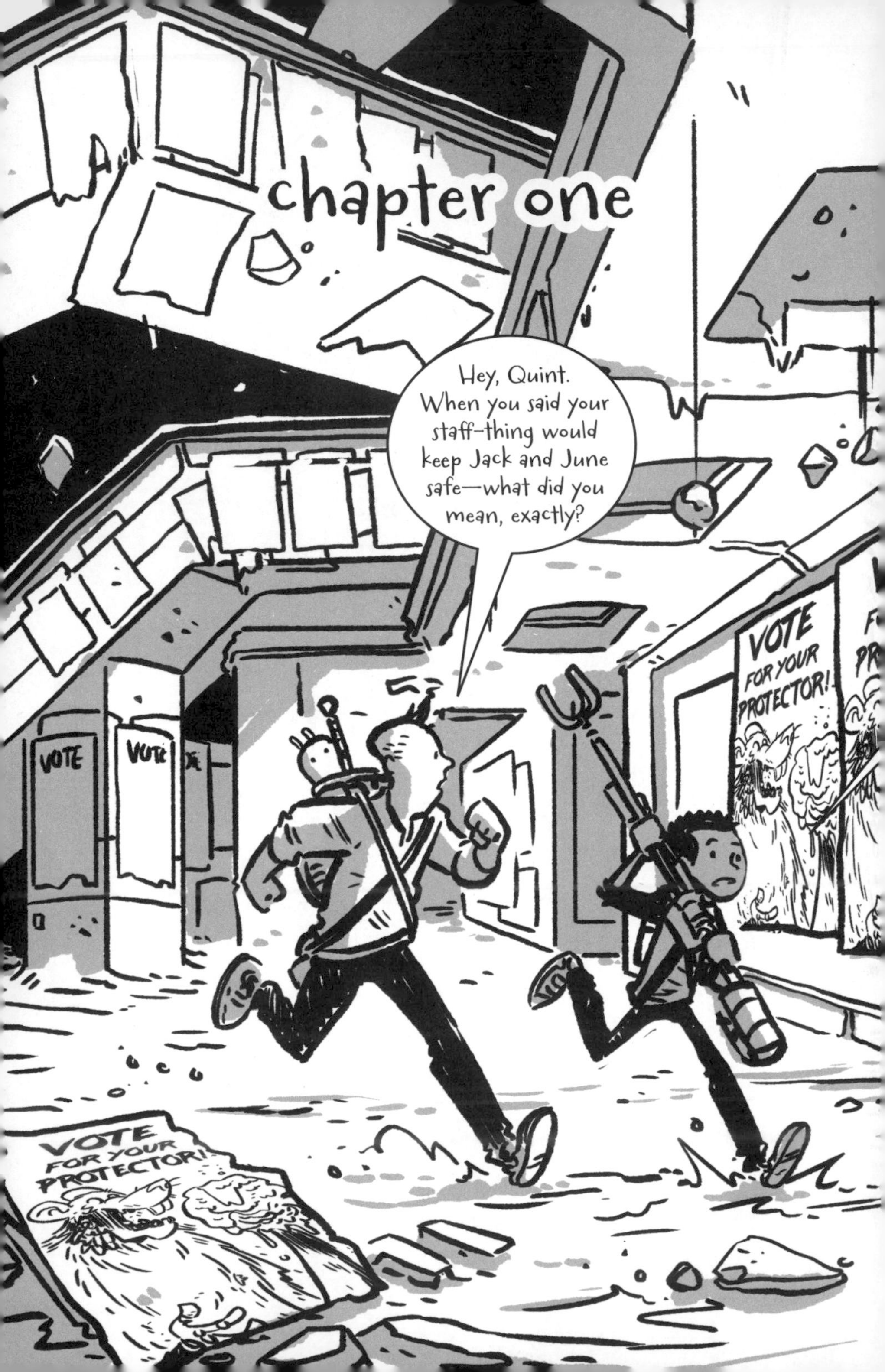
Hey, Quint. When you said your staff-thing would keep Jack and June safe—what did you mean, exactly?
VOTE
VOTE
VOTE FOR YOUR PROTECTOR!
VOTE FOR YOUR PROTECTOR!

"But what did you actually *learn* from Yursl?" Dirk asks as he vaults over a crushed sunglasses kiosk and dodges a fallen VOTE FOR GHAZT banner.

"It was mostly . . . conceptual," Quint says. "The big ideas. You see, the conjuring done by those from the monster dimension is not all that different from science in our dimension."

"That conceptual junk better be good for fighting, 'cause fighting is about to happen . . ." Dirk says. Then he shuts up so he can just *run*.

At this moment, Quint and Dirk are speeding through the Millennium Super Mall. Their destination? The parking garage. Why? Because that's where the Bone Howler, loyal servant of the villainous Thrull, is headed.

A battle awaits.

And it's crucial the battle goes well, because the Bone Howler's goal is a vile one: stop the mall's monster residents from escaping—by any means necessary.

Yup. The Bone Howler is bad news . . .

SKREE!

Bone Howler being bad news

"We gotta hurry!" Dirk barks as he catches a flash of movement outside. Through a gash torn in the mall's side, he spots the charging Bone Howler. "It's gonna be at the parking garage soon! Quint, please tell me Yursl gave you, like, a tutorial for how to beat this dude?"

"Maybe . . ." Quint says nervously. "Possibly."

Reader, she did not.

Dirk races up a broken escalator, taking the steps three at a time, and Quint follows. Their sneakers squeak and squeal as they speed inside a Lids store. There, a broken window gives them a view of the parking garage and the fractured pavement and train track graveyard beyond.

"Carapaces!" Quint cheers, pointing to the garage. "The evacuation is underway."

Sure enough, three of the crab-like creatures scurry out of the garage's exit tunnel. Atop each carapace is a car or truck—the carapace's shell—and inside each shell-vehicle are monsters: the residents of Mallusk City.

Soon, another carapace scuttles out of the tunnel. Then another, and another, until dozens are marching out of the garage, out onto a hunk of uprooted parking lot concrete. It looks like the world's most bizarre homecoming parade.

"And look who's leading the getaway . . ."
Dirk says, grinning.

Johnny Steve, the newly elected mayor of
Mallusk City, hurries alongside the carapace
caravan, directing the escape. Or . . . attemping
to . . .

Right now, Quint and Dirk are clueless to the state of the battle raging inside the mall. They only know their best friends, Jack and June, are locked in a desperate battle with Thrull. But here, at least, everything is going according to plan. Until—

PSHOOM! PSHOOM!

The sound of bone crashing against concrete—pounding hooves.

"Here it comes . . ." Quint says, and then—

The Bone Howler explodes into view! The evil beast is a nightmare of vine and skeleton.

"All right then," Dirk says, drawing his sword. "No matter what, we don't let that thing reach the carapaces. We're too close to victory."

Quint replies, "I'm not certain that fleeing in fear counts as victory."

"We're fighting an other-dimensional skeleton army," Dirk says. "I count another ten seconds of breathing as a win."

"Let's aim for fifteen," Quint says.

And with that, Dirk cries, "HANG ON, DROOLER!" and *jumps*. He hits the ground hard, landing squarely in the path of the charging Bone Howler. Dirk's hand flashes, and his sword, dripping with Ultra-Slime, slashes upward.

The wet blade slices through the Bone Howler's snout, shearing off a hunk of bone and vine. The skeletal beast recoils, then draws back a talon in a furious rage.

"Dirk, watch out!" Quint shouts, rushing into the fray. But the warning comes too late . . .

The Bone Howler's claws lash out, snapping forward, and—

CLANG!

Dirk's sword is smacked from his hand! The blade sails, end over end, before plunging into the ground, tip first, like a deadly exclamation point.

Quint glances back at the garage and the parade of escaping monsters, then swallows. "Dirk," he says softly. "Right now, you and I are the only thing preventing the Bone Howler from tearing apart every last citizen of Mallusk City."

"Hey, don't forget Drooler," Dirk says. "It's his Ultra-Slime that can actually *hurt* this thing."

The Bone Howler's midnight eyes flash. A whistling snarl escapes its half-severed snout as it takes a heavy step forward. But suddenly—

SCREEECH!

The spine-scraping squeal of speaker feedback blasts through the air. The Bone Howler jerks. Quint winces. Dirk cups his hands tight over Drooler's earholes.

"Hey, citizens of Mallusk City . . . It's Jack."

Huh? Quint thinks, looking up at the intercom speaker, listening to Jack's voice from inside the mall . . .

Earlier, I said a real leader won't lie to you. So here's the truth: today has not been the best. Don't know if I'll be seeing you again.

If I don't, please remember . . . This fight . . . If you work together, you can fight back, and you **can** win. That's the truth, too.

And then the speaker goes quiet. The monsters sit atop their carapaces, frozen.

Just minutes earlier, inside the mall, Jack had convinced the monsters to abandon their home and flee—so they might live to fight another day. So that maybe—*someday*—they might triumph.

But—without a single word being spoken— the monsters seem to be deciding that *someday* is actually *this day.*

From across the parking lot, Quint locks eyes with Johnny Steve. They share a knowing glance, then Johnny Steve turns. He bravely walks back into the garage—into the mall, to the battleground where Jack and June are doing their best to hold off Thrull.

One carapace turns to follow Johnny Steve. Then another. Soon, the entire fleet is making its way back inside. They're heeding Jack's call—just not in the way Jack intended.

But the Bone Howler won't simply *allow* the Mallusk City monsters to reenter the fight. The monster's eyes find Dirk's sword, jutting out of the pavement—and the beast knows that the two humans are unarmed . . .

Quint's hands tremble. Sure, he's studied with
a real conjurer, but Yursl only taught him one
incantation: Kinetic Crescendo. And it's not like
he ever actually *performed* it.

But moments before the Battle of the Mallusk
began, Yursl *did* say to him: "You now have all
you need to do what must be done."

Yursl's words were unnecessarily cryptic, and Quint doesn't know what she meant, exactly. But she does give off a sorta all-knowing vibe, so if she said he has what he needs, then he must have what he needs. *Maybe,* Quint thinks, *all that's left is the courage and confidence to **do it**.*

The Bone Howler stomps forward, snorting and snarling, like a boxer approaching the center of the ring . . .

"Dirk, you might want to step back," Quint says, as he levels the conjurer's cane at the monster. He flicks a toggle, and the cane hums.

This is it, Quint thinks. *Our one and only shot to defeat the Bone Howler and save the mall's citizens.*

He eyes Yursl's foam Nerf mini-basketball, hanging in its net. The basketball is the other-dimensional object that provides the energy needed to perform conjurations.

Before Quint can hesitate another nanosecond, the Bone Howler explodes forward!

Dirk pulls Drooler close and cries, "Do it!"

And Quint does. He squeezes the cane's trigger switch, and—

Many things happen at once.

A swirling, purple burst of energy envelops Quint, Dirk, Drooler, and the Bone Howler. Everything goes pin-drop silent, like someone pressed mute on the world.

Quint winces. He feels like his body is being

flattened. It reminds him of the summer he went to space camp and rode the anti-gravity chair, pulling 9 Gs. He didn't enjoy that experience one bit. He enjoys this one even less . . .

Dirk feels the ground beneath his feet seem to drop away. Like that moment on the Pirate Ship ride at Fun Land, when the ship has swung all the way back and just hangs there for an excruciatingly long moment, before it crashes forward, catapulting your stomach into your throat.

The silence ends—replaced by the sounds of ripping and shredding and a primal, agonized scream.

And then the smoke clears.

Where Quint and Dirk were standing, there is now only a smoldering crater, and one-half of the Bone Howler . . .

chapter two

"Oooh . . ." Quint groans. His head is buzzing, like a bunch of hornets are throwing a party inside his skull.

Dirk wipes his stinging eyes. "Smells like burnt Eggos."

As the purple mist begins to thin, Dirk stares, slack-jawed. It takes a moment, but the sight before him is unmistakable: the Bone Howler, sprawled on the floor, sliced cleanly in two.

"And I'll be taking *this*," Dirk says, wrenching his blade from the ground. But as he does, he realizes the ground is no longer the cracked concrete of the mall parking lot. It's *different*.

Dirk glances at Drooler, perched on his shoulder, and sees something like concern on the little monster's face. "You OK, champ?"

Drooler *meeps* nervously. And with the fog now clear, Dirk sees why—

There is no mall. No parking lot, no garage, no caravan of carapaces.

Dirk's glee evaporates. "Hey, Quint. Uh. Where are we?"

"What do you mean?" Quint manages. He's on the ground, like his knees have given out. He looks a bit like Yursl did after she blasted the Howler off the Mallusk.

Then Quint's eyes pop open and his legs go rigid as fear forces him to his feet. "Oh *no*. The conjuration . . . went wrong. I didn't perform it properly, and I think I . . . Well . . ."

"What?" Dirk asks.

"I think I, um, *teleported* us . . ."

"Teleported . . ." Dirk says. "Is that why I felt like I was getting turned inside-out a minute ago?"

Quint presses a hand to his stomach, like he's trying to force himself not to barf. "Yursl warned me about this! She specifically said, *The wrong mixture of science and spell, and your entire molecular structure could be displaced—transported to another location.*"

Dirk presses a finger into his palm. "I don't check in on my molecules that often, but they all seem to be accounted for."

The duo takes in their new surroundings. They're in a castle hall with a vaulted, triangular ceiling. Long, colorful carpets cover the floors, and tapestries drape the stone walls. Nearby, a turkey leg the size of a bowling pin sits on a silver platter. It looks fresh—glistening and golden.

"Buddy, I don't know how to tell you this," Dirk says, "but I think you did more than transport us to another place. I think you transported us all the way . . ."

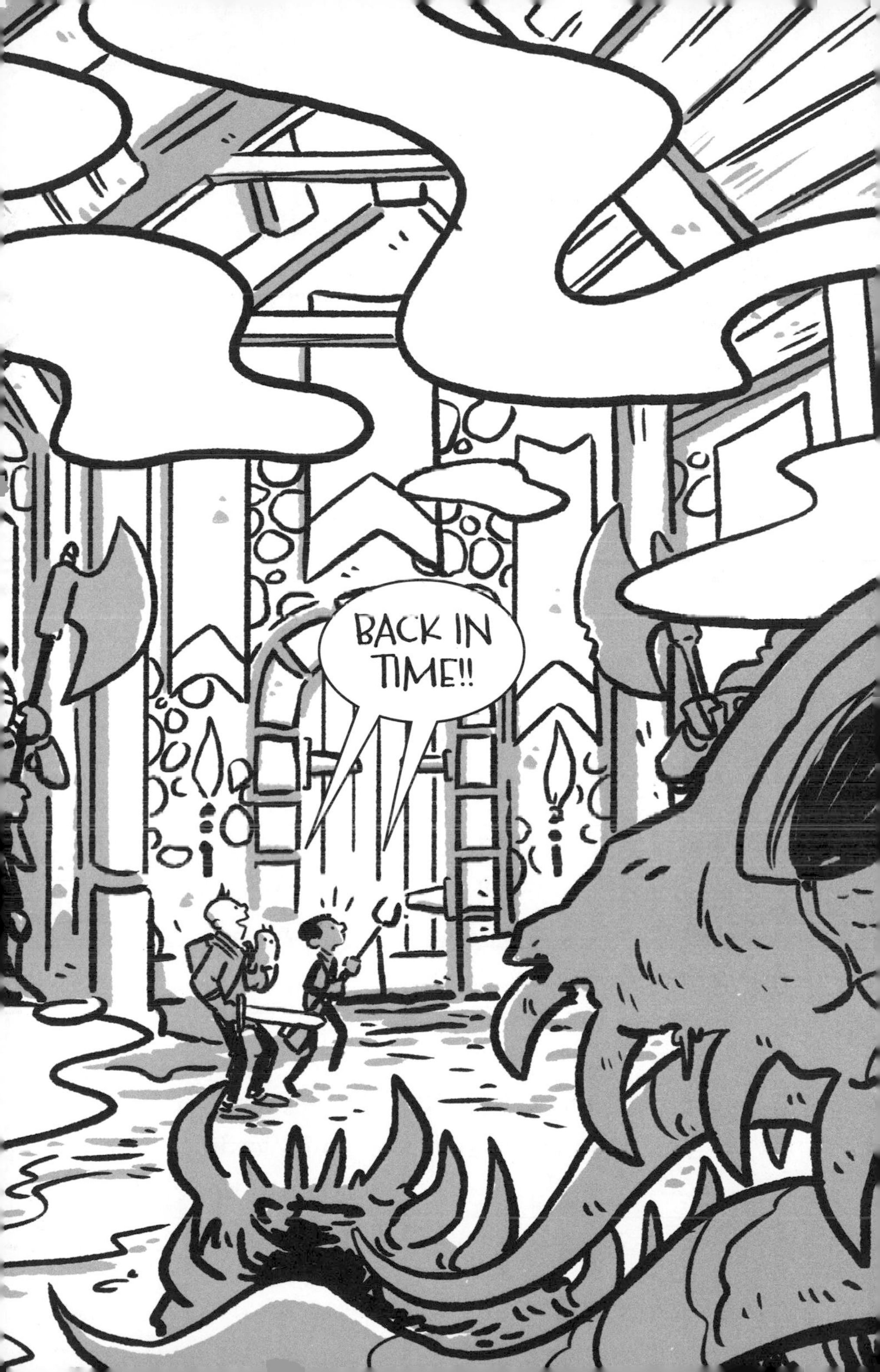
BACK IN TIME!!

The conjurer's cane drops from Quint's trembling hands, and he makes no move to pick it up. It now feels like something cursed, something not fit for human use.

"The consequences of this . . ." Quint says softly. "One mistake, and we could shatter the space-time continuum. Like *Back to the Future*!"

Dirk stares blankly for a second, then his face lights up like a neon sign. "Oh! I get that reference! Yeah, you guys watched that movie a *ton* during our tree house days. Not my favorite, but I always paid attention when that cool hero guy, Biff Tannen, was on-screen."

"Biff Tannen is the bad guy," Quint says. "The bully."

"No, I don't think that's right," Dirk says, shaking his head. "No one with a four-letter first name and a six-letter last name could ever be a bully."

Quint groans.

"But hey—maybe your awful magic did something good!" Dirk exclaims, as he begins to excitedly pace the room. "Remember Biff Tannen's big plan to save the day? We should do that! First thing: we find a sports almanac!"

Quint shakes his head. "Dirk, it's the

apocalypse. Money no longer means anything.
Remember Jack and June's million-dollar hats . . ."

"Also," Quint adds, "Biff Tannen's *actual*
scheme was to retrieve a sports almanac from
the *future*, in order to—"

"Get rich!" Dirk exclaims. "We are gonna

get *so rich*! It's simple. We find an old sports almanac, the older the better, like *ancient*. And when we get back to our regular time—which we will, 'cause you're Quint and you'll figure it out— we bring the sports almanac with us. When the world returns to something like normal, we'll be gazillionaires! I mean, just imagine if we had a book telling us who won the 1960 World Series!"

"The Pittsburgh Pirates won the 1960 World Series," Quint says flatly.

Dirk gasps. "Do your sorcerous ways know no ends!?"

Quint takes a deep breath, trying to remain calm. "What I'm trying to say is, anything we do here, in the *past*, could have dire consequences in the future. One wrong sneeze, and—"

"Argh!" Dirk roars. "I hate magic so much . . ."

"For the last time, it's called *conjuring*!" Quint says. "I messed up, but conjuring is not all bad."

"No, it is. *All magic* is *all bad*," Dirk says. "Look, I never told you this, but . . . something happened at Angela Bianucci's ninth birthday party."

"Huh?" Quint asks.

"She had this magician: Tricky Tim. And you know what Tricky Tim did? He sawed Angela Bianucci's father IN HALF! MR. BIANUCCI'S LEGS OVER HERE, MR. BIANUCCI'S UPPER STUFF OVER THERE. I ran outta there so fast . . ."

THIS IS NOT A PARTY . . . THIS IS MADNESS!

"And after that," Dirk says, "I swore I would steer clear of magic *forever*."

"Wait one second . . ." Quint says, suddenly sounding extremely concerned. "Angela Bianucci's mom told my mom the party was canceled on account of inclement weather. *That liar!*"

"I need to sit," Dirk says, collapsing into a chair that looks more like a king's throne. He lands hard, and then—

"Whoa, whoaa!" Dirk cries.

The throne tumbles back, smashing into the wall—and the entire wall topples over. And Dirk topples with it.

"Dirk!" Quint exclaims, rushing toward him. There's a sound like concrete dominoes crashing as another wall falls, then another, finally revealing . . .

"Wait . . . " Quint says. "This is a movie set!"

"We're not back in time!" Dirk exclaims.

"We're just idiots!" Quint adds.

"I've never been so happy to be an idiot," Dirk says.

23

Stepping over the fallen wall, Dirk spots a towering sign that reads FLEEGHAVEN. He figures that's the name of the town.

"You know, I think I recognize this place . . ." Quint says as they start down the cobblestone street that runs the length of the town. Except it's not *real* cobblestone—more like cheap vinyl.

They pass taverns and horse stables and endless stores and shops: a blacksmith, an apothecary, an undertaker, a store offering spells and magic items, and a sword shop called the Stabbin' Hut. But the stuff inside is clearly set decoration—not real. Some buildings are only front halves, held up by wooden poles.

"The *entire town* is fake," Dirk says.

"Indeed," Quint replies. "Fleeghaven is a fantasy movie set on a massive scale."

"And it's in worse shape than we are," Dirk says, noting the ashen craters in the ground, gashes in the building facades, and trampled star wagons. "Although right now, I'm just happy we're not back in time."

But Dirk's happiness is short-lived.

A monstrous roar cuts through the silence of the abandoned movie set town, sounding eerily hollow as it bounces off artificial storefronts and empty half buildings.

chapter three

The Bone Howler—or rather, *half* of the Bone Howler—is climbing out of the collapsed castle. It's like some alien entity crawling from the smoldering crater of a just-crashed meteor.

"Uuh, I thought you killed that thing?" Dirk says, reaching for his sword.

"Not entirely, it would seem," Quint answers. "The vines and bone were sheared through, but it's still going."

The Bone Howler's dead eyes dart around with a mixture of confusion and anger, like someone just jostled it out of a peaceful sleep.

"And it looks peeved," Quint says.

"I'd be peeved, too, if a kid conjurer sliced me in half."

"Ooh, *half*," Quint says. "We should call it the Bone-Halfer now."

The monster must not be a fan of the new name—because at that moment, it attacks! The beast's powerful front legs catapult it forward over the fallen walls. It barrels through a table marked CRAFT SERVICES—CREW ONLY!, sending a moldy frittata flying as it charges toward Quint and Dirk.

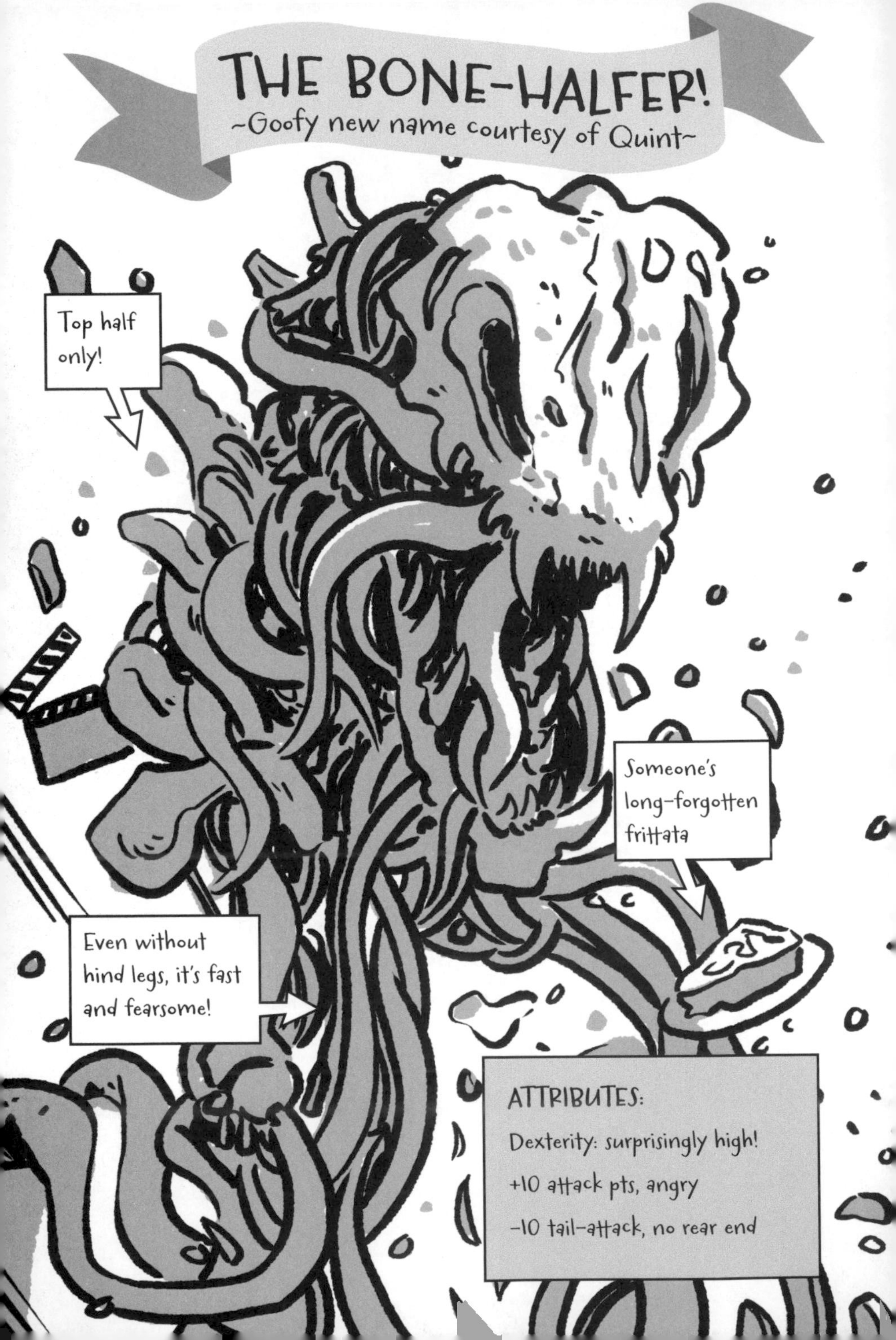
THE BONE-HALFER!
~Goofy new name courtesy of Quint~
Top half only!
Someone's long-forgotten frittata
Even without hind legs, it's fast and fearsome!
ATTRIBUTES:
Dexterity: surprisingly high!
+10 attack pts, angry
-10 tail-attack, no rear end

"Drooler, buddy, we've got some more fighting to do," Dirk says. "It wasn't always like this, I swear."

Drooler chirps cheerfully in response.

Quint peers down at his cane: the battery indicator shows that it's zapped, on empty. Relief fills Quint as he realizes he *can't* use his cane, and therefore doesn't have to risk royally messing up *again*. "Oh, fiddlesticks!" he says with a little too much gusto. "My cane needs time to recharge."

"You don't gotta use it for wizard stuff!" Dirk says. "Use it for Dirk stuff!"

"What's Dirk stuff?"

"Bashin' monsters!"

"That I can do!" Quint says, cocking back the cane—and just in time . . .

The bounding Bone-Halfer leaps! In a flash, Dirk and Quint are locked in mortal combat with the other-dimensional beast . . .

With every stab of Dirk's sword, Ultra-Slime splashes, melting the vines that give the dead monster life. One swing knocks two of the Bone-Halfer's front fangs loose. Another sends a bony hoof flying, crashing into a giant plastic horseshoe that hangs outside the town's stable.

The Bone-Halfer roars, swiping at Dirk, then twisting to avoid Quint's jabs. It's like a teenager slapping away a pair of annoying little brothers.

"Hey, Quint, quick question," Dirk says, mid-swing. "If we're fighting the monster's *head* right now, d'you think Jack and June are back at the Mallusk fighting the monster's *butt*?"

Quint shakes away the image. "If they are, they got the better part of this deal . . ."

The Bone-Halfer whip-smacks a director's chair, sending it pinwheeling into Quint.

"Oof!" Quint cries, tumbling end over end, finally slamming into the town apothecary: The Potion Pantry.

As Quint waits for the air to return to his lungs, he sees the store's facade looming over him—and notices the large, open window on the second floor. An electrical cord dangles from a giant-sized stage light on the roof. Quint thinks back to black-and-white movie Monday with his parents. It was his favorite night of the week.

"IDEA!" Quint exclaims, rising.

He reaches for the electrical cord, his mind turning quickly as he does the math. He eyes the open window, takes two steps back, does a few more calculations, then takes a half step to the side.

"Dirk!" Quint calls. "Send that thing my way!"

"Happily," Dirk shouts, swinging his sword into the Bone-Halfer's broken wing, half spinning the monster. The Bone-Halfer spots Quint then, and something flashes in the monster's eyes. Something like, *Hey! There is the human creature who sliced me in two!*

It charges at Quint.

Quint steels himself. He hopes his math is right. Hopes he remembers how the stunt from black-and-white movie Monday worked.

The shrieking Bone-Halfer's hideous mug is only a dozen feet away, closing fast, when—

Quint pulls! And the front wall of the Potion Pantry begins to fall . . .

Quint wants to run, flee, but he holds his ground, staying perfectly still as the wall crashes down and—

SLAM!

PERFECILY NOT A MISS!

PERFECT MISS!

The open window comes down around Quint, while the rest of the wall, including the heavy spotlight, crashes atop the Bone-Halfer.

"I can't believe that worked . . ." Quint gasps.

The monster tries to rise, struggling to lift the storefront facade on its back, but then—

"Where do you think you're going, buster?" Dirk says, bringing his sword crashing down.

Vines disintegrate. Bones collapse. The Bone-Halfer wheezes, long and slow, then goes still.

Dirk is heaving, exhausted, but manages a crooked smile. Quint starts to smile, too, when—

"THEY ARE THE HEROES!" a voice suddenly cries out.

Quint and Dirk whirl around, startled, murmuring, "What? Who? Not us, right?"

From all around them, monster-creatures appear, coming out of hiding: stepping from doorways, rising from behind fake horses.

"I guess the town isn't abandoned after all," Quint whispers.

"Uh, hi," Dirk says, throwing the monsters a half wave. "Um . . . We come in peace!"

At that precise moment, the Bone-Halfer lets out a final, pained death gasp.

"Uh, not counting the non-peaceful monster

killing we just did," Dirk says. "Besides that, though, we come in peace."

Quint eyes the approaching monsterfolk. Their appearance mirrors the town's: beaten down, battered, *in bad shape*.

It's clear something is awry here. Very much awry. Fleeghaven, Quint realizes, looks like a town under siege.

"Hold on! Please, one moment!" Quint calls, struggling to step out of the throng. "The *real* reason we're here is because . . ."

But Quint trails off, because the answer is not one that he likes. They're here because his first attempt at conjuring failed in a major way. And now he and Dirk are who-knows-how-many hundreds of miles from their friends . . .

"Wait, did one of you say *Drakkor*?" Dirk asks. "'Cause that *kinda* sounds like dragon. Is that what's got you folks all skittery?"

Instead of answering, the monsterfolk begin shuffling aside, making way. Something's coming. The sun's harsh glare hides the approaching *something* in a blinding shadow.

"It's a carapace," Quint realizes.

This carapace's shell is a battle-scarred—yet perfectly polished—white Jeep Wrangler.

Behind the wheel sits a teal-shaded monster with floppy ears that make Dirk think of a mutant bunny. She stares them down as the carapace continues forward.

"Are you just into making dramatic entrances?" Dirk asks. "Or are you the one who's gonna tell us what's going on here?"

"Not gonna tell you," the monster answers. "Nope. I'm gonna *show* you . . ."

chapter four

THE BRAIN POKER!

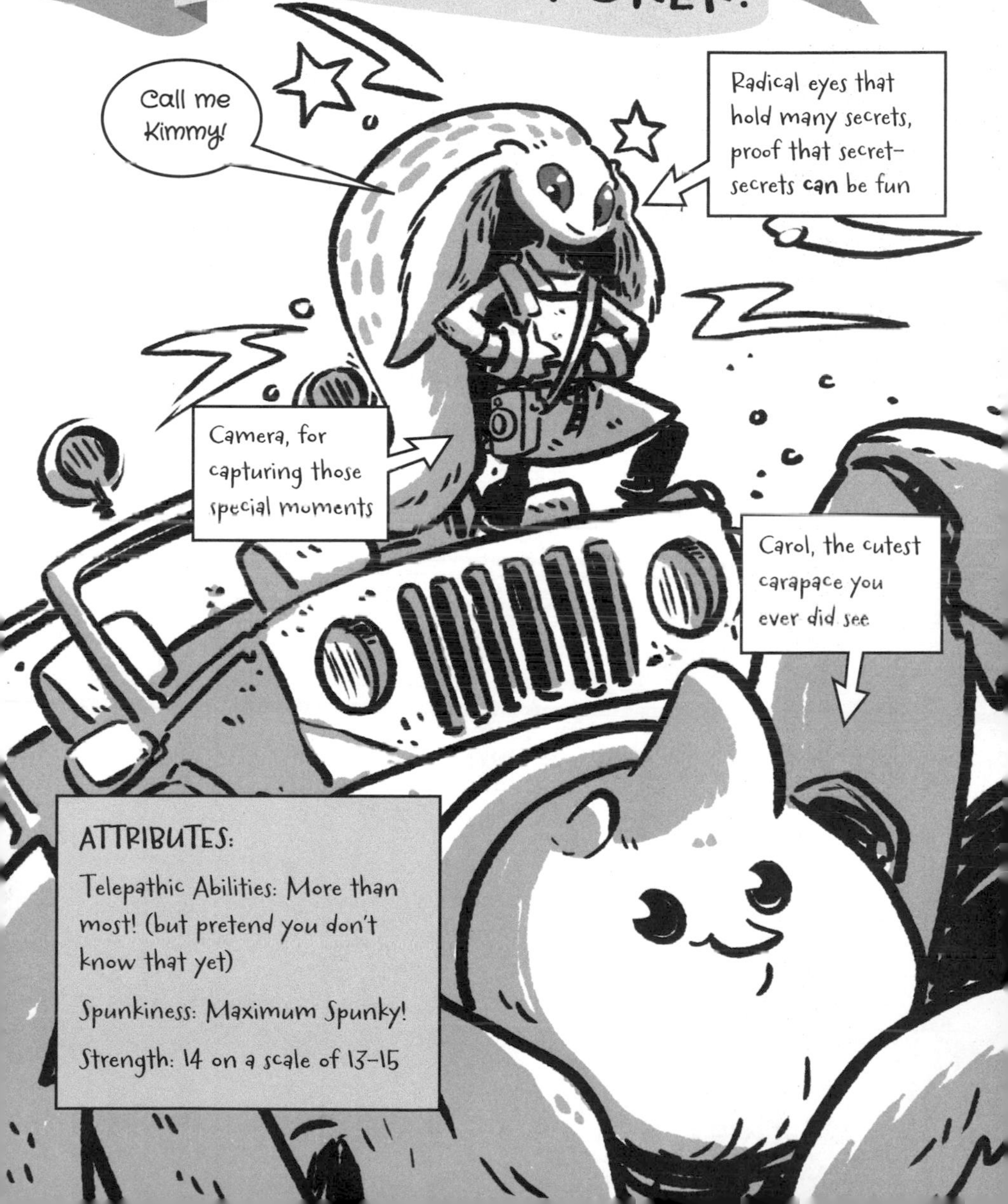

Call me Kimmy!
Radical eyes that hold many secrets, proof that secret-secrets **can** be fun
Camera, for capturing those special moments
Carol, the cutest carapace you ever did see
ATTRIBUTES:
Telepathic Abilities: More than most! (but pretend you don't know that yet)
Spunkiness: Maximum Spunky!
Strength: 14 on a scale of 13–15

A big, bright smile shines on Kimmy's face as she vaults over the Wrangler's door and to the ground. "I mean, sure, I could *tell* you—but showing is more fun, right?"

With that, Kimmy's ears bend forward. Her eyes go cloudy, turning a creamy pink color, like Froot Loop cereal milk. And then—

"WHOA!" Quint cries out.

A horrifyingly ferocious beast rises behind Kimmy! Its shadowy body, hovering in the air, seems to have appeared outta nowhere—plucked from the ether. The monster is big and growing bigger—first the size of a VW Bug, then a school bus, then a jumbo jet.

Aahh! A sorta see-through dragon thing!

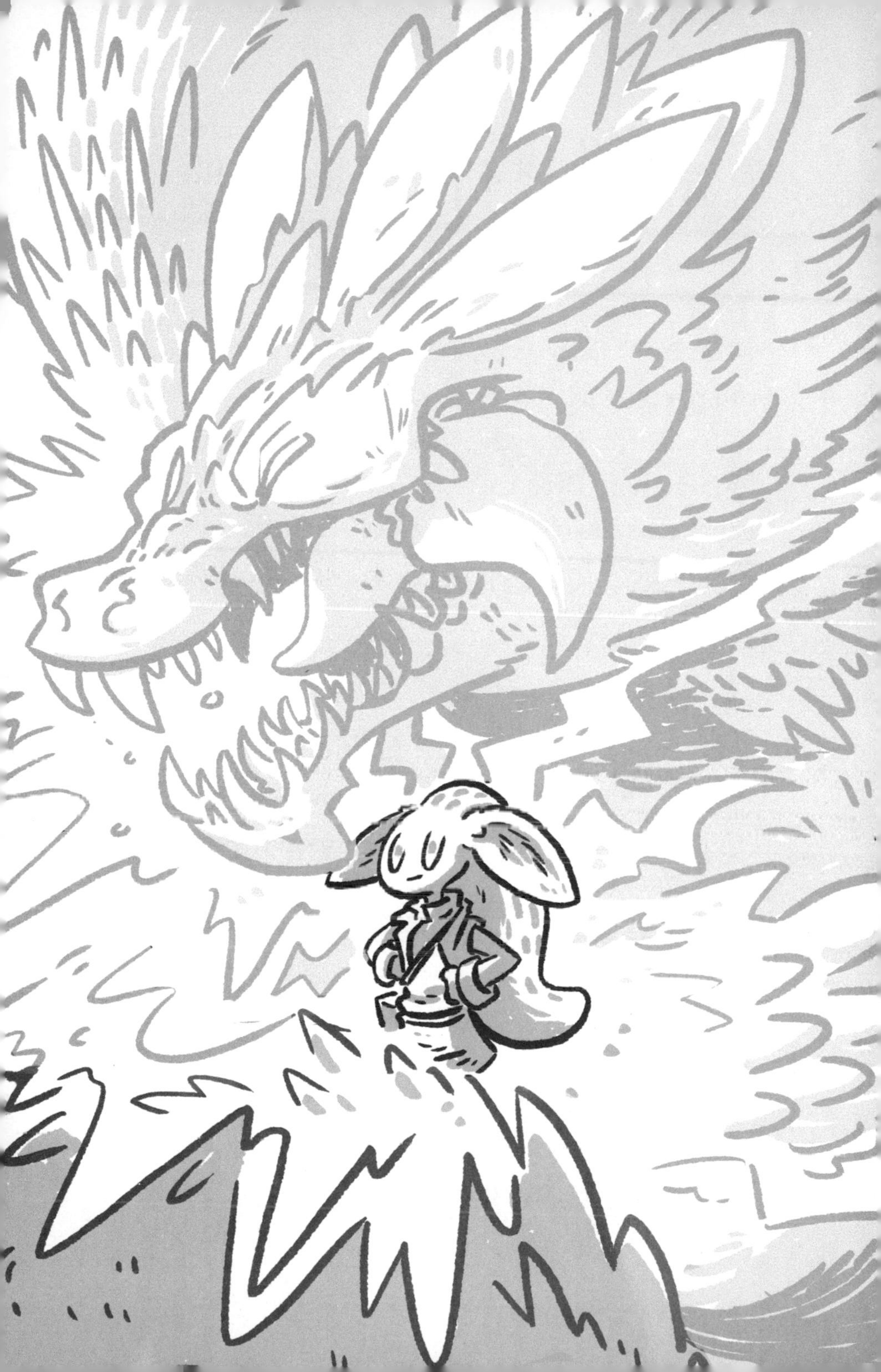

Quint braces himself as the monster crashes into him—but, oddly, he doesn't *feel* anything. He whirls around, confused, as—

POOF! The monster disappears in a puff.

A few monsters chuckle.

"Quint?" Dirk asks, cracking open one eye and peering up. "Did we just die?"

"No. It wasn't real," Quint answers, reaching down to help Dirk to his feet. Dirk dusts himself off while scowling at the giggling monsters. But then he sees that Drooler is also giggling and he can't help but grin.

"How did that—" Quint starts, before Kimmy cuts him off.

"Brain poker," she says, tapping the side of her head. "Projections instead of yakity-yak-yak. Like I said: *show*, don't tell. It's always, like, *whoa*, more effective."

"Brain poker . . ." Quint repeats. Then suddenly, "You're a telepath!"

Dirk slowly massages the bridge of his nose. "So. Much. Magic," he grumbles.

Kimmy boosts herself up onto the Jeep's hubcap. "The monster I just showed you is . . ." Kimmy pauses and clicks her tongue. "Y'know what, you probably just ought to hear the whole story from the start. The story of Fleeghaven and the Drakkor . . ."

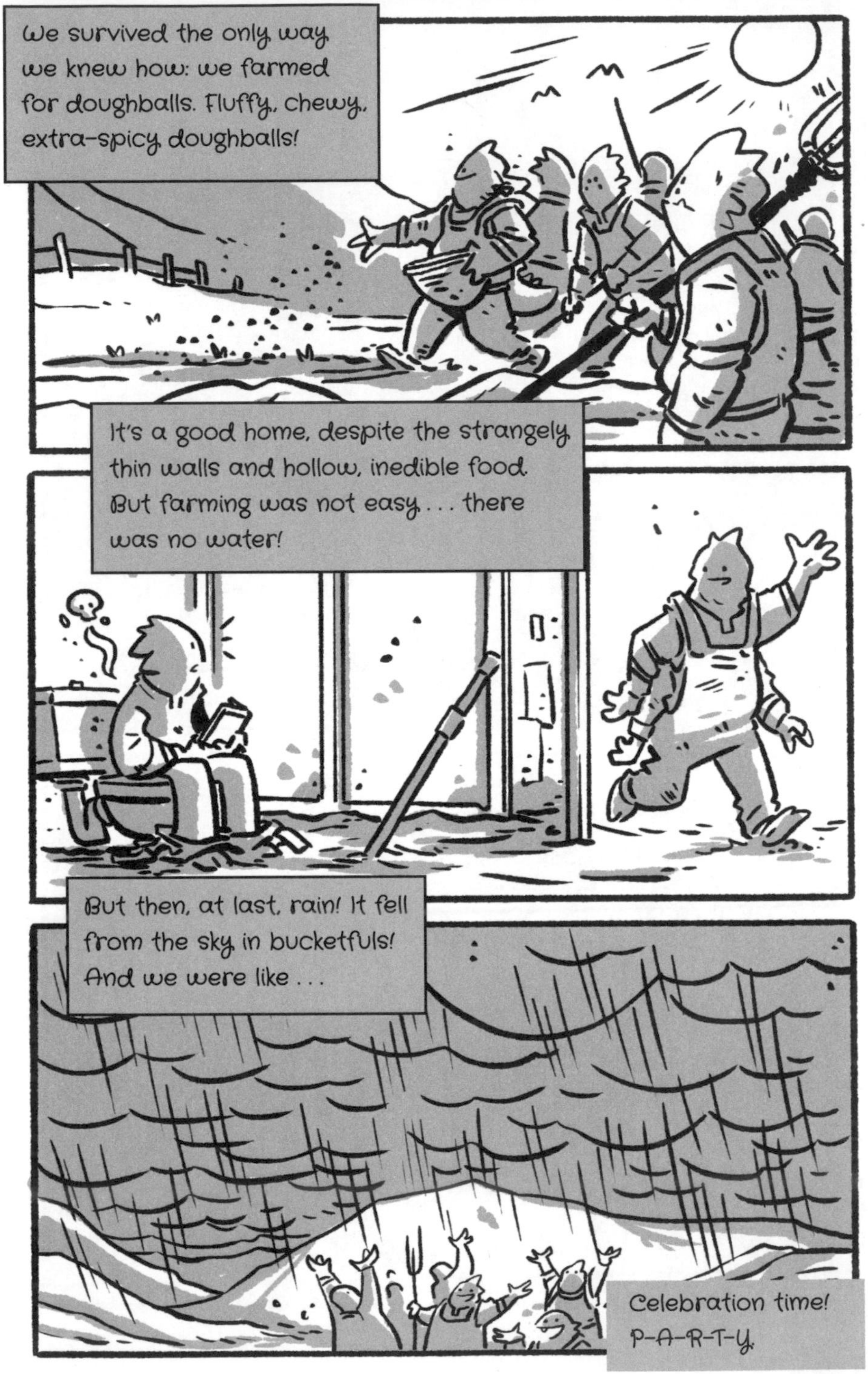
We survived the only way we knew how: we farmed for doughballs. Fluffy, chewy, extra-spicy doughballs!
It's a good home, despite the strangely thin walls and hollow, inedible food. But farming was not easy . . . there was no water!
But then, at last, rain! It fell from the sky in bucketfuls! And we were like . . .
Celebration time! P-A-R-T-Y.

But farm first.

After we finished farming, we turned it UP with a blowout bash! Super lit, lots of splashing in the fountain, and Neat-O Buzz Energy Juice flowing! Y'all should've been there. But I didn't know you then. So, sorry not sorry.

But our shindig caught the attention of a guest. A guest who did **not** RSVP. A guest who could not have RSVP'd because that guest was a **not-invited guest**. That guest was ...

The Drakkor!

The monster crashed our party—literally!—unleashing horrible terror upon our town and popping my favorite party balloon.

And then—as quickly as it had arrived—it left.

42

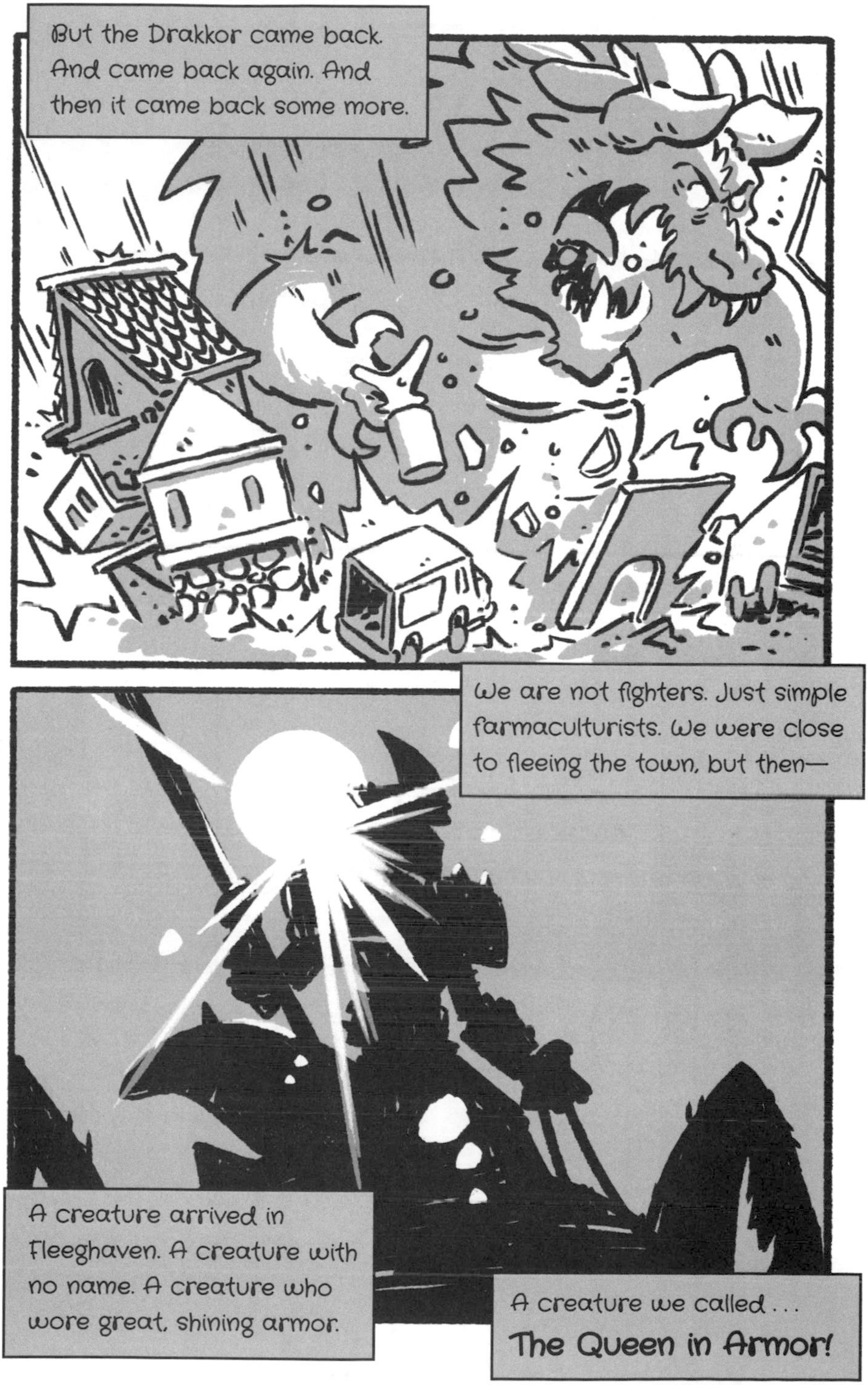
But the Drakkor came back. And came back again. And then it came back some more.
We are not fighters. Just simple farmaculturists. We were close to fleeing the town, but then—
A creature arrived in Fleeghaven. A creature with no name. A creature who wore great, shining armor.
A creature we called . . .
The Queen in Armor!

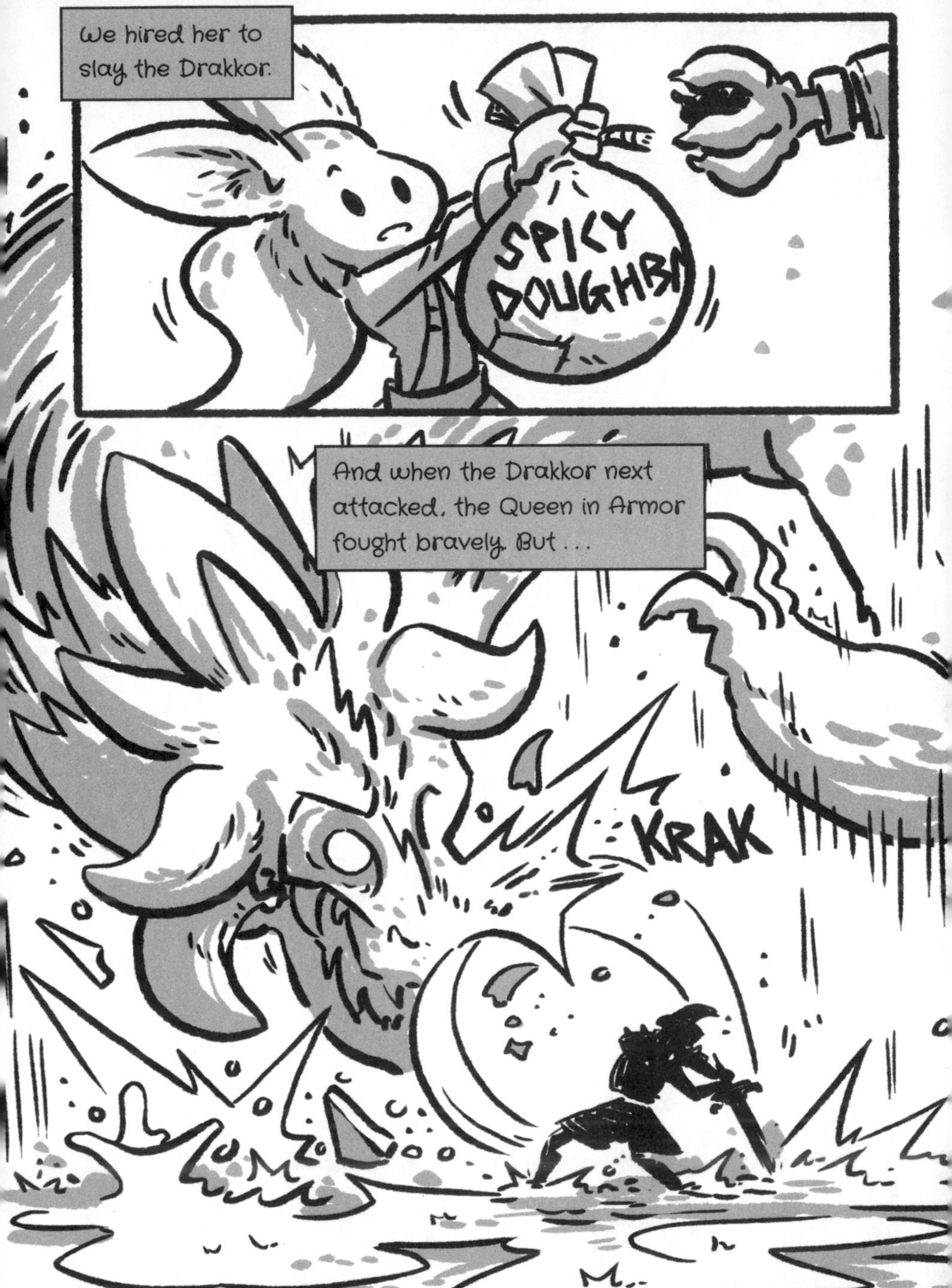
We hired her to slay the Drakkor.
SPICY DOUGHB
And when the Drakkor next attacked, the Queen in Armor fought bravely. But . . .
KRAK

She was wounded. And the Drakkor took her! Took her to its dark, foul lair in the lands beyond.

And with the Queen in Armor gone, we have had no one to help us. Until now . . .

With that, Kimmy crosses her arms and leans against the carapace. Story time over.

A deeply distressed monster suddenly exclaims, "The Drakkor has attacked thrice since taking the Queen in Armor. Thrice! That's two more than once! One more than twice! And thrice more than I can take . . ."

"Each assault is worse than the last!" another monster cries out.

Kimmy nods. "Just look there!" she says, pointing to a small cemetery hill in the distance, dotted with cracked and crumbling headstones.

"And the Drakkor *always* comes with the rain," squeaks a tiny monster. "So random."

Kimmy nods. "Yupper, that's true. And we can't withstand another attack. Each time it returns, it's *meaner*. Bigger, too."

"How big?" Dirk asks.

"Larger than a bread bucket, smaller than the moon. So . . . You guys in? You should definitely be in. Say you're in."

"In?" Quint asks.

"In for slaying the Drakkor!" Kimmy says. "What do you think I told you that whole dumb story for? Use your context clues! We need two heroes who fight monsters." Kimmy hooks a thumb at the dead Bone-Halfer. "And clearly, you two fit the bill. So whatcha say?"

Suddenly, the carapace scurries toward Quint, mouth open like a puppy dog, saliva-slobber splashing the ground.

"Whoa, whoa!" Quint shouts, backpedaling, taking a dozen quick steps before tripping over something called Roland's Rolling Wagon of Fortunes and Futures. The carapace leaps on top of the wagon, drool dripping from her mouth.

"Down, Carol!" Kimmy barks, patting her thigh. "You OK back there, hero? Sorry about that. Carol's just a pup. She must smell chocolate. You got chocolate on you?"

"Huh? Oh," Quint murmurs, checking his pockets while keeping his eyes on the carapace looming over him. "I might have something . . ."

He fishes out a Snickers bar. Carol immediately snatches it and starts eating.

But while digging in his pockets, Quint finds something else . . .

"Whatcha got?" Dirk asks as he steps around the wagon. "A book?"

Quint turns the book over: it's totally normal, like you'd find in any library or bookstore. But when he opens it, the jacket slips off, revealing a sort of second, *secret* cover.

"This is a tome from the monster dimension!" Quint realizes. "A guide to conjuring!"

"But when . . . ?" Quint wonders. "How . . . ?"

Confused, he flips to the first page and finds a scrawled message from Yursl: "For Quint— *This* will guide you. As I said, when I secretly slipped this into your pocket, unawares: *You now have all you need to do what must be done."*

Whoa. It's like a message from beyond, Quint thinks. Or *worse*—and this next realization makes Quint's stomach roll—a message that could, in a way, be from *beyond the grave.* Because Quint doesn't know what happened at the Mallusk after they left. Yursl could be a prisoner of Thrull's, or worse . . .

"That should be helpful," Dirk says. "And we need a helpful thing like that, 'cause, dude, these folks need *our* help."

"But we left our friends in the middle of battle. With *Thrull*," Quint says. "We need to get—"

"Helloooooo! Guys?" Kimmy calls. "I can totally hear you. *Brain poker*, remember? But also, you two just talk super loud. Ever try whispering? I'm not a big fan, but if you wanna be all hush-hush, maybe give it a spin?"

Quint and Dirk sheepishly step back into view.

"Listen," Kimmy says as Carol bounds back to her side, "I didn't want to resort to bribery, because bribery is for stinkers. But if you help us, I will give you . . ."

Everyone waits while Kimmy rummages through her coat, then dramatically reveals . . .

"THIS!"

"A rubber chicken?" Dirk asks.

"Whoops," Kimmy says, glancing at the dangling bird. "I was playing rubber chickens earlier. I meant . . . THIS! A mapparatus!"

But you can have a rubber chicken, too, if you want it. I have, like, a thousand. But you can't have this one. This one is my most favorite.

Quint has to stop himself from rushing forward and yanking the object straight from Kimmy's hands. "A mapparatus is like a crystal ball mixed with a map!" he tells Dirk. "Yursl told me that functioning ones are very rare."

"More like the *rarest-est*," Kimmy says. "And this one's all yours . . . *if* you slay the Drakkor."

The monsterfolk are growing impatient. "Why do they delay in accepting the quest?" one cries.

Another shouts, "Are they not the heroes foretold, who would be coming this summer?"

Dirk leans toward Quint. "Accept the quest? Coming this summer?? What are they talking about???"

By way of answering, Kimmy points to a wardrobe truck parked in a nearby alley.

Quint's eyes light up, and for one moment all thoughts of getting home and all fears of conjuring are pushed from his mind. *"Hero Quest 5*! I knew I recognized this place! I saw leaked photos online! This is the set! This is the *real* Fleeghaven! Well—'real'—y'know."

"Hero Quest?" Dirk asks.

"Only the *greatest, cheesiest* mid-budget sword-and-sorcery film series ever!"

Dirk just shrugs and stares at the movie poster. "Well, I can see why they think we're the heroes foretold, or whatever. I mean, I bear a striking resemblance to that warrior guy. And you totally have a Professor Weird vibe going on."

"I believe you mean Dr. Strange," Quint says.

"OK, listen, buddy," Dirk says, like he's plotting the final play before the buzzer. "We can find our way back to the Mallusk, but it might take a *long* time. I used something like that map, though, way back when I battled those Rifters—and it'll get us back *quick*."

Quint presses his lips together tight, thinking: This is the *right* thing to do. And they're *always* doing the right thing 'cause doing the right thing is kinda their schtick now . . . But how many opportunities do they get to do that without Jack's running commentary or June being all, "I'M JUNE! LET'S LISTEN TO MUSIC!"

Here, now, they can do the right thing—and do it wizard and warrior style. Hero Quest style.

He's nervous, for sure, but there's also something like excitement beginning to bubble in his chest. Dirk sees it on his buddy's face, sees that he's made his decision, and gives him a hearty slap.

"Here's the deal, monsterfolk! We're not gonna lie to you!" Dirk calls. "We're not those heroes—not exactly. But . . ."

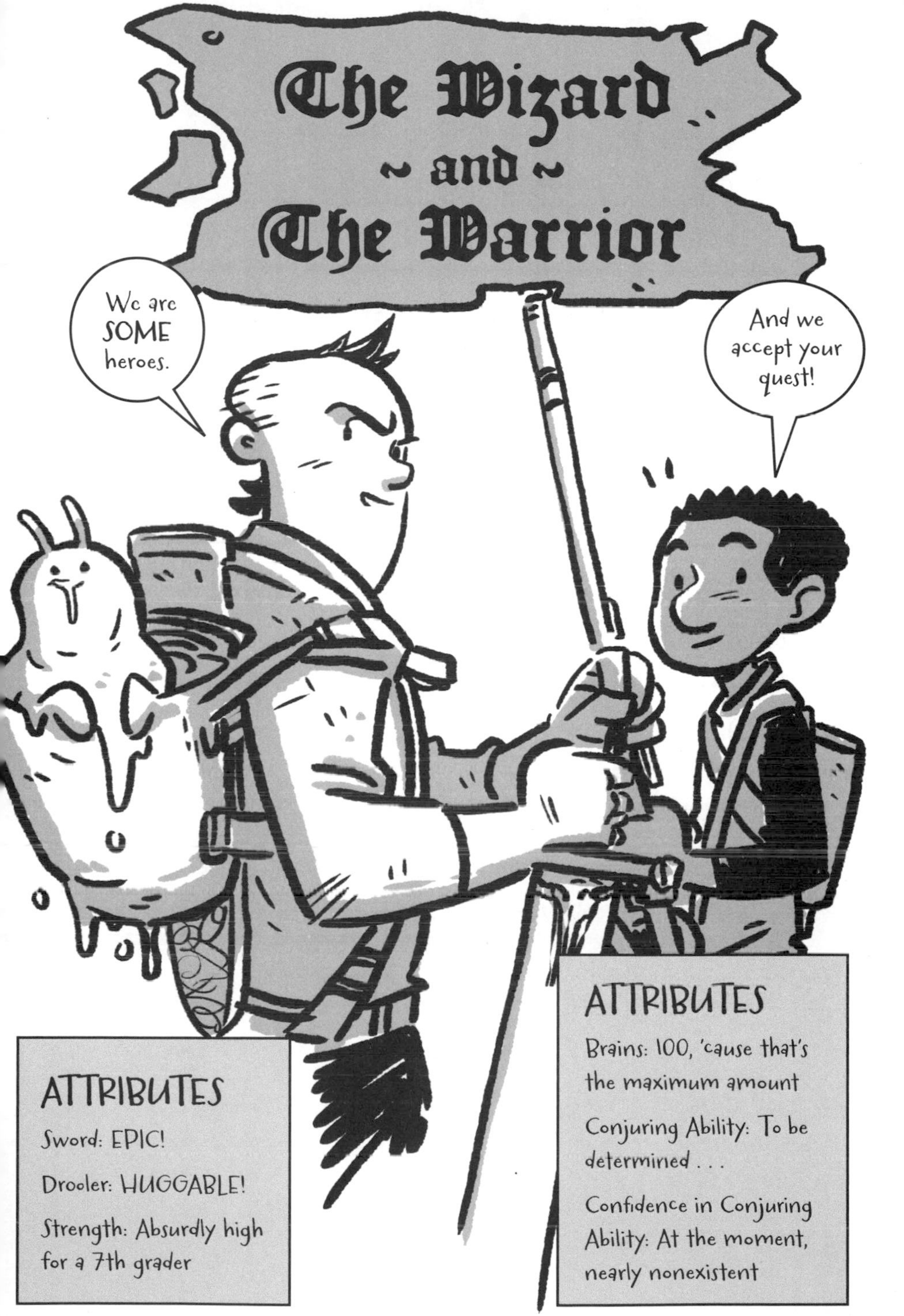
The Wizard ~ and ~ The Warrior
We are SOME heroes.
And we accept your quest!
ATTRIBUTES
Sword: EPIC!
Drooler: HUGGABLE!
Strength: Absurdly high for a 7th grader
ATTRIBUTES
Brains: 100, 'cause that's the maximum amount
Conjuring Ability: To be determined . . .
Confidence in Conjuring Ability: At the moment, nearly nonexistent

"Now point us in the direction of the Drakkor," Dirk calls. " 'Cause we're gonna slay the pants off that thing."

"The Drakkor doesn't wear pants," Kimmy says.

"Then we'll slay the socks off it."

"No socks."

"Well, what does it wear?" Dirk asks.

"The blood of its victims."

"Oh," Dirk says. "Then we'll slay it, and afterward we'll power wash the blood off it!"

With that, the monsters erupt in a roaring cheer! "POWER WASH THE BLOOD! POWER WASH THE BLOOD! POWER WASH THE BLOOD!"

"Ahem, yes, there will be plenty of power washing," Quint says. "But we must embark on this quest quickly! Our friends await us."

"So tell us what we gotta know," Dirk says. "Where is this Drakkor monster's lair?"

Kimmy flashes a sly smile. "Oh, get ready for fun—'cause I'm gonna take you there. Yup yup, I'm comin' with!"

chapter five

NINETEEN MINUTES LATER . . .

I raided the wardrobe truck.

New helmet?

Double helmets. This one fits right on top of my everyday, zombie-chatter-blocking helmet.

Dirk proudly taps his newly acquired armor. "See, this helmet is cooler looking than my everyday helmet."

"I built your everyday helmet!" Quint exclaims.

"Exactly," Dirk says, grinning.

"Wait, Quint, I almost forgot!" Dirk suddenly says. "If we're going questing, we need epic gear. So I snagged something for you, too . . ."

And then, with a sudden whoosh, Dirk reveals—

Quint eyes the velvety fabric and plastic gems sewn into the collar. He *wants* to wear it—it's the *actual one* from Hero Quest! But . . .

"No," Quint says quietly. "I can't wear that. Even if it's only a costume, I haven't earned it."

Dirk frowns. "Dude, are you—"

HONK!

HONK!

Dirk's interrupted by Kimmy, in the Jeep, laying on the horn. "Guys! Over here! Can you see me? I'm the one in the Jeep, honking! Oh good. You're looking at me. Let's goooooo!"

"I will happily saddle up," Quint says, climbing up into the carapace. He needs to dive into the book, ASAP—and reading while walking inevitably ends with walking into a stop sign.

"Then I'll be hoofin' it," Dirk says. "Wanna stay as far away from Quint's conjuring as possible."

Quint glances back. All of Fleeghaven has gathered to watch their departure. He sees monsters sitting on storefront porches, leaning over rooftops, and perched on wooden barrels. And on their faces—faint glimmers of hope.

This entire town has placed their faith in us. In me, Quint thinks. *I really hope they're not all making a horrible mistake.*

And with that, this odd band of humans and monsters sets off, traveling down Fleeghaven's long main street, then out into the strange, wild wasteland beyond.

Their hero quest has begun . . .

As Quint flips the pages, he begins to feel nervous again. The book is jammed full of diagrams and drawings, but he can't read the instructions alongside them.

Learning how to become a conjurer with this book is **not** *gonna be easy,* Quint thinks. *It's like trying to assemble a Lego Death Star when I only have the instructions for a Lego microwave.*

"What's a Lego microwave?" Kimmy asks.

Quint glances up, confused. "How did you—?"

"Do I need to get 'brain poker' tattooed on my forehead?" Kimmy asks. "Ooh, I should!"

Quint feels frustration mounting—and the increasingly loud yowling from the Wrangler's stereo isn't helping. "Uh, Kimmy!" he calls, straining to be heard. "The music?"

"That's Pete!!" she shouts back. "He's a star, dude. The tunes are actually the sound of food moving through his digestive tract!"

Quint's about to ask who Pete is and why he sounds like talons on a chalkboard, but then he sees: the Wrangler has no actual stereo. Instead, a tiny cricket-looking monster sits on the dash, wearing a bottle cap as a hat. A headphone cord is plugged into his belly.

"Might it be at all possible to lower, uh . . . Pete?" Quint asks. "This volume doesn't quite lend itself to studying."

Kimmy's ears twirl slowly, like she's rolling her eyes. "You guys are such olds."

Dirk glances up. "*Olds?* How old are *you*?"

"Only four hundred nineteen," Kimmy says. "Which is roughly sixteen in human years."

"Well, ha," Dirk says. "We're still younger."

"You don't *seem* younger," Kimmy says. Still, she gives Quint the break that he requested. "Pete, take five."

Pete flicks the wire from his belly and slithers across the dash.

I JUST FEEL THE MUSIC IN MY GUT, MAN.

Finally, there is something like quiet, and Quint is able to focus. Unfortunately, the quiet lasts for all of six seconds.

"So, you guys said something about Thrull?" Kimmy asks. Then, a moment later, "Sorry, I don't do awkward silences. Just awkard conversations!"

"We're gonna stop Thrull from building the Tower," Dirk says. "Save the dimension from Ṛeżżő̌ch. Stuff like that."

"Wait . . . you guys are tangling with *Rężžőcħ*?" Kimmy asks, impressed. "Does that mean you know . . . *the Blarg Slayer*?"

Quint lowers his book. Dirk misses a step.

"I'm sorry," Quint begins. "Did you say—"

"The Blarg Slayer?" Dirk repeats.

Kimmy nods. "Yeah, y'know: 'Big Sully.' 'Captain Jack.' *Jack Sullivan, the Blarg Slayer!*'"

Quint and Dirk stare at Kimmy, jaws slack.

"*Fine . . .*" Kimmy says, and her eyes fog over as an image forms in the air—

Quint and Dirk exchange a stunned, indignant look. "OK, first," Dirk says, "*no one* calls Jack the Blarg Slayer. Or, like, any other cool nickname."

"And we more than *know* him! He's my best friend!" Quint exclaims.

Kimmy frowns. "So weird, 'cause I for sure haven't heard of you guys *at all*. You said . . . Quitter and Dunk? Those are your names? I'm really racking my brain here . . ."

"No, I am Quint Baker! Scientist, inventor, and holder of a record seven straight years of perfect class attendance."

"And," Dirk adds proudly, "*my* attendance was so lousy the school made up a special award for it . . ."

Just then, Carol begins to slow. A dark thicket of trees lies ahead of them.

"The Forbidden Forest of Foreboding," Kimmy says, wrapping her ears around her face like a scarf. "It's a spooky bad time. But it's the only path to the Drakkor's lair."

Kimmy and Quint hop out of the Wrangler, and Carol leads the way into the forest. In moments, they're engulfed by darkness.

Slowly, though, small flashes of light begin to flicker through the trees. Glimpses of color, like a sunbeam passing through a prism.

They walk for a few minutes in sheer darkness—then suddenly come upon a section of forest where the overgrown ground glows and the trees' thick trunks glimmer.

"Snareghul splatter," Kimmy explains. "Also known as crystal-crust."

Quint is about to ask her to explain further when they circle around a wide, shimmering oak tree, and his heart nearly explodes as he comes face-to-face with three zombies—

AHHH!

MEEEEEEEP!

Once Quint and Dirk's very brave, very heroic screaming finally ends, they realize the zombies are no threat: they are frozen inside crystal-crust.

Quint's heart rate returns to something like normal, and he says, "It's like they're encased in glass." Looking around, he adds, "Much of this place is. Like a petrified forest . . ."

"Oh, it's petrifying, all right," Dirk adds. "Let's pick up the pace."

The heroes, now fully freaked out, journey deeper and deeper into the otherworldly forest. Everything is eerily quiet—until suddenly, it's not. An odd, singsongy tune calls out from a clearing beyond.

"A siren's call?" Quint asks.

"A wounded banshee?" Kimmy suggests.

"Wait . . ." Dirk says, holding his breath so he can hear better. "That kinda sounds like . . . *singing*?"

Ahead, they see a break in the shimmering, post-apocalyptic trees. Rays of light shine down, and the entire forest seems to sparkle, like morning sun reflecting off fresh snow.

"Check that out," Dirk whispers, nodding to the clearing ahead.

They see a strange cage, hanging from the long branch of a crystal-encased tree. The cage is unlike anything from this dimension: its bars are fleshy and dotted with sharp, spiny tendrils.

"Looks like a trap," Dirk says, carefully moving forward.

"I believe it most certainly *is* a trap," Quint whispers. "But one that's already been sprung."

The cage gently sways and turns in the breeze. Inching closer, they discover the source of the singing: a creature, huddled and bent inside the cage. The creature's off-pitch song fades into a soft, wet sort of blubbering.

"I don't believe it . . ." Kimmy says with an annoyed sigh. "Galamelon?"

"Who's there??" the caged creature—Galamelon—exclaims, startled, accidentally banging his head on the top of the cage.

"Kimmy, you *know* this crooning monster dude?" Dirk asks.

"Ahem!" Galamelon says. "What you thought was singing was actually meditative chanting. I am preparing to conjure an escape from this Snareghul's foul trap." He jabs a finger toward the ground, where—two dozen feet away—a bus-sized monster lies still, asleep.

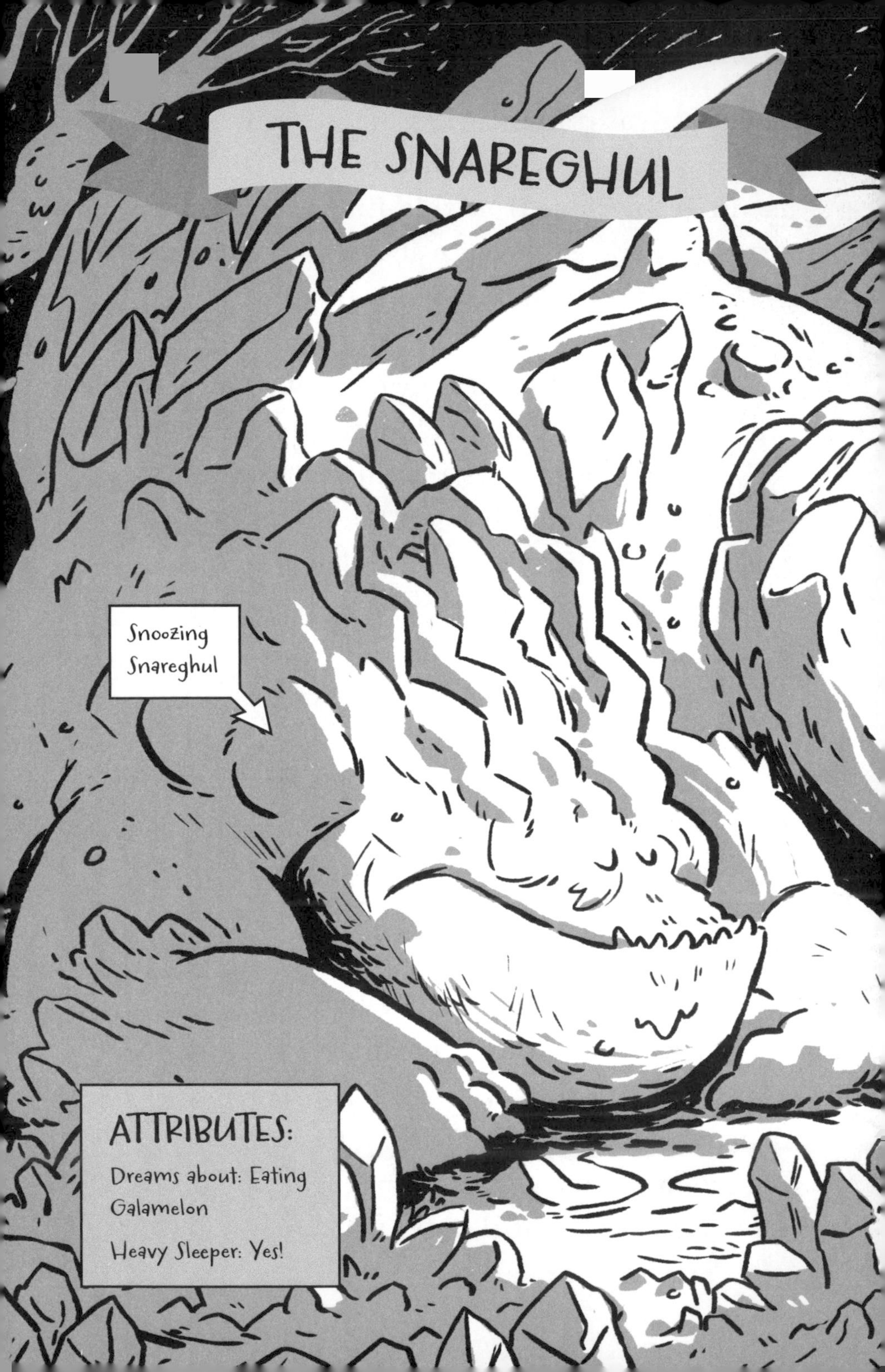
THE SNAREGHUL
Snoozing Snareghul
ATTRIBUTES:
Dreams about: Eating Galamelon
Heavy Sleeper: Yes!

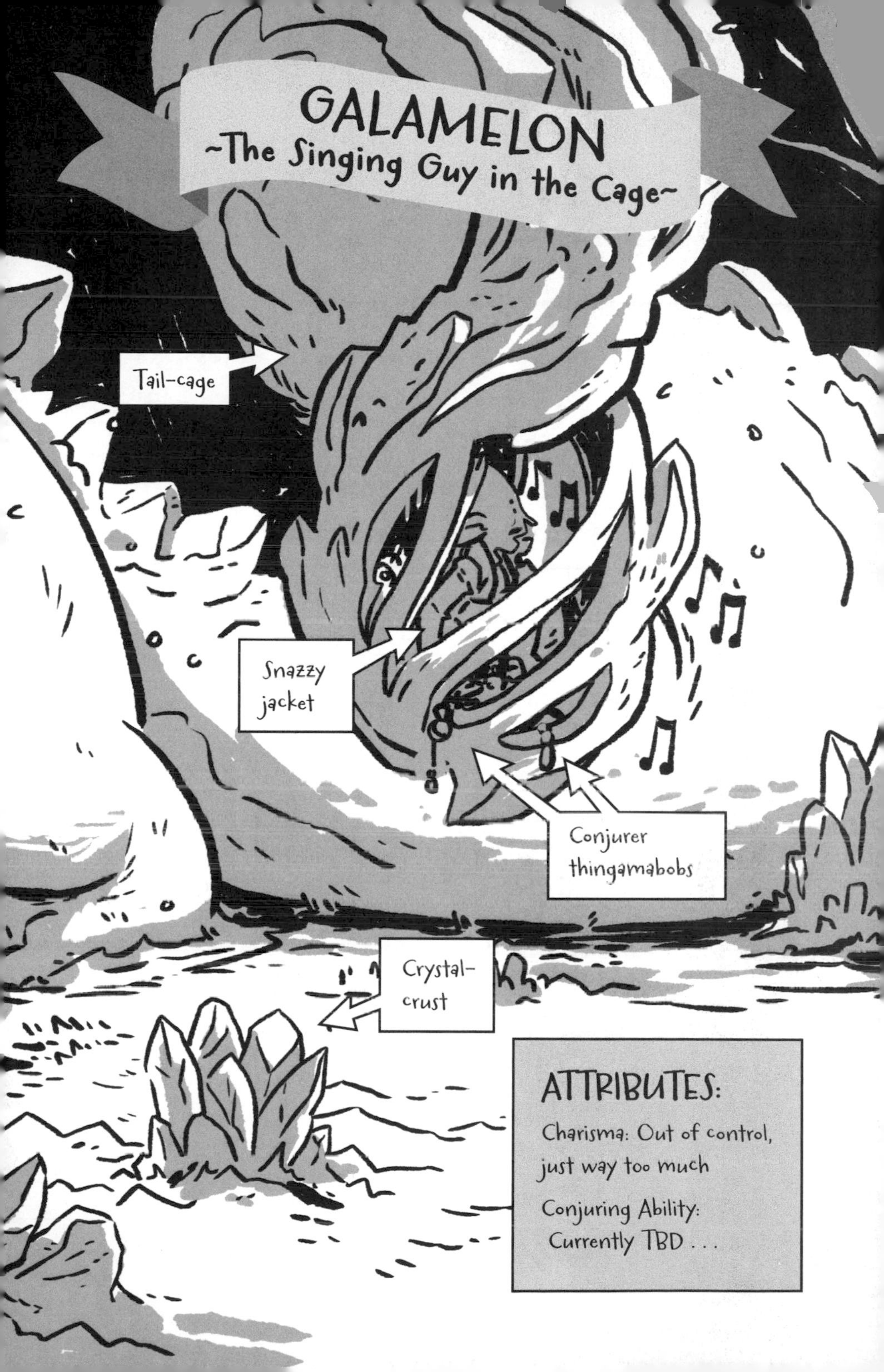
GALAMELON
~The Singing Guy in the Cage~
Tail-cage
Snazzy jacket
Conjurer thingamabobs
Crystal-crust
ATTRIBUTES:
Charisma: Out of control, just way too much
Conjuring Ability: Currently TBD . . .

Dirk eyes the entire setup, then turns to Kimmy. "Lemme guess. If we try to free this Galamelon guy from that cage, then that beast— the Snareghul—wakes up?"

"Yep," Kimmy says. "And a Snareghul *always* wakes up hungry. C'mon, we'll let it enjoy its breakfast. Catch ya later, Galamelon!"

Galamelon wipes dirt from his eyes, squinting—then suddenly jams his cheeks against the fleshy bars. "Wait . . . KIMMY! Buddy, pal! I'd hoped I'd run into you again!"

"And I'd hoped you were dead."

Dirk looks at Kimmy. "You two aren't exactly pals, huh?"

"Not even frenemies. Long story short: We hired him to slay the Drakkor, but . . ." Kimmy trails off. "Look, he's just *the worst*, OK."

"Wait . . ." Quint says, stepping toward Galamelon. "Are you a . . . *conjurer*?"

"Sure, guy!" Galamelon says. "Best conjurer in—"

"Baloney!" Kimmy says. "You couldn't conjure your way out of a paper bag."

"False! I have conjured my way into—*and out of*—dozens of paper bags! Now just listen," he pleads, gripping the bars. "I'll make you a deal.

Deal of a lifetime! Never gonna get a chance at a deal like this again!"

"What sorta *deal*?" Dirk asks, crossing his arms.

Galamelon's bulging, desperate eyes dart across the adventurers. "Oh, it's a good one. A real good one. You get me outta this cage, and in return, I can offer something that's, um . . . that is—that is—"

Galamelon's eyes suddenly fix on Quint—and the book in his hands.

"*That is*"—Galamelon finally finishes—"a very rare book!"

"You . . . know what this book is?" Quint asks.

Oh, indeed I do . . . And I know more than that. I know you need someone to help you unlock its secrets . . .

chapter six

Dirk stalks to a nearby rock, plops down, and immediately slides off its glassy shell. "Stupid slippery rock. Stupid spooky magic,"

he grumbles. "This whole business gives me the heebie-jeebies. Don't wanna see any magic being done—and definitely *not* in front of Drooler."

Galamelon flashes Quint an overeager smile, showing way too many teeth. "I'm guessing your journey has left you famished. Might I offer . . . some sustenance?"

With a flick of his wrist, a bag of Cheetos appears in Galamelon's hand! Right out of thin air.

"Wow!" Quint's eyebrows shoot up. "*That* is the sort of conjuring I need to learn. Well, that, and also how to go about teleporting us back to the Mallusk. And maybe, probably, also how to slay a Drakkor and free a queen."

But one step at a time, he thinks.

"Catch!" Galamelon says, as he drops the bag through the bars.

Quint does not catch. The bag falls to the forest floor.

"Don't touch it, Quint!" Dirk calls from his spot by the stone. "No touching magic Cheeto bags!"

Quint ignores his friend. Tentatively, he picks up the bag. But . . . "It's empty."

Galamelon frowns—but only for an instant.
"Course it's empty! It's a two-part conjuring.
Didn't I say that at the start? First I conjure the
bag, and now . . . the actual Cheetos!"

And as if from thin air, they appear . . .

Dirk suddenly stalks over to Quint, grabs him,
and pulls him to the rock. "Quint, this dude is
giving me serious used-car-salesman vibes."

Quint nods. "I admit, he does seem a little . . ."

"Full of it? Untrustworthy? Full of untrustworthiness?"

"I was going to say *unpolished*," Quint whispers. "But, Dirk, I need the help of a real conjurer—and here one is, offering to mentor me. It's like it was fated! A step on our hero quest! Look, we don't know what happened at the Mallusk after we left. We don't know what happened to Jack and June . . ." Quint trails off, not wanting to give words to the worst-case scenario.

Dirk's face goes tight. They're both imagining the same horrors.

"And we don't know *what* we'll be facing when we return. So I . . ." Quint's voice quivers. "I can't fail again . . . I *need* to crack this conjuring thing. And I can't do it alone. At a minimum, I need someone to help interpret the book!"

Dirk rubs his jaw, thinking. He glances at Drooler. Drooler blinks twice, then sneezes. "Drooler," Dirk says. "You are wise beyond your years."

Dirk whips out his sword—so lightning-quick that Quint leaps back. Dirk stomps toward Galamelon, raises the sword, and swings—

KLONK!

Dirk's blade slams into the living cage and the entire thing snaps open with a wet *schlorp!* An instant later, Galamelon is falling to the forest floor.

REEARRRAGH!

The Snareghul has snapped awake—and is instantly on the attack.

"Ah, hamburgers, now we're in for it," Kimmy says. "Carol, time to skedaddle!"

"Watch out!" Quint shouts. "Snareghul cage-tail on the attack!"

The monstrous tail *whooshs* through the air, then there's a loud *crunch* as the cage slams into a tree. A flash of silver-white erupts from the Snareghul's tail, splattering the tree-trunk with crystal-crust.

"Everyone, get on!" Kimmy shouts, as she scrambles into the Wrangler. "Now!"

Dirk hoists himself up as Carol starts picking up speed. Galamelon grabs hold of Carol's tail, pulling himself up, hand over hand.

"Wait!" Dirk yells. "We don't have Quint!"

Dirk spots Quint speeding after them. He's nearly at the Wrangler—until suddenly he trips over Galamelon's conjured Cheeto bag and falls face-first into the brush.

The snarling Snareghul stomps toward Quint, tail snapping back! Quint scrambles to his feet and swings his cane like a hockey stick, slapshotting a dozen Cheetos—

"Wait up, guys!" Quint calls, running full throttle now, feet pounding the forest floor.

But Carol is galloping free—and Kimmy can't slow her.

The Snareghul has quickly recovered from the eye attack. Its tail is swinging wildly, gathering momentum, about to come crashing down on Quint.

"Wait UP!" Quint cries again, and then—

"Hauling!" Kimmy shouts back as Carol careens faster through the forest.

The Snareghul's furious roar echoes through the woods, shaking the trees with a powerful rage. There's a deafening *SMASH* as the Snareghul angrily slams its cage-tail down, splashing the ground in splatter.

"You saved me!" Quint says to Galamelon, still catching his breath.

"I'd check your pockets," Kimmy grumbles. "That no-goodnik probably stole your wallet."

"Course I saved ya," Galamelon says, fiddling with the seat recline lever. "It's what I do. Not only great at conjuring—also great at saving."

Dirk frowns. He's slightly less skeptical of Galamelon—but only about 6 percent. Still 94 percent skeptical.

But Galamelon did save Quint—which counts for a lot. So, Galamelon is part of their hero quest. For now . . .

"So, where's this band of heroes headed?" Galamelon asks, leaning back and slipping his hands behind his head. "Or are we a fellowship? An adventure party? A syndicate of swashbucklers, perhaps? What are we calling ourselves?"

chapter seven

Dirk cocks his head and glances at Drooler.
"Actually, there's a lot about Drooler I don't know.
A lot I'm still learning. But that's all part of—"

Dirk is interrupted by a sudden commotion coming from the Wrangler. Dirk and Kimmy wheel around, just in time to see Galamelon poking at Quint's cane.

"Galamelon, wait!" Quint suddenly cries. "Don't touch that lever or—"

FWOOM

LIME HOUSE BBQ & GRILL

MAGICAL MISFIRE!

"HEY!" Dirk barks. "Watch where you're pointing that thing!"

Galamelon frowns at Dirk, then returns his attention—and the conjurer's cane—to Quint. "Your staff isn't like any I've seen before," Galamelon says.

"Because it's not," Quint replies. "I built it using materials from *this* dimension. The mini-basketball gives it a magical nudge—but it's technology that allows me to wield it. Yursl taught me all I know about this stuff."

"And I can tell you know a *lot*," Galamelon says.

Quint shakes his head. "Not enough. The first time I used the cane—it went, well, poorly. I tried to destroy a monster using Kinetic Crescendo. But I only sliced it in half—"

"Sliced it in half! That's fantastic, guy!"

"Ehh, no. I also mistakenly teleported us."

Galamelon nods wisely. "Yep, that'll happen. Incantations of destruction aren't easy. For master conjurers like *me*, they're a breeze. But tougher for a novice. Best left to the experts."

"*I* need to be an expert," Quint says.

"And that's why you got me!" Galamelon says, flashing a wide, crooked grin. "Now let's see what we're working with here . . ."

Galamelon opens the book and begins flipping the pages. He shakes his head at conjuration after conjuration, until he finally says, "Bingo! This one! We'll start with something simple."

Quint frowns at the otherworldly text. "But I can't read that."

Galamelon waves a hand dismissively. "Pssht. It's a ton of words anyway—no need to bother with them. All you *really* need is the name of the conjuration: Ňåżž Œŭl. Which, in your language, translates to 'Orb of Protection.' Just do the movements in the little doodle, there, and then say those three words. You were born to conjure this conjuration, guy!"

Quint stares at the page. Maybe he *can* ignore the words. Maybe it's like ordering from the menu at Denny's, the ones with all the pictures. And when you can't decide between the Triple-Chocolate Super Slam or the Lean Lumberjack Trio, the pictures always steer you in the right direction.

"OK," Quint says. "If you say so . . ."

He begins swinging the cane in a wave pattern, and as it begins to hum, he shouts, "Orb of Protection!" and pulls the trigger-switch.

Something like Day-Glo silly string explodes from the tip of the cane, and . . .

SCHLA-BOOM!

Galamelon rolls his eyes—but Dirk's hard glare catches him, and he grudgingly clambers into the back of the Wrangler. "Don't pay any attention to those two," Galamelon says, as Quint follows him. "What matters is that ya did it!"

"*Did* I, though? What I conjured didn't look like this," Quint says, tapping the page. "The image depicts something more akin to a protective bubble . . ."

"Protective bubble, oodles of noodles, same difference," Galamelon says. "Now, c'mon—we're off to a grand start. Let's keep it going, guy!"

And thus begins . . .

𝕬 𝕮𝖔𝖓𝖏𝖚𝖗𝖊𝖗 𝕿𝖗𝖆𝖎𝖓𝖎𝖓𝖌 𝕸𝖔𝖓𝖙𝖆𝖌𝖊— led by 𝖂𝖎𝖘𝖊 𝕮𝖔𝖚𝖓𝖘𝖊𝖑𝖔𝖗 𝕲𝖆𝖑𝖆𝖒𝖊𝖑𝖔𝖓!

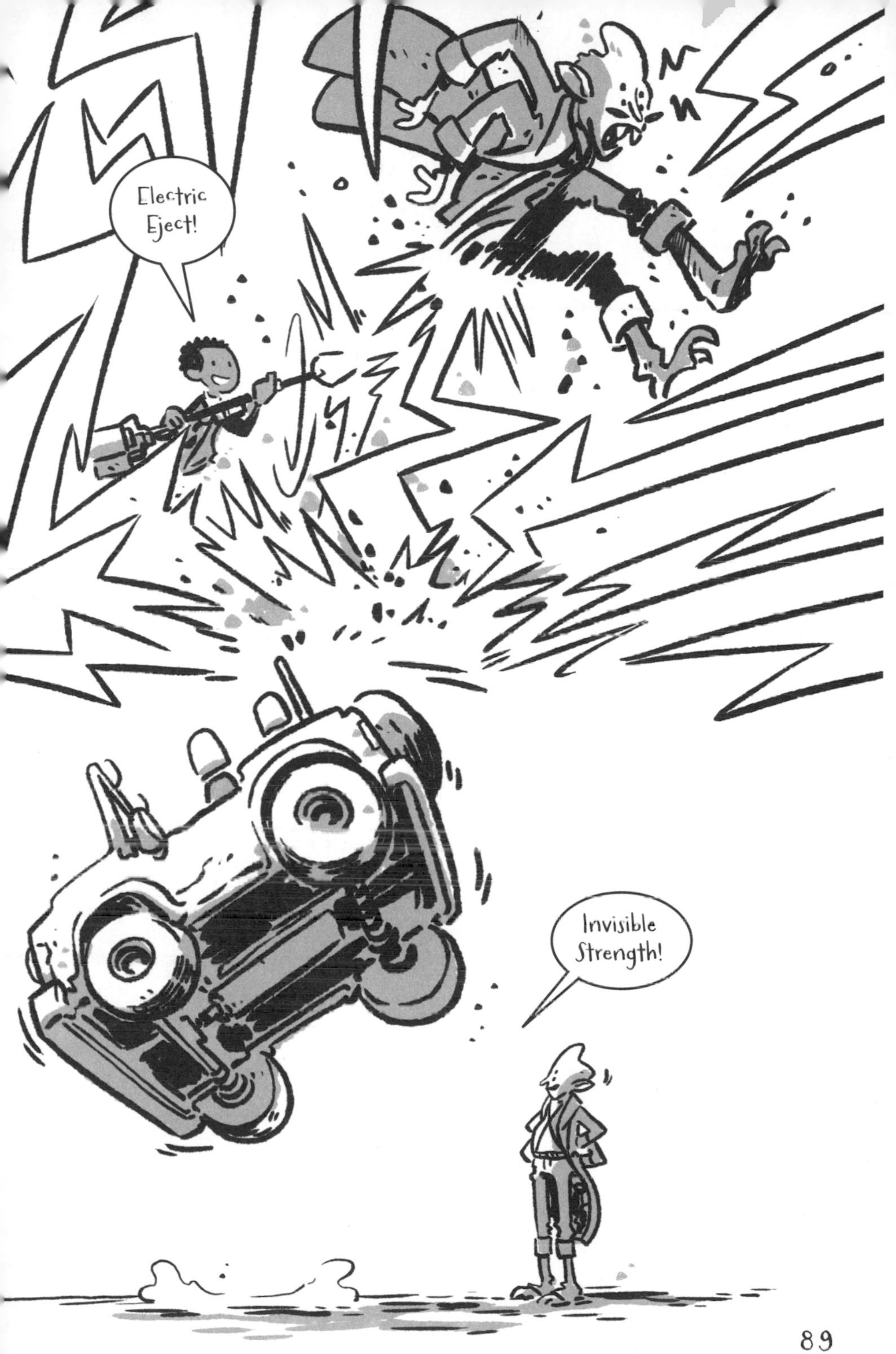
Electric Eject!
Invisible Strength!

The odor of electricity and sweat fills the air. In less than three hours, Quint has performed roughly thirty-seven conjurations.

"You're making tremendous progress, guy!" Galamelon cheers. "You're a born conjurer!"

Quint frowns. "But none of those conjurations were performed as intended. And none of these are going to help me slay a Drakkor."

"Well, it's like I was saying: incantations of destruction are hard. Can take *years* of training."

"I don't *have* years!" Quint exclaims. "I have a Drakkor to slay, like, *tomorrow*."

"Time is a tricky foe indeed," Galamelon says. "So jump ahead in the book—to the good stuff."

"Skipping ahead seems dangerous . . ."

"You know what your problem is, Quint?" says Galamelon. "It's your confidence!"

Quint eyes Galamelon. "If you truly are a great conjurer, why didn't you slay the Drakkor?"

Galamelon hooks a thumb at Kimmy. "Those monsterfolk were holdin' me back! Wouldn't let me unleash my full potential! Never let me cut loose—see, I'm a cut loose guy, like you—"

"I'm not really a cut loose guy."

"Exactly what I was about to be saying! I'm a cut loose guy, like you are *going to be*!" Galamelon says. He pulls Quint close. "You see, folks fear what they don't understand. Conjurers like us, we gotta rise above that. Block 'em out."

Quint bites his lip, thinking about Dirk's fear of all things conjuring. "I guess that makes sense . . ."

"Course it does! Now let's go. Skipping the boring parts, straight to the big stuff!" Galamelon cheers, flipping the pages. "Have a go at this one: Daggers of Doom."

Quint focuses, follows the drawing, and—

KRAKA-ZOOP!

A beam of smoldering plasma blasts Galamelon out of his seat and clean off the Wrangler. He hits the ground in a heap.

The sun is sinking behind the horizon when Kimmy says, "The Drakkor's lair is just beyond the next town. But it's too dangerous to travel in the dark. Also, I don't like driving at night."

"I'll drive!" Galamelon says, waving an arm around.

"No ya won't!" Kimmy replies, waving *two* arms around in response.

She tugs on the gearshift, tap-taps her foot, and steers Carol toward a motel just off the road. "All right, crew," she says. "We'll rest here for the night. Group sleepover! Get cozed!"

They all clamber out of the Jeep and glance around: they're at the rundown remains of a no-star, roadside dive called the Scandinavian Inn . . .

"It is decimated," Kimmy explains. "The Drakkor has been here—he's destroyed this place. And this is—"

"OOH!" Galamelon exclaims. "I spy video blackjack!"

Galamelon rushes off while Quint and Dirk wait patiently for Kimmy to continue.

Kimmy swallows hard. "This is what Fleeghaven will look like, soon, if you don't slay the beast . . ."

Quint swallows. *I need to master my conjuring skills. Fast.*

"Galamelon," Quint calls, stepping down into the pool. "My cane has finished charging. Shall we get a few hours of late-night cramming in?"

Galamelon springs to his feet. "Absolutely, Quint. Too bad—I was just about to summon a hearty banquet for our companions. But, mentor duty calls. Let's leave them to their sad, not-fancy foods. You've got training to do."

Dirk shoots Kimmy a skeptical glance as Quint and Galamelon hike up and out of the sloping pool. "So, Kimmy, tell me," Dirk says, as he chomps into a triple-decker, orange peanut butter vending machine cracker sandwich. "What are we looking at tomorrow? You said the Drakkor, like, levels up between attacks?"

"Sure does!" Kimmy chirps, peeling a hunk off a large ball of dough and popping it into her mouth. "Gets bigger, scarier."

"Wish we still had Big Mama . . ." Dirk says, sounding mournful. "Or our BoomKarts. Or any of the crazy Quint contraptions we had back in Wakefield, at our tree house."

"You must miss home," Kimmy says gently.

"Eh. Only a little. Home is wherever my buddies are—"

"OPEN WIDE!" Kimmy suddenly exclaims.

"Huh?" Dirk glances up just as Kimmy tosses a fresh glob of dough in Dirk's direction. Dirk opens his mouth, but—

Drooler gulps down the intercepted hunk of dough, and doesn't even have the decency to look ashamed. He emits a high-pitched BURP, followed by a mischievous little giggle.

"Never seen him do that before," Dirk marvels. "Little guy learns something new every day."

Kimmy nods. "Me too! I learned that your dimension has *a lot* of mattress stores. Like, way more than seems necessary? And you guys have these things called *families*, which is just b-a-n-a-n-a-s."

"Well, Kimmy," Dirk says. "Let's hope Quint is learning as fast as you and Drooler . . ."

Quint is *not* learning as fast as Kimmy or Drooler. At that moment, he is nervously staring down a rusted snack shack, which Galamelon has modeled into a makeshift conjurer's shooting range. A single soda bottle sits atop the cash register.

"This one's *extra* simple," Galamelon says, slapping Quint on the shoulder. "Just swing your cane in a tri-circular motion, say 'Arcane Jab,' and blast that bottle to bits. It's a low-level conjuration. A total cinch job."

Quint takes a deep breath and focuses on the bottle. He begins swirling the cane, and then—

"ARCANE JAB!"

"What?? Everyone loves big and destructive! Like I always say, 'No such thing as *too big* or *too destructive.*' That was my yearbook quote."

Quint shakes his head. "Why can't I do this? I don't even feel like myself."

Galamelon sets a hand on Quint's shoulder. "Maybe you're *not* yourself anymore. Think about it! Spooky, huh? And on that note . . ." Galamelon fishes an eye mask from his pocket. "Bedtime! I'm bushed. Sleep tight!"

Quint is left standing there with his mouth open and his cane hanging limply from his hands. He watches Galamelon descend into the mostly empty motel pool, cursing the condition of their chosen sleeping spot, before finally flopping into a half-inflated unicorn pool float.

"You OK, bud?"

Quint turns and sees Dirk walking around the edge of the pool. "No! I am going to let Kimmy down. I'm going to let *everyone* down."

"Quint—"

"I was doing multiplication at age four! Trigonometry at age seven. They were going to send me to the high school to take advanced biology, but I refused because the high school smells like cologne and tuna casserole!"

"You done?" Dirk asks.

Quint sighs heavily and nods.

"Good. Now listen," Dirk says. "I never crammed for a test. I don't think I ever even opened a textbook. And look at me now."

"You look like bootleg He-Man."

"Exactly! I turned out fine!"

"Fine won't cut it," Quint says, his voice heavy as he plops down on a rusted lounge chair. "I need an A+ in conjuring, and I need it now. Dirk, I've always been able to succeed at everything."

"Ehh, have you though?" Dirk asks. "Little League? Dodgeball? That week you tried to get into curling? Or—"

"OK, fine, not everything. But everything I ever *tried* to be good at!" Quint says. "So why is this so hard?"

"'Cause it doesn't come natural," Dirk says. "And that's OK. You'll figure it out. Just like Jack figured out how to talk to girls, even though that *definitely* doesn't come natural to him."

"Oh, it most certainly does not," Quint says with a laugh. "I was there the first time he tried to talk to June . . ."

"Yep, that sounds like Jack, all right," Dirk says, laughing a bit as he takes a seat on a tiny poolside table. "I hope Drooler never goes to him for advice . . ."

Dirk looks up at Quint. He's about to tell his friend not to stress, to just relax. But when he catches Quint's eyes, he sees real fear there. Quint needs serious, legit conjuring skills— skills he doesn't have.

"HEY, YA PAIR OF NIGHT OWLS!" Kimmy shouts. She suddenly appears at the pool ladder, head peeking up—and Dirk's happy for the interruption. "You oughtta get some snooze time. You'll need your energy—tomorrow afternoon, the clock strikes Drakkor-slaying, queen-saving o'clock."

Kimmy starts back down the ladder, then pauses and pokes her head up again. "Don't forget . . . We're here because you guys are *heroes*. You two dudes better not let me down. 'Cause if you do, I'm gonna look *so* dumb."

Kimmy then slips from the ladder and splashes into the water below. A moment later, she calls out, "Even dumber than that!"

Quint and Dirk, left alone, stare out at the terrifying wasteland beyond. The towering

Viking monument looms over them. Quint and Dirk both feel a chill as they think about the Drakkor, awaiting, somewhere out there.

"Get some sleep," Dirk says finally. "Kimmy's right, we're gonna need our energy . . ."

And that word —"energy"—gets Quint thinking. As soon as Dirk climbs down into the pool, Quint returns to his book. And he has a plan . . .

chapter nine

Dirk jerks awake at the sound of a loud *SCHWOOM* followed by a *BANG*!

"Whazzat?" he grunts, half-asleep but already kicking off the flea-bitten motel bathrobe he was using as a blanket. Drooler *meep-meep*s good morning as Dirk grabs his sword.

Coming out of the pool, Dirk spots Quint. He's standing with his conjurer's cane on the pool's uprooted diving board, masked in silhouette by the morning sun.

"Dude, you're already up?" Dirk asks, still rubbing gunk out of his eyes.

"More like . . . *still up*!" Quint says with a sly—and slightly unnerving—grin.

"Did you get *any* sleep?"

"Oh, sure! Got a solid three minutes. I slept standing up. Like a horse!"

Dirk peers at Quint sideways, noticing he looks a little twitchy, like he pounded ten movie theater–sized fountain sodas. "Are you all right, bud?" Dirk asks. "I haven't seen you this wired since that time you tried to control Big Mama with your brain . . ."

"That would have worked if you hadn't stopped me," Quint says, flashing a way-too-wide smile. "Now, to your point—I may be a bit over-energized, yes, but I feel GREAT. I crammed HARD, friend. And I believe I have mastered ONE conjuration: Kinetic Volley. It is the second level of the Kinetic Dynamo conjuration tree."

"Wait . . . Kinetic Dynamo? Isn't that the one that teleported us??"

"Close! It was Kinetic *Crescendo* that teleported us—that's the seventh level of the Kinetic Dynamo conjuration tree. But the technology in my cane allows me to adjust the *energy*—the power, if you will—of the conjuration. Do you follow?"

Dirk scratches his chin. "Uh, yeah, I follow. Maybe. But explain it again for Drooler."

Quint beams, happy to continue. "Every conjuration has levels—just like a skill-tree in a video game! At its maximum level, Kinetic Dynamo produces enough energy to teleport, like you saw. But at a lower level, it's akin to a small laser blast. By adjusting a few dials and knobs, it becomes a less powerful—and less teleporty—conjuration! Behold!"

Drooler *meeps* once. "Uh-huh, Drooler," Dirk responds. "*Whoa* is right."

Just then, Kimmy shambles over. Her tall ears are sticking out at wild angles, like monster bedhead. "Too early," she mutters. "Awake bad."

"Look who's up!" Quint calls cheerfully. "Hey, sleepyhead, you ready to slay a Drakkor?"

Kimmy cocks her head, a little surprised by Quint's energetic eagerness, then grins. "Ooh, yesyesyes," she says, suddenly all business.

They rouse Galamelon, who missed all the commotion thanks to a crude pair of chewing gum earplugs. "Just a little bit longer . . ." he mumbles. "I'm in the middle of a powerful dream. Dreams often foretell the future, and as a conjurer, I must heed the dream's call. It may hold much meaning . . ."

"You talking about *this* dream?" Kimmy asks, projecting for all to see . . .

"You're here to help Quint," Dirk growls, grabbing Galamelon's eye mask and yanking him to his feet. "So get up and start helping. Unless you wanna handle the Drakkor alone?"

"There is nothing I would desire more," Galamelon says. "However, I promised to guide Quint—so I must restrict the usage of my own powerful abilities. No easy task for a master conjurer like me—but I am being disciplined."

"You can be disciplined in the Jeep," Dirk says. "C'mon."

———

Carol gallops hard down sunbaked streets, speeding through the thick, humid air. The sun is midway in the sky when, at last, the adventurers reach the Drakkor's lair.

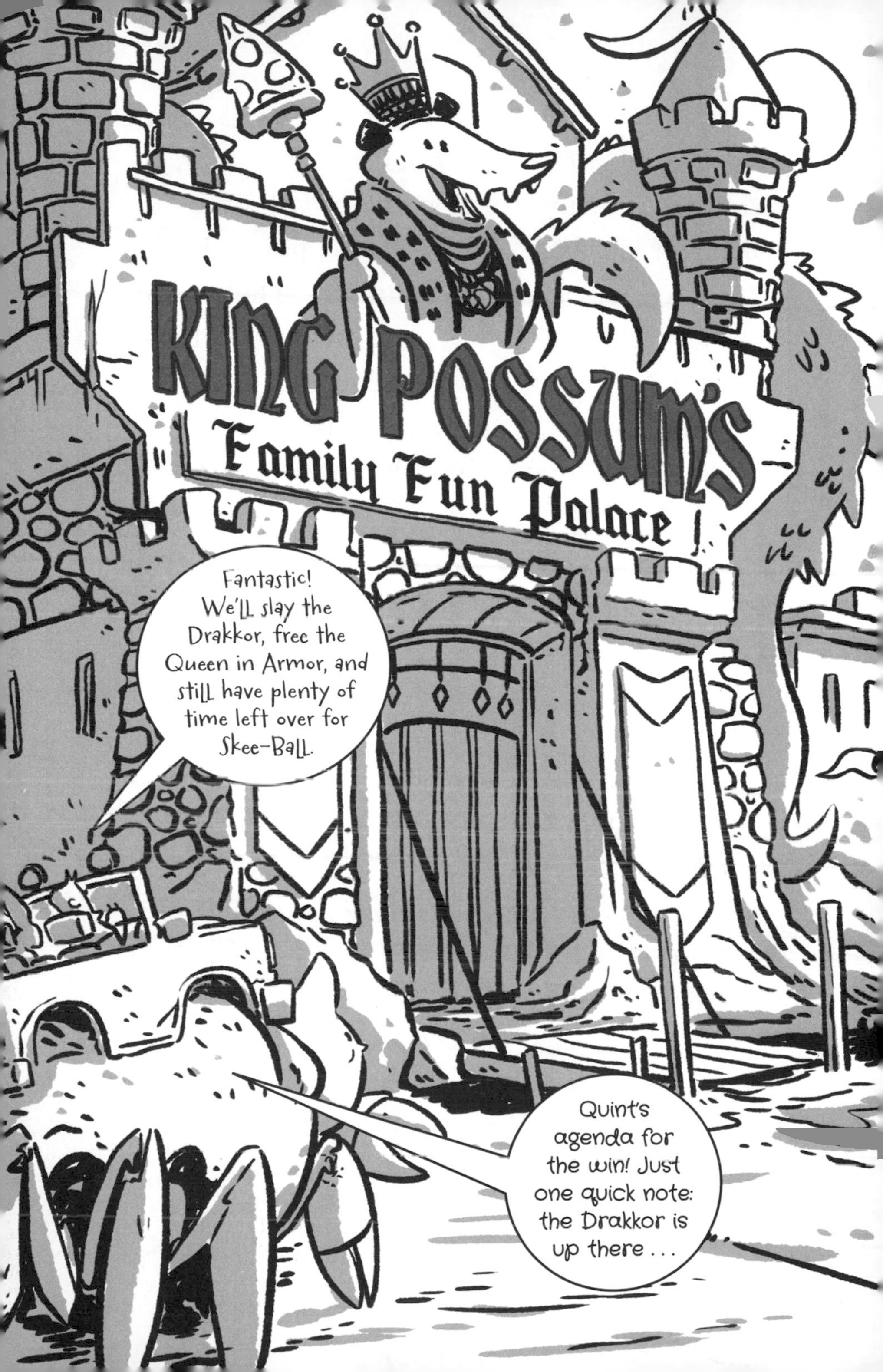
KING POSSUM'S
Family Fun Palace
Fantastic! We'LL slay the Drakkor, free the Queen in Armor, and stiLL have plenty of time left over for Skee-BaLL.
Quint's agenda for the win! Just one quick note: the Drakkor is up there . . .

Squinting, they see the Drakkor's spiked tail hanging over the side of the palace, snaking through gaps in the parapet. The rest of the monster is obscured by a plastic, paint-chipped spire. A raspy snoring sound can be heard, and the sleeping beast's tail rises and falls with each breath.

"So what's y'all's big plan?" Kimmy asks.

But Quint doesn't hear her. Staring at the palace, full of conjuring confidence, he can only think about *success*. "Dirk, when we pull this off—we're gonna be even more heroic than the actual Hero Quest heroes! They'll make a real movie about *us*, maybe! *Hero Quest 6!*"

Dirk grins. "Hey, you're right! And there'd be Dirk and Quint collectable popcorn buckets!"

"We'd get our own breakfast cereal!" Quint exclaims. "It'll be so bad!"

"Meep!" Drooler squeaks excitedly. "Meep!"

"I want in on this," Galamelon says. "T-shirts, beach towels, the whole shebang."

"Hellooooooooo," Kimmy says, interrupting their ill-timed brainstorming sesh. "You're supposed to be thinking about *slaying the Drakkor*. Not licensing opportunities! Although I would totally buy all that junk of yours . . ."

With that, Kimmy casts four very
embarrassing daydreams into the air . . .

Before Galamelon can explain that he was only eating them because they were part of a well-balanced breakfast, Carol yips and bolts toward the palace.

"That puppy isn't gonna live to see adulthood if she keeps that up," Dirk says, as they race after the runaway carapace.

They speed across the Family Fun Palace's parking lot and find Carol outside a plastic drawbridge, absolutely *devouring* candy from a toppled-over vending machine.

"Look," Galamelon says, waving toward the entrance. "Our host awaits us."

Crossing the drawbridge, they find an animatronic possum in royal attire: King Possum.

"I'll handle this," Galamelon says. "Gotta know how to talk to these highborn types."

"Dude," Dirk starts, but—

"Watch and learn, guy," Galamelon quips, procuring a card from his pocket.

King Possum, of course, says nothing.

"Ah," Galamelon says, winking at Quint. "A stoic ruler. He needs more than buttering up. Take notes, young apprentice . . ."

"LET US IN, MY MAN!" Galamelon shouts, then begins waving his hands, and follows that with a limp roundhouse kick, then a bow—which turns into an unintentional split.

While Galamelon's on the ground, groaning about a pulled hammy, Dirk presses a sun-faded SPEAK TO ROYALTY button on the animatronic king.

King Possum's voice is staticky and slightly robotic. "Greetings, peasants! If thou hast reservations for the Pizza Theater, journey upstairs. If thou desire a visit to the Home Run Dungeon, travel downward. And remember King Possum's one and only decree: HAVE FUN!"

"Thank you, O wise and benevolent king!" Galamelon booms, as he awkwardly rises from his accidental split. "In return for your hospitality, I shall perform a conjuration—one that will reward you with a lifetime of good fortune and—"

ZZZ-KRAK!

Before Galamelon can finish, the animatronic figure short-circuits: the king's eyeballs spark, his fur catches fire, and his head pops off like a busted jack-in-the-box.

"Entry granted!" Galamelon says. "Another success by the master conjurer . . ." Then, as he rushes inside, he squeaks, "If anybody asks, that thing with his head never happened!"

"Carol, you're on lookout duty. Hang here, 'K?"
Kimmy says, waving to the parking lot. "But don't
let that stop you from having fun! King's decree!"
With that, she follows the heroes in to the
Drakkor's lair . . .

So, let's get some fresh ideas going! No bad ideas! Except y'all's original ones, 'cause those weren't ideas, they were goofy daydreams.

The Home Run Dungeon sounds like the sort of place you'd keep a prisoner. Galamelon and I will go there—and use our conjurer abilities to free the Queen in Armor!

Then Kimmy and I will head up—and see what this Drakkor is made of . . .

I hoped to face the Drakkor, one-on-one, in a battle of magic versus might. But I reluctantly agree to partake in the queen-rescuing piece of the plan.

Quint and Dirk—the wizard and the warrior—bump fists. Dirk looks carefully at Quint. "You good, pal?"

"I'm a little hungry," Galamelon replies.

"Not *you*," Dirk sighs. "I'm asking my *actual* pal. Quint."

"I *am* good!" Quint says, with way-too-wide eyes. "Amazing! All that late-night studying is about to pay off."

Dirk notices Quint is bouncing on his toes and tap-tapping his cane. Dirk's not sure if his friend is too tired, too awake, or has *actually* become the world's most confident conjurer overnight.

"All right, then," Dirk says. "Be safe, OK?"

"*You* be safe, guy," Quint says, giving Dirk a too-hard poke in the shoulder. "Hero quest!"

Dirk swallows. Everything in his head is telling him Quint isn't ready for this. But he's also pretty darn sure that doubting Quint would be a mistake.

Quint's grin wavers for a moment, so Dirk quickly says, "I'll see you soon, then! You won't be able to miss me—I'll be the one lugging the Drakkor carcass."

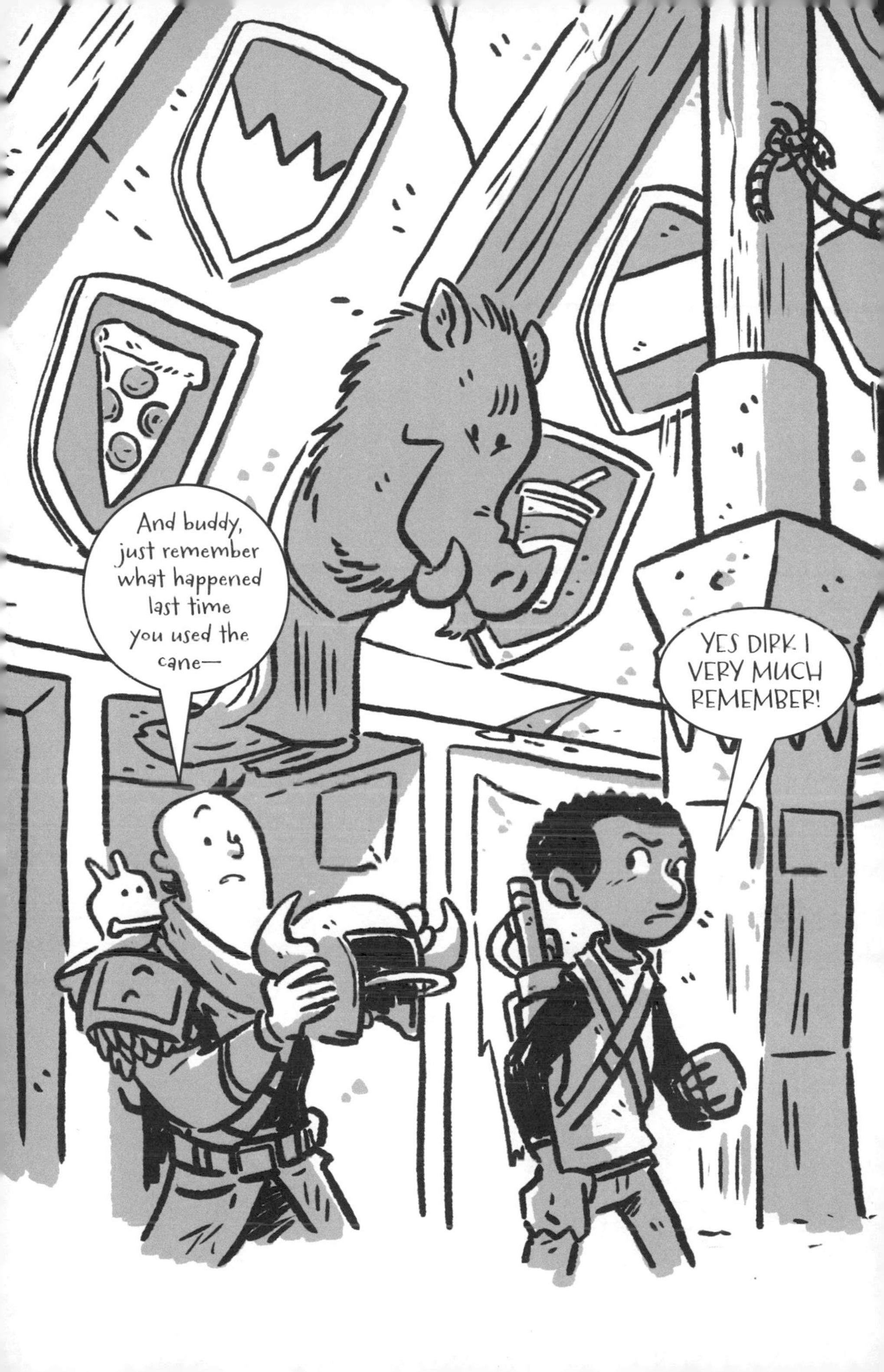
And buddy, just remember what happened last time you used the cane—
YES DIRK I VERY MUCH REMEMBER!

chapter ten

Quint and Galamelon make their way down a series of sloping hallways, each more dimly lit than the last. Battery-powered candles flicker in plastic sconces, revealing black oil-goop dripping from cracks in the ceiling, trickling down the walls.

"Smells like monster blood," Quint says. "And it's getting so dark I can hardly see . . ."

Galamelon pulls a necklace from under his shirt, there is a sudden *SNAP*, and then neon pink light fills the hall.

"Ooh!" Quint says, in awe. "What conjuration is that? Can you teach me?"

Glow stick necklace. Made it myself. Never know when a party might break out.

Oh.

But . . . I did not have it on me until just this moment. I summoned the necklace with one flash of my mind—and now, here it is, around my neck.

Before Quint can give that claim the thought it deserves, a sound stops them in their tracks.

"A strange noise ahead . . . Weird mumbling . . ." Quint says, peering down the shadowy hall. The walls are cracked—like something big squeezed its way through: *the Drakkor*, Quint thinks.

Galamelon nods. "My conjurer's ear does hear a muttering anear."

They press on, emerging into a cavernous hall filled with batting cages: the Home Run Dungeon.

The discomforting sound is clearer now: a crazed, nonsense sort of rambling.

"I must admit," Quint says. "That is one of the most unsettling sounds I've ever heard . . ."

MEANWHILE, DIRK AND KIMMY HEAD TOWARD THE PIZZA THEATER . . .

119

"Hey!" Dirk exclaims, suddenly processing what Kimmy said. "That's not fear you're hearing. It's readiness. Steely readiness. We're almost at the Pizza Theater, so I'm preparing myself. And stop reading my mind!"

"Okey dokers. I understand mind-reading consent," Kimmy says. Then a second later, she says, "Sooo, whatcha thinkin' 'bout?"

"Thinkin' about slaying a Drakkor. And how *not* nervous I am about doing that," Dirk says, and he doesn't care one iota if Kimmy can read that lie.

Black oil-goop drips down the walls of the winding staircase that leads to King Possum's Pizza Theater. The steps are littered with bones, and every few moments, there's a *CRACK* as one is crunched beneath Dirk's boots. There is one final *CRACK* as Dirk and Kimmy reach a pair of red double doors.

"Let's do it, do it!" Kimmy chirps. "Pizza Theater time!"

Dirk grunts and nudges open the door, revealing a large, circular auditorium. Rings of dining tables encircle a large center stage: a theater in the round.

Light seeps through fake stained-glass

windows—and Dirk sees discolored, discarded strips of *something* that are scattered and draped across the theater.

"Oh man," Dirk says. "I think that stuff is . . ."

"It does *not* smell nice," Dirk grumbles, yanking his shirt collar up over his nose. "It smells like that black oil-goop stuff."

Kimmy picks up one of the long strips and slowly rubs a finger over it. "This is *old*."

Dirk leans in, eyeing the strip. "Looks like a snake's skin, after it's molted. You said the Drakkor keeps getting bigger, right? Maybe it sheds this when it levels up. When it gets more evil."

"Doesn't taste evil!" Kimmy says, stuffing a balled-up wad of the skin into her mouth.

"You are so weird, Kimmy."

She pauses, chewing. "Huh. In fact, if I had to say . . . it tastes more like—"

"No, do NOT tell me. Just—*no*."

A soft, steady rumbling can be heard from overhead. Their gazes jerk upward, just in time to see bits of dust from the ceiling.

"I think the Drakkor's asleep directly above us," Dirk whispers.

Kimmy points across the theater to a door labeled ROOF ACCESS: EMPLOYEES ONLY. "Then that's our path to the Drakkor. Ahh, bummer— we're not employees."

"Pretty sure we'll be OK," Dirk says.

"That's the quest!" Dirk continues, trying to keep his voice to "don't wake the dragon" volume. "We are on a *Drakkor-slaying quest.*"

Kimmy's ears flick forward twice, like she's blinking. Dirk sighs. "OK, look, I don't love it either. But if we don't end this thing on the rooftop, then it's going to be bad for a *lot* more innocent creatures. I mean, I stepped on a *lot* of bones on our way up here. For real, once this is done, I'm gonna have to plop down on the curb and spend like twenty minutes digging bone out of my boot treads."

"Can I help with the boot tread bone digging?" Kimmy asks.

"Sure."

"Great! Then I'm in!" Kimmy says, starting across the room. "C'mon. Let's slay this snooze head nightmare."

MEANWHILE, IN THE HOME RUN DUNGEON...

"A nightmare," Quint says. "That's what that creepy garbled nonsense reminds me of . . . somebody murmuring, mid-nightmare."

Only one batting cage is closed—but they can't see inside, because piled against it are dozens of monster bones: rib cages, claws, and jagged tails.

"The sound is coming from that cage," Quint says. "I bet it's the queen, trapped inside!"

"I'll handle this part," Galamelon says, beating dust off his long coat, wiping dirt from his shoulders, and attempting to smooth out his shirt. "I'm an expert at talking to queens."

But before Galamelon can display his queen-chatting proficiency, a fresh round of mad shrieking erupts from the cage. He freezes.

When the noise finally ceases, it's Quint who steps forward. As he approaches the cage, he feels a mix of conflicting emotions: hesitant to discover what he'll find, anxious about what he might have to do, but still loaded with eager energy from his all-nighter cram session.

Peering through the piled bones, he can just barely make out a figure.

"The Queen in Armor! It must be her!" Quint cries. He clasps his hand around a bone—roughly the size of a T. rex's femur—and tugs.

The emotions inside Quint shift from conflicting to outright *colliding*. Quint feels like he's about to spontaneously combust as he considers Galamelon's advice.

At last, Quint releases his grip on the bones. "See, here's the problem," he says quickly. "The incantation I studied was Kinetic Volley."

"Then Kinetic Volley it up, guy!"

Quint shakes his head. "I wish! But if I don't perform it with perfect precision, I could annihilate the entire cage—queen included!"

"I see your conundrum." Galamelon nods.

Quint's throat is tight as he says, "Galamelon, I . . . I think I'd rather you handle this one."

Galamelon swallows hard, then glances around the dungeon. He eyes the hall, from where they came, then the bathroom, the ticket booth, an emergency exit, and then back to Quint.

"Hey. Hey, hey! No more of that face!" Galamelon says. "Now, it goes against my every instinct as your mentor—but I will allow you to sidestep this task."

Quint breathes a sigh of relief—then quickly tries to cover the sound with a fake cough. "Thank you," Quint says softly.

"You betcha! Now . . . the first thing I'll need is *that*," Galameon says, tapping Quint's cane. "Normally, I'd make do with my ol' magic fingers, but this conjuration calls for *pizazz*."

Quint hands his cane to Galamelon, and—

Galamelon drops it. "Ah. Heavier than I remembered. Er . . . heavier than conjurer canes from my dimension, I mean."

Galamelon fiddles with a knob. He flips a toggle switch up, down, up again, back down again for good measure, then finally decides he prefers it up.

"Now, the readying exercises," Galamelon says, beginning a walking lunge.

With that, Galamelon levels the cane at the bones blocking the cage's door. A large bead of sweat rolls off his eyebrow and plops onto his mustache. He begins uttering a series of other-dimensional words that, to Quint's ears, sound like advanced-level incantations; but in fact, roughly translate to, "You got this, Big G. You're gonna smack this one outta the park. Doorway blocking bones—prepare to meet your maker . . . Right *NOW*!"

Galamelon jerks the cane's trigger-switch so hard that it nearly snaps in two. Untold gigawatts of power erupt from the battery, surging down the length of the cane!

"Uh-oh," Galamelon whispers, as—

BZZZ-ZAP!

Wild, undirected energy explodes from the cane, filling the room with blinding white light!

"I can't see!" Quint cries, throwing his hands up to shield his eyes.

"Oh, good!" Galamelon shouts. "I was afraid it was just me!"

Blinded, neither Quint nor Galamelon sees the zipping stream of electricity miss the bones and the batting cage entirely—and instead slam into a nearby circuit breaker. There is a sudden electrical crack as a backup generator clicks on, restoring power to every level of the Possum Palace—including the Pizza Theater . . .

MEANWHILE, IN THE PIZZA THEATER ...

Dirk and Kimmy are crossing to the roof-access door when a booming voice suddenly fills the room—

"Welcome to King Possum's Pizza Theater! Put your hands together if you're ready for a show!"

Dozens of overhead spotlights flash on, showering the stage in green and orange light. Music erupts: a high-pitched, carnival-like tune. There's a loud rumble, and the palace shakes and shudders as the stage slowly starts to rotate.

A dozen animatronic figures come into view. They look like members of King Possum's extended family—a posse of mechanical rodents with lifeless, too-big eyes and dirty, matted fur.

"Who turned on the power?!" Dirk exclaims.

"I bet *they* did!" Kimmy exclaims, gleefully clapping her hands. "They love dancing and singing so much that they brought themselves to life!"

Dirk frowns.

"Pssht, whatever," Kimmy says. "Your friend has a magic cane, and I'm crazy for thinking robot animals can bring themselves to life using only the power of love?"

The characters' beaks and mouths flap open as they break out in song . . .

Suddenly, the theater trembles. Dust rains down and ceiling tiles crash to the floor.

"Uh-oh," Dirk says. "Think all the singing and stage-spinning woke the Drakkor . . . "

Kimmy says. "Drat. There goes your shot at a big, brave sleep-murder."

"Don't call it a sleep-murder!"

The turntable stage is spinning faster now, and the MC's voice booms again: *"And here comes King Possum's royal court! Cheesy Chipmunk, Eddie Spaghetti, Frankie the Funky Ferret, and all their animal pals!"*

"Ooh, a platform is rising from beneath the stage," Kimmy says. "Neato!"

"Not neato," Dirk says, watching as three costumed characters appear. "Those dudes do *not* look animatronic. Look at those huge, puffy getups—that's like Disney stuff. But, like, the bootleg Times Square version."

"Maybe we'll see the famous Nearly Nude Wild West Guitar Bard!" Kimmy exclaims.

For a split-second, Dirk thinks he's about to confront the first real live humans he's seen since the start of the monster-zombie apocalypse—not counting his friends or Evie Snark.

But then he sees that their puffy costumes are torn and splattered with monster blood. The bobblehead tops of their costumes tilt and sway and finally tumble off, revealing the faces underneath: foul and rotting, with flesh-hungry eyes.

They're not human. Not anymore.

"Zombies . . ." Dirk says. "Weird pizza show zombies."

MURGHH!

At once, the zombies attack! Kimmy grabs a microphone stand from the edge of the stage, twirls it twice, then swings!

"Don't beat 'em up too bad!" Kimmy shouts while spinning to plant the microphone stand's base into Frankie Ferret's chest. "We must follow the Code of the Blarg Slayer!"

Dirk rolls his eyes. *Freaking Jack . . .*

RRRR-RIP!

Dirk's gaze shoots upward. The ceiling is being torn apart—peeled open like a sardine can.

"The Drakkor!" Kimmy cries as a blade-like claw rips the ceiling fully open, flooding the theater with daylight.

Dirk reels back, shielding Drooler, as the Drakkor plunges through the opening!

CRASH!

The force of the Drakkor slamming onto the spinning stage feels nearly nuclear. Chunks of bone and half-eaten monster carcasses fall with it, raining down like a hailstorm of rotten flesh. For a moment, it feels like the entire palace might collapse.

A torrent of dread fills Dirk as he sees the Drakkor, up close, for the first time . . .

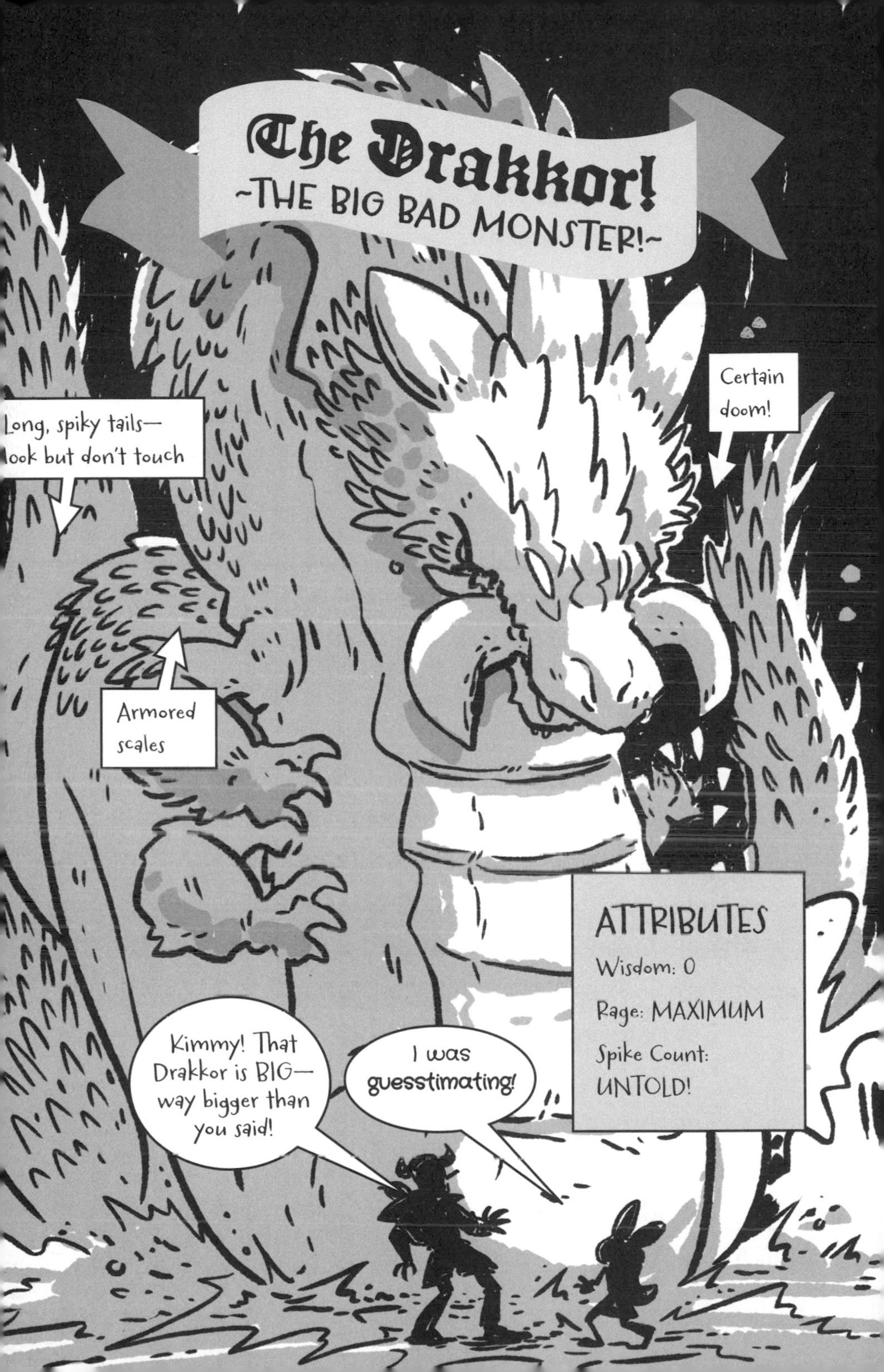
The Drakkor!
~THE BIG BAD MONSTER!~
Long, spiky tails—look but don't touch
Armored scales
Certain doom!
ATTRIBUTES
Wisdom: 0
Rage: MAXIMUM
Spike Count: UNTOLD!
Kimmy! That Drakkor is BIG—way bigger than you said!
I was guesstimating!

MEANWHILE, IN THE HOME RUN DUNGEON...

Galamelon's conjuration was BIG—way bigger than Quint expected. He pulls his hands from his eyes and blinks. Relief floods through him: bright spots fill his vision, but his sight is returning.

He sees everything *shaking*—like the palace is a ship caught in the storm of the century. The batting cage trembles, the bones rattle, and then—*CRASH!*

The Flintstones' rack-of-ribs-size bones blocking the cage's door clatter to the ground.

"You did it!" Quint cheers.

"I DID?" Galamelon shouts, unable to hear much over the loud *WHAP* sounds now echoing through the room: baseballs being rocketed out of newly powered-up pitching machines.

Galamelon looks down at the cane, up at the cage, and then down at the cane again. "I mean . . . I did! The conjuration is complete . . ."

But before they can celebrate—

"FREEDOM IS MINE!"

The queen BURSTS out of the batting cage! In an instant, her hands find Galamelon's throat.

"AIEE!" Galamelon shrieks. "HER HANDS ARE SMALL BUT SQUEEZY!"

The Queen in Armor is a fast-moving blur of dust and bonemeal, but Quint manages to make out a few details: a stubby tail, bone earrings, and spike-hair. And he's heard that raspy voice before.

Right then it hits him . . . he *knows* the Queen in Armor. He knows her very, very well . . .

Presenting . . . **Skaelka, the Queen in Armor!**

Armor . . . that looks oddly familiar?

Hand (which should be hold-ing an axo)

YOU ARE LUCKY I AM WITHOUT MY AXE, STRANGE MONSTER! IF I WAS NOT, YOUR LIFE WOULD ALREADY BE FORFEIT!

ATTRIBUTES

Love of Axes: Infinity

Happiness: −9, due to loss of axe

Sadnesss: +9, due to loss of axe

No axes anywhere!?

Durability: +74, on account of the cool armor

Royal Lineage: ZERO

137

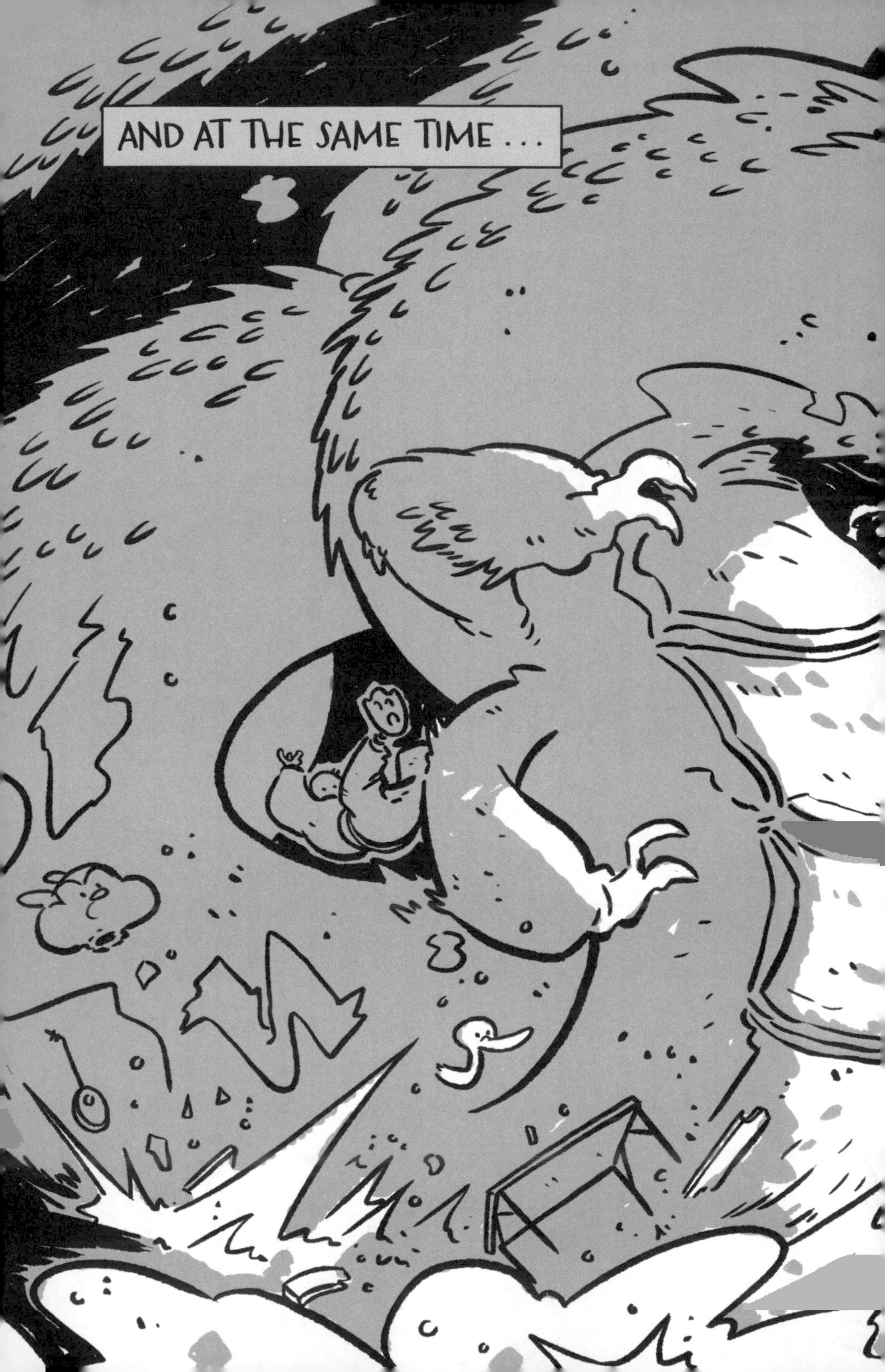
AND AT THE SAME TIME . . .

I really wish the Queen in Armor was here! Without her, our life is forfeit!

chapter eleven

In the now roofless Pizza Theater, sunbeams bathe the Drakkor in warm light. The monster glows like some creature from the depths of the ocean, orange framing its body in a halo.

"KIMMY!" Dirk barks. "The Drakkor is BIGGER than BIG. This isn't what we signed up for!"

"It's just the angle. Makes it look big. It's all perspective."

"IT'S RIGHT THERE!"

"OK, yeah, it's true, it's huge," Kimmy admits. "But you guys wanted the cool mystical map, and cool mystical maps don't come cheap!"

Suddenly, a massive claw flashes as the Drakkor smacks Dilly Armadillo, rocketing the creature toward Dirk like a sparking meteor.

The Drakkor's claws swipe again! Cymbals clash, a drum thuds, and more animatronic animals—the king's "royal band of rock-and-roll rodents"—are sent spiraling toward Kimmy.

"Incoming!" Dirk barks, swinging his sword at an advancing armadillo. But quick as lightning, Kimmy swoops in and—

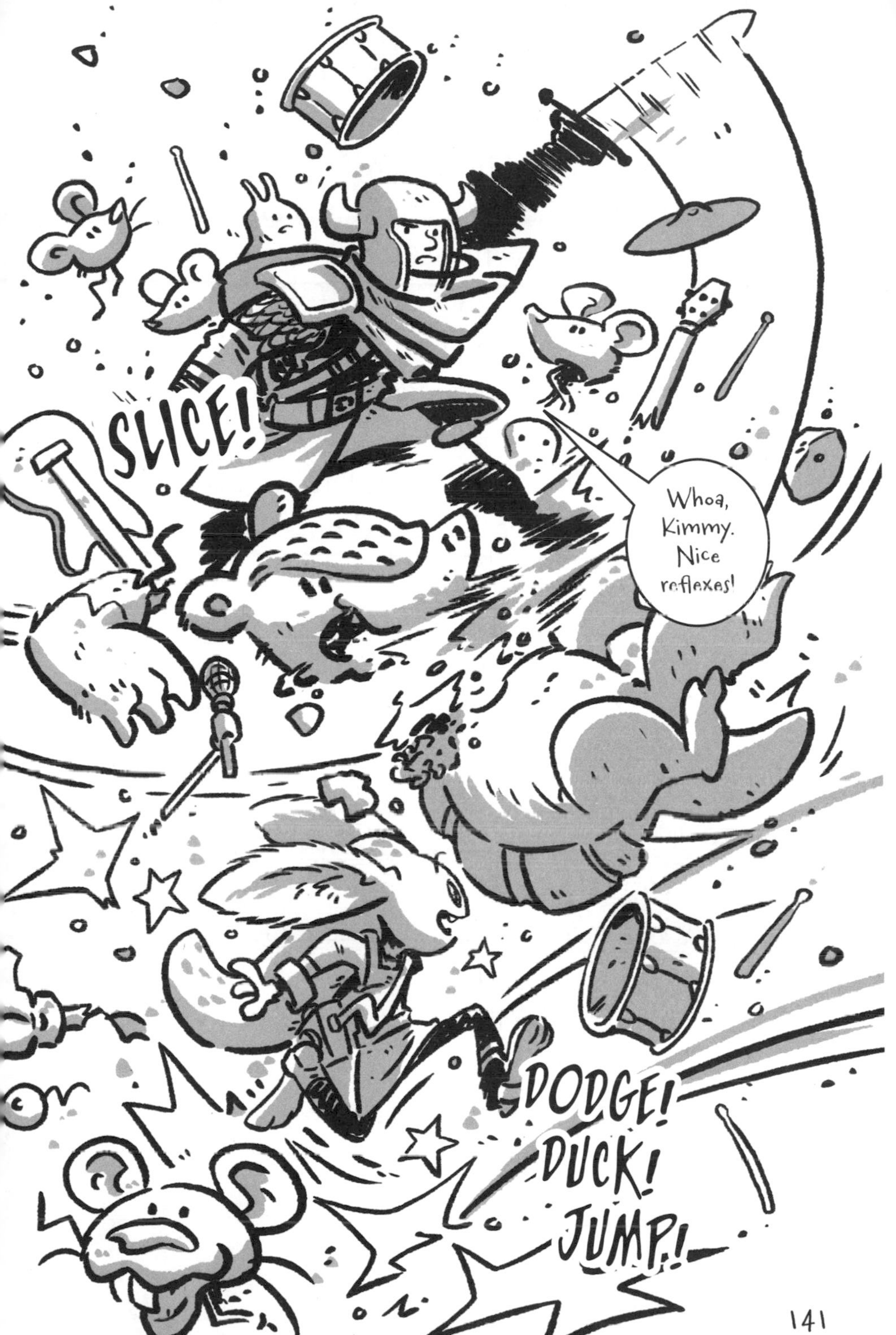
SLICE!
Whoa, Kimmy. Nice reflexes!
DODGE!
DUCK!
JUMP!

Drooler *meeps* twice. "I know, champ . . ." Dirk says. "She's ridiculously fast."

"*Brain*—and I cannot stress this enough— POKER!" Kimmy yells back. "I know where big ugly's aiming before it attacks. I get *inside* its mind, so I can see what's . . . uh-oh . . ."

Kimmy doesn't finish her sentence.

She's suddenly frozen.

"Kimmy!" Dirk calls. "What are you doing??"

Dirk watches her eyes swirl pink as her brain-poking focus on the Drakkor intensifies. And the Drakkor glares right back. It's like they're duking it out in the staring contest semifinals.

"KIMMY!" Dirk shouts. "You gotta move!"

But she doesn't move—not an inch, not half an inch. It's like her feet are nailed to the floor.

Dirk doesn't know exactly what's happening, but he can take a guess. Kimmy and the Drakkor are locked in some kind of mind meld—and Kimmy can't pull out of it.

It's like she's snared—trapped in a trance.

Dirk watches, in utter horror, as the Drakkor gnashes its teeth and takes a heavy step toward the unmoving Kimmy . . .

MEANWHILE, IN THE HOME RUN DUNGEON...

Quint watches, in utter disbelief, as the Queen in Armor wrings Galamelon's neck.

"Skaelka!" he finally manages. "*You're* the Queen in Armor? But . . . you're not a queen!"

"I know no Quints," Skaelka scoffs.

"Sure you do!" Quint says. "You know *me*! And I'm a Quint! And you know June and all the other monsters from Joe's Pizza . . . Look, you're even wearing—wait . . . *MY ARMOR!?*"

And as he says that, it hits him: none of this makes *any sense*. Quint's brain starts spinning.

The last time Quint saw that armor, it was inside Big Mama, many miles and many days ago. He assumed the armor was lost forever when Big Mama was destroyed inside the Museum of Histories and Ancient Antiquities.

He didn't think he'd ever see it again—and he can't fathom how he's seeing it now or how Skaelka came to be wearing it.

Galamelon suddenly lets out a strangled shriek as Skaelka digs in her nails—and Quint is snapped out of his reverie.

If Quint doesn't do something quick, Skaelka's going to choke the life out of Galamelon—and then what??

That's when Quint spots a wheeled cart, half-filled with baseballs. With no other choice, Quint heaves the cart toward Skaelka. "Galamelon, we're getting out of here!"

MEANWHILE, IN THE PIZZA THEATER . . .

"How do I get her out of there?!" Dirk exclaims, watching Kimmy, still trapped inside the Drakkor's thoughts.

The Drakkor's eyes remain locked with Kimmy's, using her power to its advantage. Its massive, clawed feet pierce the stage floor as it prepares to launch itself, but then—

"DROOLER, HANG ON!" Dirk blurts as he crashes in, tackling Kimmy to the floor.

Kimmy's pupils morph, and the pink color in her eyes fades away. "What . . . ? Where . . . ?" Kimmy murmurs, her mind all ascramble. Then she sees the looming Drakkor and remembers. "Oh, right. Impending death."

In a flash, Kimmy is up—and yanking Dirk to his feet.

The rotating stage turns again, spinning faster, and the Drakkor struggles to climb off. Its fangs snap while its claws swipe at Dirk.

"Too slow!" Dirk says, jumping backward out of reach, then dashing forward as the stage brings the monster's tails within striking distance.

Then—

"I'm not sure I'm glad . . ." Kimmy says as the Drakkor lets out another ear-splitting *roar*.

Just then, more costumed zombies appear! Staggering across the stage are a zombie astronaut, a zombie hot dog, and a zombie soda can!

"Why does this show have so many characters?" Dirk asks. "And what even was the plot?!!"

"Lady Mouse and Sir Pizza battle the stars, I'm pretty sure," Kimmy says.

The stage is spinning faster and faster, like an out-of-control Tilt-A-Whirl. Dirk can see what's coming—the centrifugal force is about to *launch* the zombies off the stage.

"This is an unwinnable battle!" Kimmy shouts, just as—

I wasn't! It doesn't take a mind reader to know that WE SHOULD SCRAM!

Unwinnable battle, yeah. I was just thinking the same—hey! I told you to STOP READING MY MIND!

The zombies land *hard*—crashing onto tables, slamming into chairs, and tumbling across the theater. But they quickly stagger to their feet, then charge toward Dirk and Kimmy, arms raised.

"Drooler, it's your time to shine," Dirk says, then swings his blade in a wide arc, showering the zombies in Ultra-Slime.

With the zombies momentarily blinded, Kimmy and Dirk run full throttle into the Pizza Theater's kitchen. They ignore the questionable grease stains and never-been-washed griddles as they race toward a server's door, down a back staircase, then finally burst out into a hallway.

"Think we lost the Drakkor," Dirk says. "For now . . ."

Kimmy stops, plants her hands on her knobby knees, and tries to catch her breath.

"That's never happened to me before . . ." she pants. "I was *inside* the Drakkor's mind, but I got stuck. I saw memories in there—and they weren't cute. The Drakkor was in some sort of fortress, ruling over it like a total boss. Look—"

Kimmy then projects an image of what she saw—

"We can chat about that later," Dirk barks. "Right now, we gotta find Quint!"

MEANWHILE, IN THE HOME RUN DUNGEON ...

Quint is watching the cart careen across the smooth concrete floor, and—

BAM!

The cart rams into the dueling duo! Skaelka is thrown aside and Galamelon is flipped up and into the cart. Galamelon glances around frantically, like a gopher peeking out of a hole. "Gotta get out of here, gotta get out of here . . ."

"No, Galamelon!" Quint shouts from across the dungeon. "You gotta get outta *the cart*!"

Quint is interrupted when Skaelka grabs a monster claw, long since severed from its body, from the batting cage floor. She raises it high, like a pseudo-axe. "Ha! Skaelka has acquired a new weapon: the Limb Cleaver!"

"Never mind, stay in the cart!" Quint yells. "I'm coming!" He catches up, pushing the cart toward the only clear exit he can see: a door beyond the batting cages.

Behind them, Skaelka is giving chase—and swinging her newfound Limb Cleaver.

Quint slams the cart into the doors and they crash open, revealing another winding hall that, he fears, will only take them deeper into the Drakkor's lair.

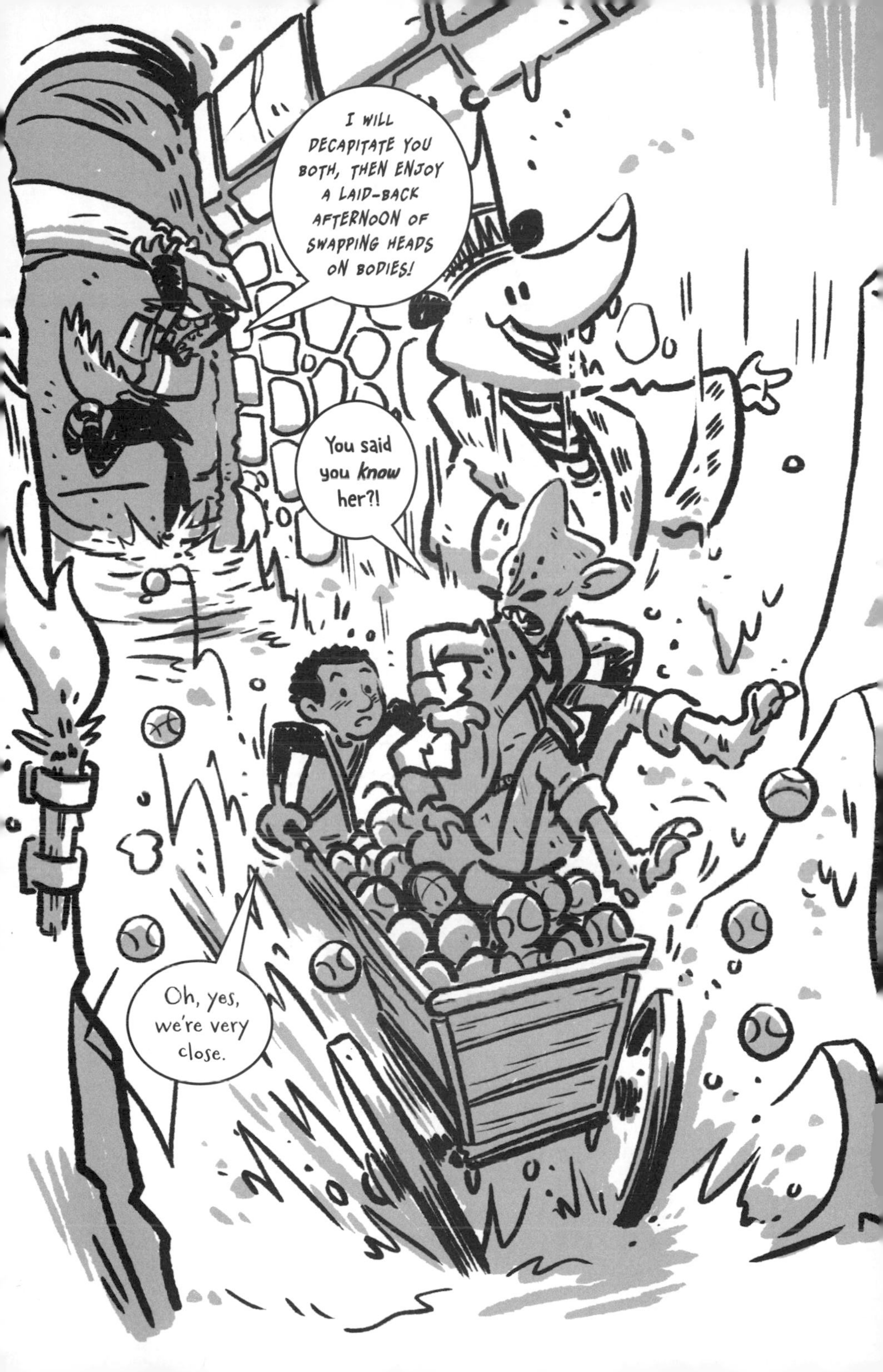
I WILL DECAPITATE YOU BOTH, THEN ENJOY A LAID-BACK AFTERNOON OF SWAPPING HEADS ON BODIES!
You said you *know* her?!
Oh, yes, we're very close.

chapter twelve

Quint bounces off Dirk and the cart topples, tossing Galamelon to the floor! "Dirk!" Quint gasps. "You're running, too? What are *you* running from?"

"The Drakkor," Dirk shouts. "It's a hulk!"

"We ditched it at the Pizza Theater," Kimmy says. "But it could be anywhere! This is its *lair*!"

"Ugh, you guys *still* didn't slay it? C'mon . . ." Galamelon groans.

"Just be happy we don't slay *you, con-man*!" Kimmy snaps.

"Wait . . ." Dirk says. "What are *you* guys running from?"

"HER!" Quint shouts, as Skaelka *bursts* around the corner—

"I am no one's Skaelka, strange boy!" Skaelka roars.

"Yeah, Dirk, about that? She's only *sorta* Skaelka . . ." Quint starts to say, grabbing Dirk and pulling. "You'll see. For now—RUN!!"

Quint, Dirk, Galamelon, and Kimmy speed down one twisty corridor after another, desperately trying to stay one step ahead of Skaelka while also searching for a way out.

"Skaelka, what are you doing?" Dirk shouts over his shoulder. "We're buddies!"

Kimmy exclaims, "You're *buddies* with the Queen in Armor?! AND the Blarg Slayer? Talk about friends in high places! When this is all over, we should hang! Like, all the time! I'm free most Wednesdays."

Suddenly, the end of the hallway ERUPTS in an explosion of plastic and concrete as—

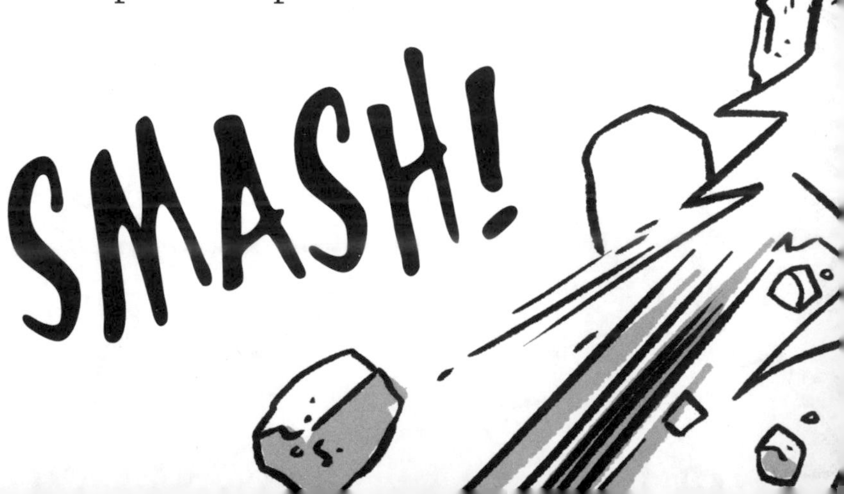
SMASH!

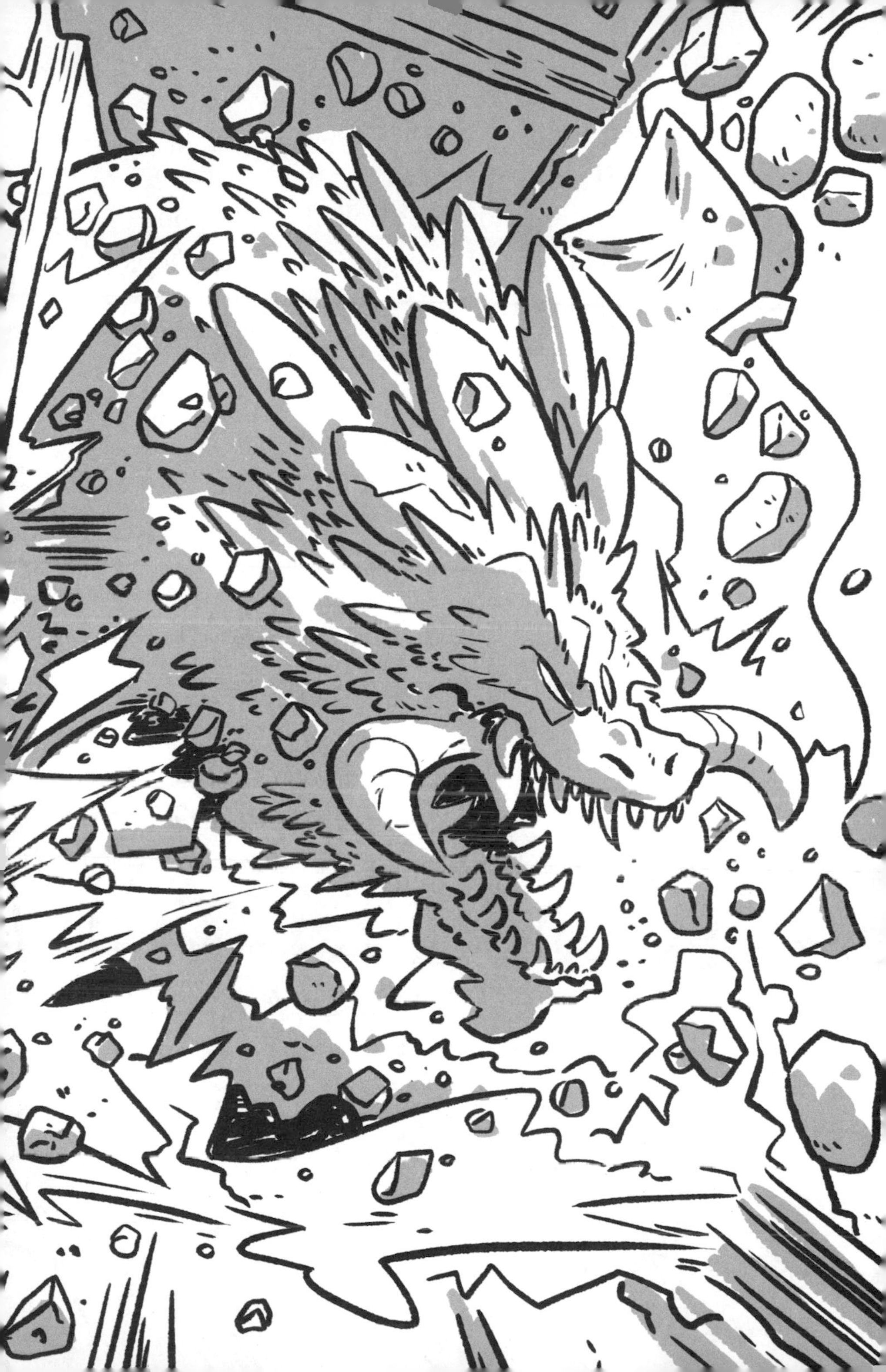

"Drakkor!" Kimmy shrieks, and at once everyone's trying—and failing—to screech to a halt. Their feet slip on the slick black oil-goo— Dirk tumbles into Galamelon, Galamelon flops in front of Quint, and Quint flips over all of them.

Only Skaelka avoids a fall, nimbly bounding up and over the heroes' backs.

"You there, Drakkor!" Skaelka barks, as she pounces onto the Drakkor's snout, unleashing a flurry of axe blows! "Skaelka is very pleased to inflict pain upon you!"

But even the great warrior Skaelka is no match for the Drakkor!

Icy cold energy begins to radiate from the Drakkor. Freakish purple light, like a strange frozen flame, flashes inside the monster.

"Uh-oh. I've seen this before," Kimmy says. "And we will *not* enjoy what happens next."

And whatever that is, Quint thinks, *I can't let Skaelka have a front-row seat.*

He lunges forward, tugging at her armor. "Skaelka, he's going to destroy you!" Quint shouts, yanking her off the Drakkor.

"Who dares—!" Skaelka cries as she topples backward.

The purple energy blazing inside the Drakkor builds, glowing brighter and brighter.

"Quint, the conjuration you were working on all night!" Galamelon says, fumbling open the book and flipping to a dog-eared page. "*Kinetic Volley. Do it.*"

Quint catches Galamelon's eye—and forces a nod. "All right," he says, though he sounds anything but sure. He plants his feet and grips the conjurer's cane in his hands.

Quint's entire body is quaking. The fear for his friends' lives—and his own—is almost all-consuming.

Remember, Quint, he whispers to himself, *use only enough energy as needed. You do **not** want another accidental teleportation.*

He flicks a toggle at the base of his cane, and a whining buzz rings out.

The smell of electricity—like an old Hot Wheels track—fills the air.

He holds the microphone close to his mouth, like a nervous kid about to belt out his first song at the school talent show. But this verse is simply two words: Kinetic Volley.

He repeats the words in his head, over and over, like a mantra. It's supposed to help him visualize the conjuration and *focus*. But instead, as he repeats the words, a terrible image manifests in his mind: he and Dirk being transported, nearly killed.

He tries to shove the awful image aside. But it's still there as the Drakkor's body radiates magenta and Quint realizes he can't wait any longer to perform the conjuration.

And that awful image and that horrible, still fresh fear—they cause Quint's finger to tremble as he pulls the trigger-switch and—

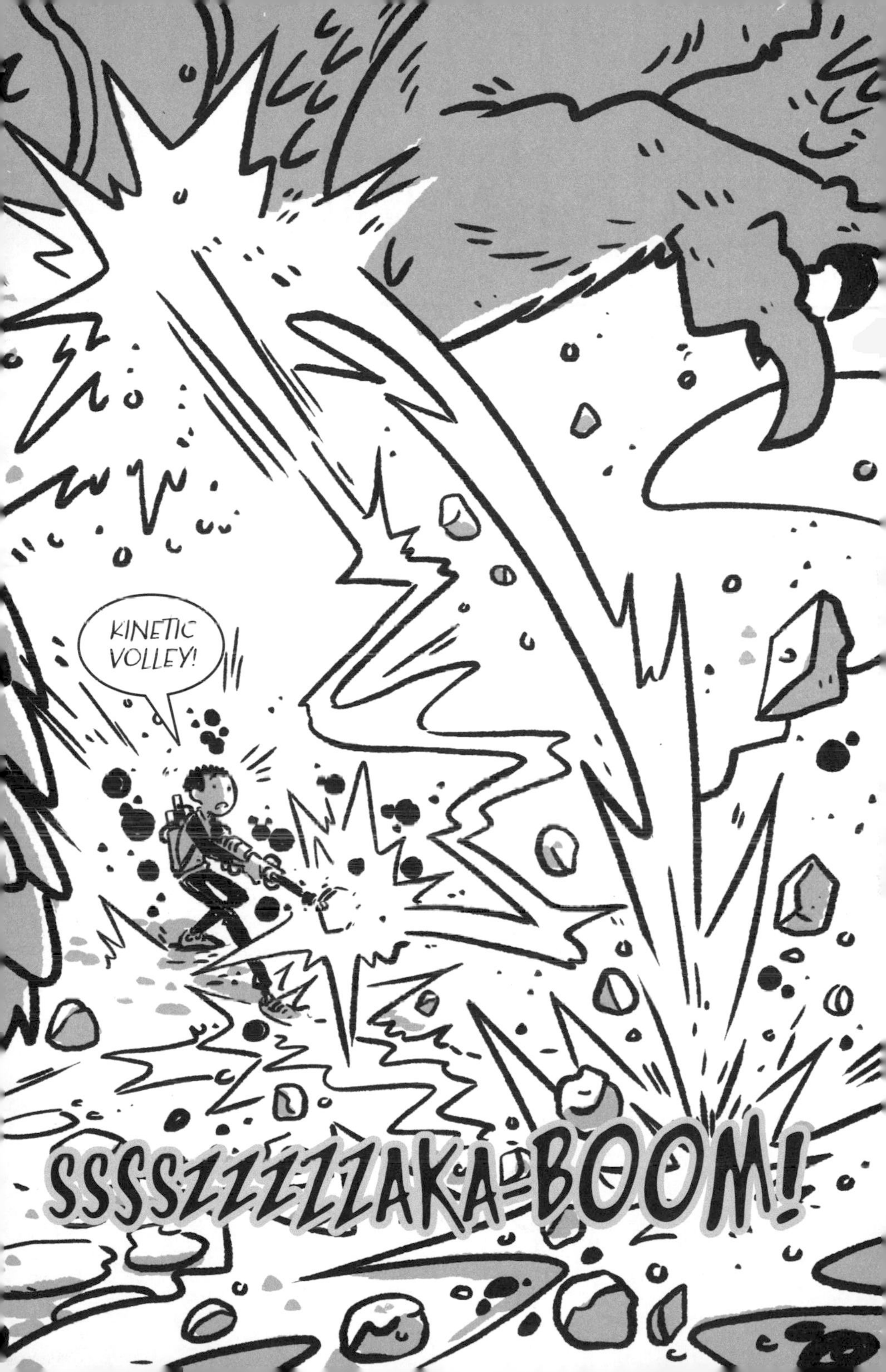
KINETIC VOLLEY!
SSSSZZZZZZAKA-BOOM!

chapter thirteen

They are suddenly falling.

Quint's incantation has blasted a blazing column of energy straight up and down, evaporating everything above and below, including the floor beneath their feet, the floor beneath that, *and* the floor beneath *that*.

Even as he plummets, Quint looks up.

Above him, he sees the swirling aftermath of his conjuration. The beam nicked the Drakkor, and the monster is howling, reeling back, black oil-goop spraying from a fresh wound in its chest.

And below them, Quint sees stuffed animals and plushies. *Thousands* of them appear to be rising up at rocket-speed as the heroes plunge through the final, just-exploded hole.

"BRACE YOURSELVES!" Dirk shouts, grabbing Drooler tight, just as—

FWOOOMP!

"I believe we fell all the way to the basement," Quint says, squinting. "Guess they store their merchandise here."

They can't see much beyond the peak of the mountainous stuffie pile—everything beyond is shrouded in shadow.

"Bravo, Quint! Rescued our rear ends, ya did!"
Galamelon cheers. "You used your conjuring
powers in our moment of need—and saved me!"

Dirk and Kimmy shoot Galamelon a glare.

"I mean . . . us!" Galamelon says, sinking
into the stuffie pile and getting cozy. "Oh, my
mentorship is going marvelously. I should open
a school after this. A whole franchise of schools!
And hang big paintings of me in the hallways!"

Quint avoids his friend's gaze. "We got lucky.
I was trying to perform a Level Two Kinetic
Dynamo conjuration. That was like Level Five!
We're fortunate to be alive."

Everyone glances around. Galamelon's right: Skaelka is nowhere to be seen. Dirk lifts a large stuffed armadillo, searches underneath, then swallows hard. Drooler *meep*s sadly.

"You sure did!" Galamelon says, again going for the high five. "Big-time vaporization!"

"NO," Dirk insists, shooting Galamelon a hard look. "Quint, you did *not* vaporize Skaelka. You just blew a bunch of holes through the building."

"But if you *did* vaporize her," Kimmy says. "I bet you at least vaporized her in one piece."

"That's not how vaporization works!" Quint cries. "If she's been vaporized, she's . . . *vapor*! Particles. Billions of—"

"Quick, Quint!" Dirk cries. "Turn on your flashlight! We gotta find a way outta here before she chops us up!"

"Nope. No way," Quint says. "Absolutely not."

Despite Skaelka screaming toward them, Quint doesn't move. "The flashlight is affixed to my conjurer's cane, and I'm never using the cane again. Galamelon, from here on out . . ." Quint heaves a heavy sigh. "I think it'd be best if *you* handle all the conjuring."

Galamelon lets out an awkward laugh-cough. "Oh, I'm flattered, but I couldn't possibly—"

SCRAAAPE!

Everyone freezes. Even Skaelka.

"You all heard that, right?" Kimmy whispers. "That heebie-jeebie noise that sounded like razor-sharp claws raking across cold steel?"

CREEEAK!

"It sounds like . . . shop class," Dirk says softly. "Like twisting metal."

They peer into the darkness, holding their breath. Slowly, a sliver of light appears.

"I think the light is coming from a door," Quint whispers. "To the outside."

"And by the looks of it, *something* is trying to come *inside*," Dirk says.

There is another scrape, another creak, and then a booming *CRUNCH!* The door is being bent, scrunched, and pulled by whatever *something* is on the other side.

"Ready yourselves," Dirk says, reaching for his sword. "That includes you, Drooler."

Drooler bravely *meep*s in reply.

The door cracks wider, jostling the stuffie mountain and causing everyone to sink down a few inches.

"I bet it's bandits," Galamelon says. "Or trolls. No, bandit-trolls. Who wants to bet? If it's bandit-trolls, I win. If it's anything else, you win. So, you can guess anything: rabid donkeys, tap-dancing fish, could even be—"

"CAROL!" Kimmy exclaims.

The door cracks open farther, revealing the young carapace.

"Nevermind, bet's off, you all took too long," Galamelon quickly says.

Carol's claws finish prying the door off its hinges—and the door pops open fully.

Suddenly, the mountain of merchandise is loosened, causing a tidal wave of stuffies that whisks the heroes out of the basement, down a loading ramp, toward daylight—

PALACE ESCAPE!

"We're free!" Galamelon cheers. He staggers out of the sea of stuffed toys. "Huzzah! Farewell, horrible pizza castle! Farewell, Drakkor!"

"BID FAREWELL TO YOUR HEAD, GIGGLE-BOTTOM!" Skaelka roars, leaping out of the pile, swinging her Limb Cleaver, before—

Carol gently lowers Skaelka, never releasing her from the straitjacket-tight embrace.

"And it's me," Kimmy says, turning to face Skaelka. "Remember? I hired you to fight the Drakkor in Fleeghaven. I'm your *friend*."

Skaelka looks Kimmy up and down. After a long moment, she says, "Yes. You are known to me, Kimbertron. But not this unheroic bunch."

"Wait, wait, pause," Dirk says. "*Kimmy* is short for *Kimbertron*?"

Kimmy's ears twirl. "Doy! What else?"

Quint takes a slow step toward Skaelka. "Hey, it's *us*. We've done, like, a *million* things together, friend. Don't you remember . . ."

"None of those happened!" Skaelka roars. "More lies!"

"Wait!!" Dirk exclaims, lighting up as a memory leaps to mind. "I can *prove* we're buds! Look!"

Dirk whips out his wallet. After a moment of scrounging, he plucks out a photo. "PROOF!" he announces, holding it out for all to see.

"Dirk, that's you and Drooler," Quint says. "From the mall photo booth."

"Whoops, ha, wrong photo," Dirk says, his cheeks turning pink. "But hey, while we're here, are we the cutest or what?"

"Meep! Meep-meep!" Drooler chirps.

"Anyhoo," Dirk mutters as he once again rifles through his wallet. Then, "OK, here we go. PROOF! AGAIN! For real this time."

Everyone leans in.

"Lookit," Dirk says. "That's us, Skaelka, back in Wakefield. And that's you, buddy, right in the middle, throwing up a peace sign. And . . . wait, Rover! What about Rover—"

"I would never give a 'peace sign'!" Skaelka snarls, silencing Dirk. "Skaelka loathes peace with every fiber of her being. That is a Photoshop!"

Quint takes a careful step toward Skaelka. "I can prove, beyond all doubt, that you know us. Here . . ."

Slowly, and only because Carol still has Skaelka in a hug-lock, Quint lifts her shoulder armor. "Look," he says, leaning in. "See that logo?"

"Though how you got ahold of that armor," Quint adds, "is a mystery . . ."

Skaelka stares at the logo for a long while—then at Quint. Finally, she says, "This armor saved my life when I dueled with the Drakkor. If you truly did construct it . . ."

She doesn't finish the sentence. But she nods once. It's not quite the Skaelka version of *thank you*—but it's close. And it seems to indicate a temporary truce. That makes Dirk and Quint *very relieved*, because it means they can focus on the *real* enemy: the Drakkor.

While Carol releases Skaelka, Dirk pulls Kimmy and Quint aside. "I don't understand," Dirk says. "Why doesn't Skaelka remember us?"

Kimmy uses her left ear to rub her chin. "When she showed up in Fleeghaven, she didn't know her own *name*. I've never met a monster I couldn't brain-poke—but I get *zilch* from her."

"Zilch?" Quint asks. "Why would that be?"

"It's like—I dunno—like there's a lock chained around part of her mind," Kimmy says. "And not a fun lock, like you use for securing your favorite rubber chicken. A bad lock—a sort of cruel, psychic seal. I could *maybe* crack it open. But right now, we've got way more urgent—"

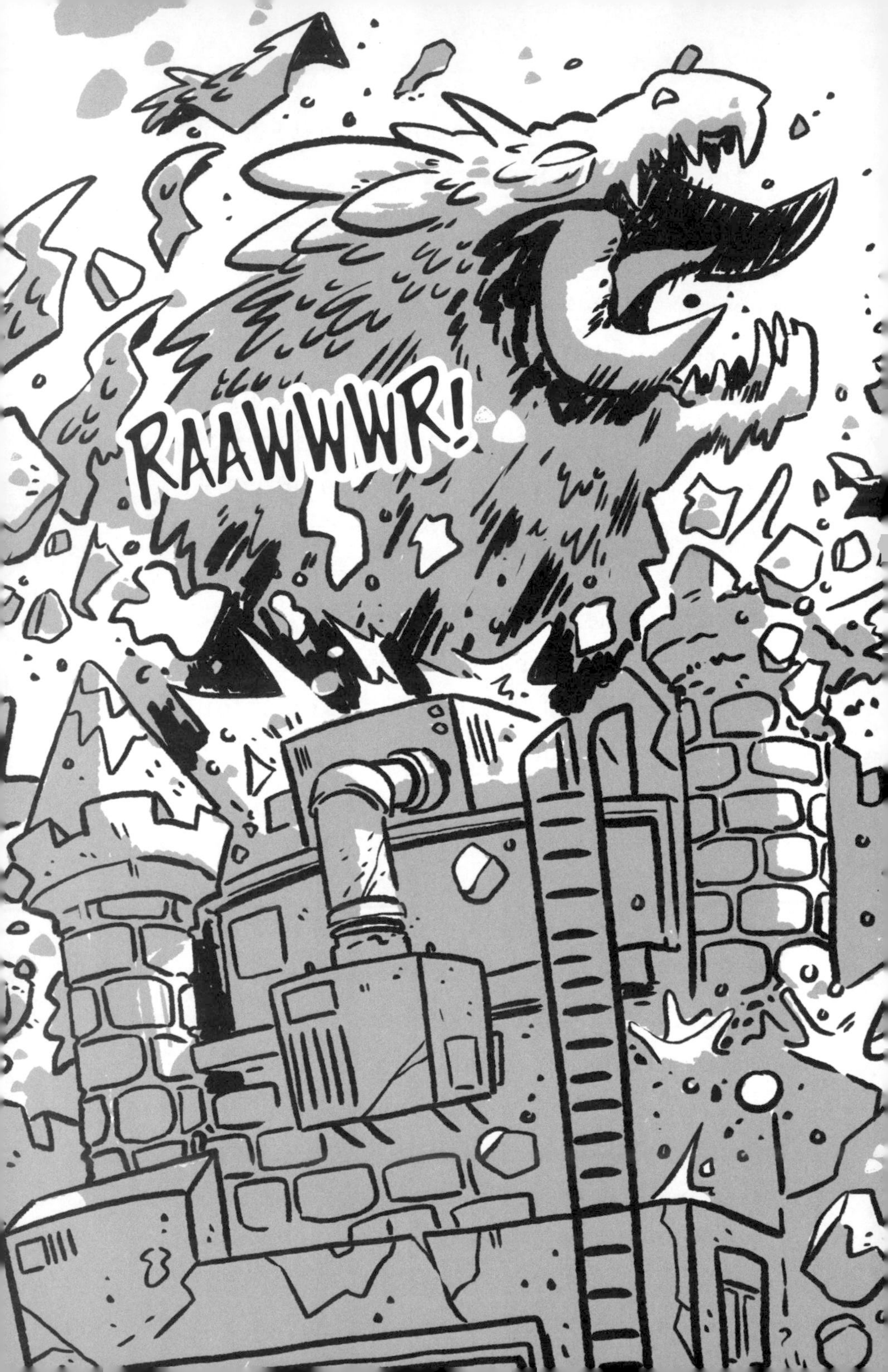
RAAWWWR!

"Well, that was good timing," Kimmy says. "'Cause I was gonna say urgent *stuff* and that urgent *stuff* is the Drakkor. We can't risk going back into the Possum Palace and *beefing it*. Fleeghaven is totally unguarded."

Drooler suddenly makes a *gorp* sound.

"Agreed, champ," Dirk says. His face is stony and his eyes are narrow. "So we go back to Fleeghaven. And make our stand there. Kimmy, we told ya we'd slay the Drakkor and save your town—and with Skaelka along for the ride, we still can."

Skaelka nods, tapping her Limb Cleaver. "I have unfinished business with that beast."

Kimmy's ears twist together in thought. "The Drakkor only attacks when it rains, remember? We *should* have time to get back."

Quint rubs his chin. "If we all hop on Carol—no tough-guy trotting, Dirk—and ride in a straight path, as the crow flies, we can make it in less than a day."

"So it's decided," Dirk says. "Back to Fleeghaven. No diversions. Straight as an arrow. . ."

But they take only two steps before spotting the towering array of signs ahead . . .

"Ha!" Dirk says. "Well, we're definitely gonna be goin' around *that*."

But at that very moment, a collective *moan* erupts; a shambling swarm of hungry ghouls—

"It's those zombified actors from the Pizza Theater!" Dirk shouts. "More of 'em!"

"Bet they brought their undead understudies," Kimmy says. "Those dudes are hungry for flesh *and* a shot at stardom."

"I question whether Pizza Theater actors have understudies . . ." Quint says.

"We have but one choice," Galamelon shouts. "ENTER THE MAZE!"

"Oh! Oh! No! I know what we should do!" Kimmy exclaims. Her arm shoots up into the air. "Call on me!"

"Um . . . Kimmy?" Quint asks.

"Go *around* the maze!" Kimmy says, and her eyes laser on Galamelon.

But it's too late. Galamelon is hopping up on the Wrangler's bumper, one foot dangling, pointing ahead. "That way, Carol! There are possum-sized Kit Kats in there, probably!"

Carol takes off like a shot—so fast that Galamelon tumbles off the back of the Wrangler. His boot gets snared on the tow-hook, and he's suddenly being dragged behind the speeding carapace like a busted tailpipe. "NEVER MIND, I AGREE WITH KIMMY!! WAAAAAIIT!"

Galamelon's cry fades to silence. In just seconds, Carol has rounded the first towering corn wall, vanished from sight.

"I'm gonna kill him . . ." Dirk growls, before quickly adding, "Pretend you didn't hear that, Drooler."

So with no other choice, Quint, Dirk, Drooler, Kimmy, and Skaelka enter the maze—leaving the Possum Palace and the zombie thespians behind . . .

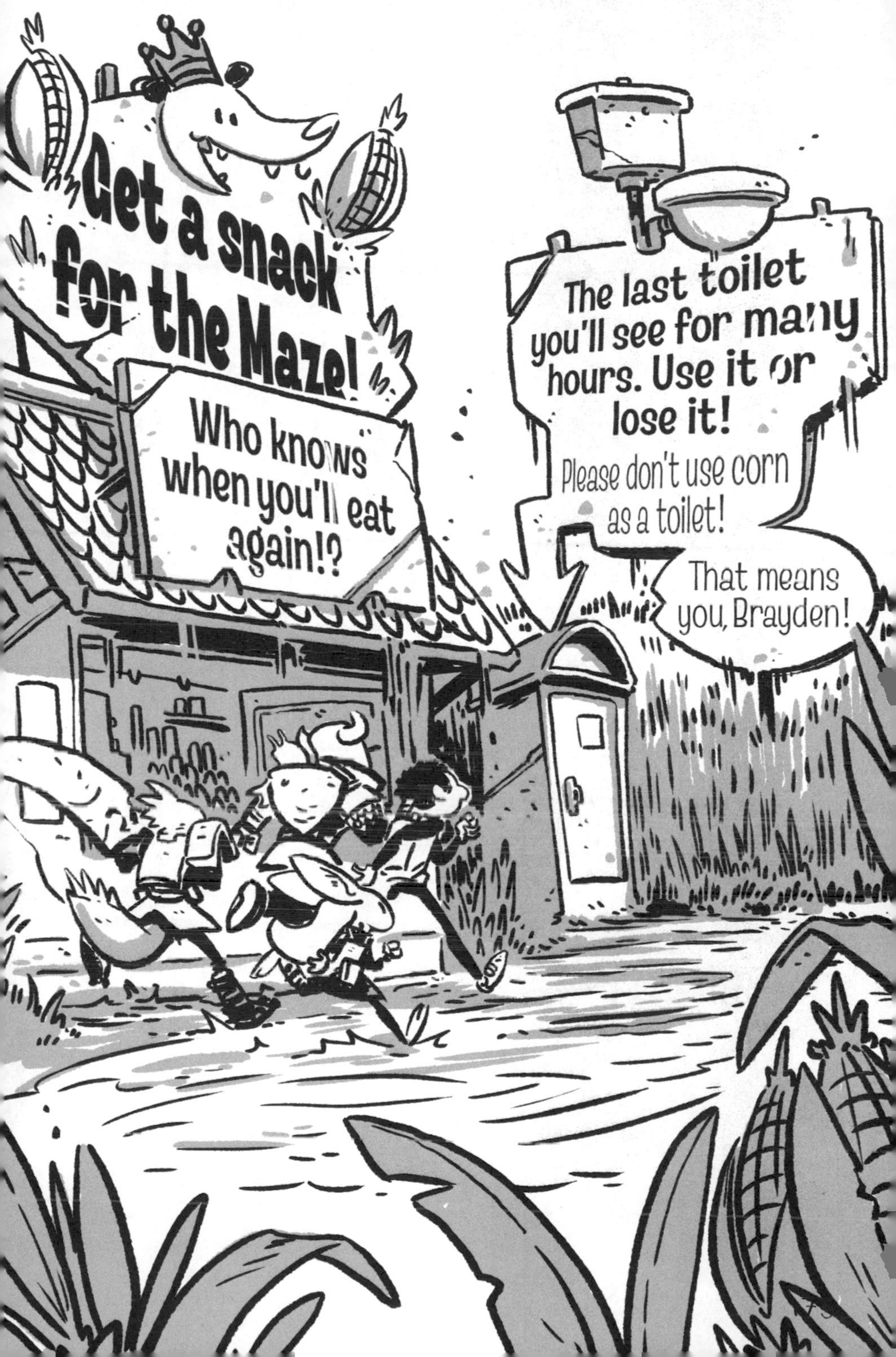
Get a snack for the Maze!
Who knows when you'll eat again!?
The last toilet you'll see for many hours. Use it or lose it!
Please don't use corn as a toilet!
That means you, Brayden!

chapter fourteen

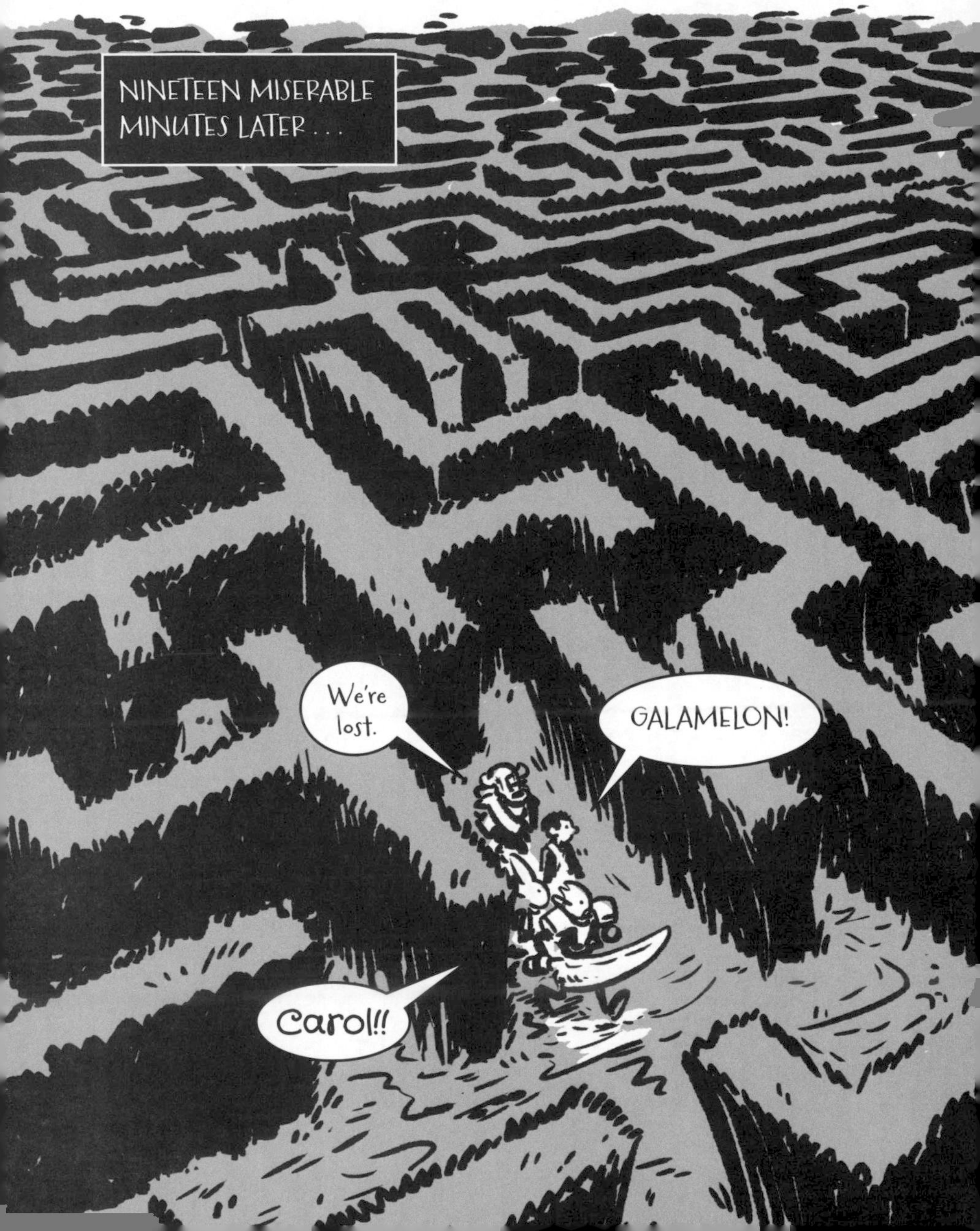
NINETEEN MISERABLE MINUTES LATER . . .
We're lost.
GALAMELON!
Carol!!

The more they walk, the more lost they become. And the longer they're lost, the more frustrated they grow.

"You know, if there are five hundred wrong paths through this maze and just one correct path, then the odds of us getting out of here are five hundred to one," says Quint. "Simple math."

"I got a math question for ya, Quint," Dirk says, nodding at the ground. "What's big enough to leave a track like *that*?"

Quint sees that the path beneath their feet is sunken and curved, like a giant bowling lane gutter, and the grass is flattened. "I'd rather not know," he replies.

Skaelka, who has been mostly stoic and silent during their trek, suddenly snaps. "An afternoon family fun maze is no match for me," she declares. "Skaelka refuses to abide the many lanes of this labyrinth! Stand aside, as I hack our way to escape!"

Skaelka swings the Limb Cleaver into the overgrown wall of corn, and—

SCHLURP!

Strands of some strange, gum-like ectoplasm suddenly grab hold of her Limb Cleaver. "WHAT MADNESS?" Skaelka barks as she's ripped forward and yanked *into* the maze wall!

"Quint, gimme a hand!" Dirk shouts, immediately grabbing hold of her. But she's being pulled deeper and deeper into the maze wall. In seconds, only her legs can be seen, kicking wildly.

"Let go of your limb-cleaver thing, Skaelka!"

Dirk cries as he tugs on her booted ankle.

Quint's hands wrap around her other leg. "On three," he says, nodding at Dirk. "One, two—"

Skaelka hits the ground with a wet flop, then instantly rises, shaking a gummy fist at the corn. She tries wiping off the substance, but there's just too much: her whole body is coated in the sticky, gloopy gel.

Quint shakes his head. "Thanks to that ecto-gum goop running through the hedges, we cannot simply climb or hack our way out of—"

GGGGRRRRRRW!

A thundering roar reverberates through the maze's endless pathways, sending a shiver through the corn husks.

"What was that??" Dirk asks, spinning. "Feels and sounds like . . . *rolling* . . ."

The sound grows *deafening* as some unseen terror closes in. The ground ripples like the earth itself might simply implode at any moment.

"It's a Squancher!" Kimmy shouts, hardly able to hear herself over the snapping and cracking of cornstalks.

"You know what it is??" Dirk asks.

"Nope! I just enjoy giving things fun names. I call potatoes 'spud lumps' and I *so* hope I get to meet one, someday! But not as much as I hope I get to meet a Squancher!"

And at that moment, she gets her wish.

The shadow of a rolling tank of a *creature* falls over them. Its ball-shaped body is massive, rising above even the tallest of the cornstalks.

But they only glimpse the creature for an instant. "Lucky us—it's not traveling down our path," Quint whispers. "It's one lane over."

The thundering sound fades as the monster barrels past, continuing through the maze.

"Nice of it not to hop over here and crush us or anything," Kimmy says. "Neato petito."

"Let's make haste," Quint says, marching ahead. "Avoid any carved-out paths—I'd like to make it out of here without meeting one of those Squanchers face-to-face."

But as they take the next corner, they discover their path is blocked. Blocked by one of the very creatures they hoped to never see up close . . .

DUN- DUN-DUUNNN!

chapter fifteen

The adventurers stand in a circular clearing at the maze center, frozen into terrified silence.

Thankfully, though, the Squancher is frozen, too. Frozen—'cause it's dead.

Up close, Dirk sees that its hard-shelled body is divided into shimmering, segmented sections. They remind him of the armored plating they saw, weeks earlier, at the history museum.

"Galamelon!" Quint cries out.

"And—way more importantly—Carol!" Kimmy exclaims as the young carapace scampers around the dead Squancher.

Quint is watching Skaelka. Her mouth is open slightly and her face is shifting from something like confusion to realization.

"You did not kill this beast, fool," Skaelka says to Galamelon. Her voice is a whispered snarl. "*I slayed the beast. Slayed it dead.*"

Quint and Dirk exchange a baffled, anxious glance. Very gently, Quint says, "Skaelka, I think you're confused. We've been together since we entered the maze. How could you have—"

THIS IS TAMMY. THIS IS MY AXE. MY AXE SLAYED THE BEAST.

QUVEACH

Oh. Well. I took care of it, like I said! I kept an eye on the monster, and I got some gunk on me in the process, sooo, points for me.

A ripe, rotting smell wafts off the Squancher, but Skaelka doesn't seem to notice. She's turning the goo-splattered axe over in her hands, eyeing it closely. Her tail twitches as she looks from the Squancher to her axe and to the Squancher again. She takes a step back, looking around—like she's seeing everything for the first time, but also like she's *not.*

When she speaks, her voice is soft—and she sounds spooked. "There is no doubt it was I who felled this unfamiliar creature. I do not know when . . . but I know that I did."

Everyone stands silent. A towering, corn-carved sculpture of King Possum looms over them—and it only further reminds Quint of his failed conjuration in the palace hall.

Drooler *meeps* at Dirk curiously, and Dirk shrugs. "Sorry, champ, no answers for ya."

"Hold on . . ." Quint says, eyes shut tight as he turns this new info over in his head. "That would mean you've been in this maze before, Skaelka. Which means you made it *through* this maze before. And could do it again!"

Kimmy's ears shoot up stiff-straight: hope!

But Skaelka grimaces. "I cannot remember!" she snaps, slamming her axe into the ground. "Skaelka's memories are lost!"

Kimmy says, "If the way out is stuck in your memory, I *may* be able to retrieve it. But I won't know for sure without getting inside that lovely brain of yours. Which means, well, I gotta get inside that lovely brain of yours. So—"

CRACK!

Just then, thunder erupts in the distance. The wind picks up, ruffling the cornstalks. They all look to the sky. Dark clouds are gathering.

"A storm is coming," Dirk says.

"Nice," Galamelon says. "My hair looks good wet."

Kimmy glares. "Galamelon. Rain means another Drakkor attack. *On my town.*"

Skaelka's body is rigid. She scowls, like allowing someone to pry around inside her brain is a violation she cannot permit, then looks down.

"Skaelka . . ." Quint says softly. "We can figure another way out. You don't have to."

Skaelka lifts her head and looks Quint in the eyes. There's something like recognition there. As if she *knows* she's heard his voice before. But then her mouth turns into a jaw-clenched scowl. To Quint, it looks like Skaelka was close to retrieving a forgotten memory—but that the memory has vanished again.

Or . . . could it be something else?

Quint wonders if maybe Skaelka's memories haven't been lost, exactly, but *stolen*? Tampered with? Skaelka has fought in countless other-dimensional conflicts and taken more battle damage than any warrior—but he's never seen her so shaken, so defeated.

And *who* or *what* could do that?

A breeze whips past them, carrying around the clearing, shaking the King Possum sculpture. Skaelka stiffens. "Kimmy, my memories are needed to help your monsterfolk, but they are also the key to discovering what has been done to me."

"I'll need the help of a conjurer," Kimmy says. "A *true* conjurer—which means you, Quint."

Quint swallows. "Are you *sure*? You've been brain-poking me and Dirk pretty successfully this entire journey."

"This is different," Kimmy says. "What I'm about to attempt—it's like nothing I've ever done before. I need you—and your conjurer's cane."

Quint catches Dirk's eye—and thinks about what Dirk was surely about to say earlier, when he showed Skaelka the group photo. Skaelka left Wakefield with Rover. But Rover isn't with her now. Which could mean that he's lost somewhere—or worse . . .

Quint knows he must do this—not just to help them escape the maze, but to hopefully learn when and where Skaelka and Rover were separated.

Kimmy clucks her tongue. "Skaelka, Quint—it is time to begin."

Dirk realizes this is a different Kimmy than they've been questing with. Her voice is heavier now—less chirp-chirpy. He takes three long steps back. "You got this, pal!"

"Quint, step closer," Kimmy says. "Place the cane's tip in the space between Skaelka's eyes and mine. Energy will flow two ways: from me into Skaelka, and Skaelka into me. You must keep that energy flow *even*, Quint. Balanced."

Quint swallows a jawbreaker-sized lump in his throat. He takes a deep breath, shakes out his arms, and raises the cane.

GET ON WITH IT! SKAELKA'S BRAIN IS GETTING ITCHY!

I'm gonna scratch that itch, Skaelka. Open your mind to me. Allow me to see your secrets.

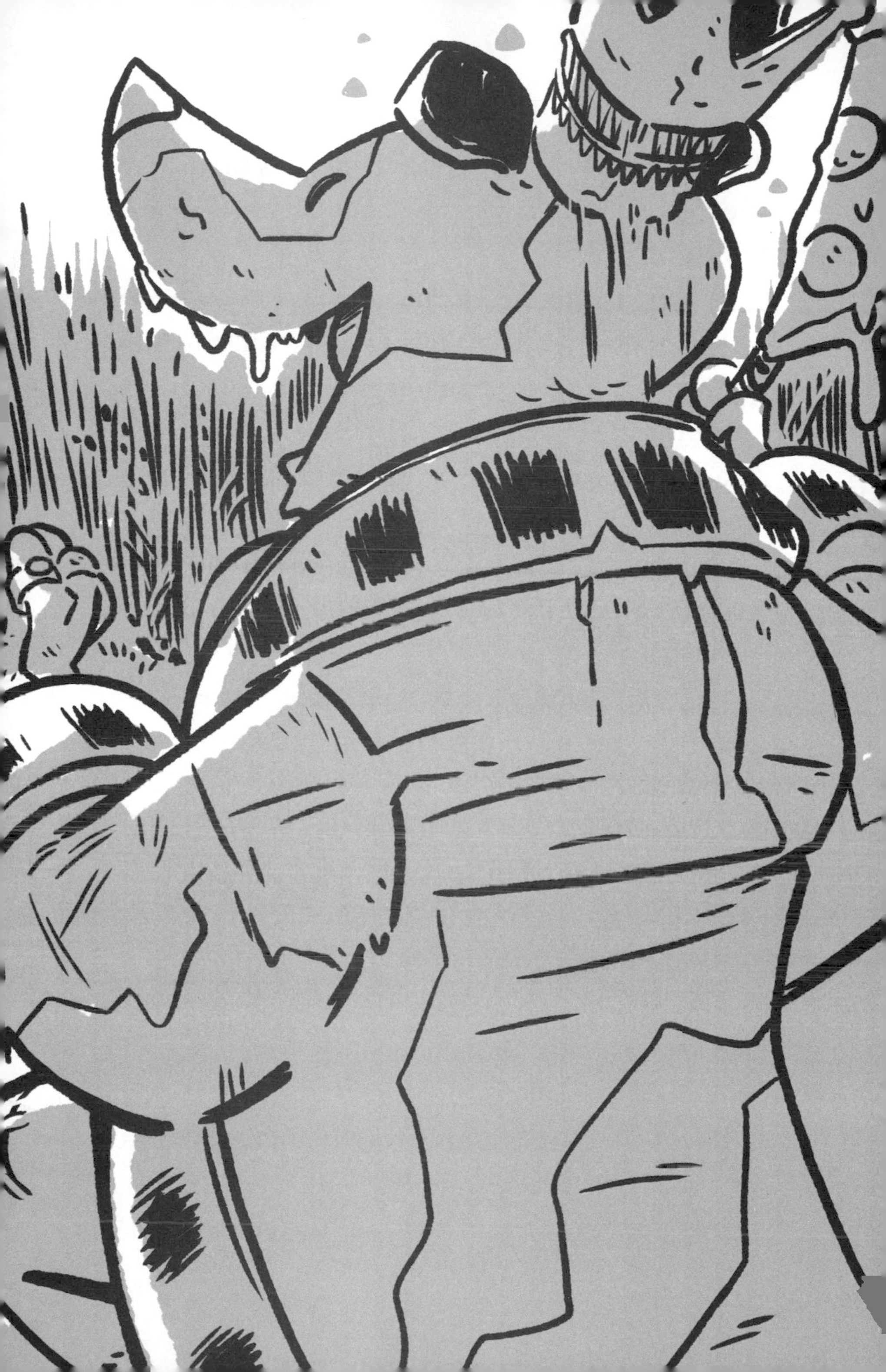

Kimmy stares intently at Skaelka until her lids sink halfway closed and her eyes turn cloudy and pink. Skaelka's body sags as she falls into a trance.

The brain-poking has begun.

Wind whistles around them. The air crackles.

The tip of Quint's cane begins to glow as Kimmy's mind reaches out, connecting with Skaelka, searching for the mental doorway she must enter.

The crackle in the air becomes a whine, gradually amplifying like an ambulance siren speeding closer until—

"ARGH!" Kimmy's eyes snap open and she slaps the ground in frustration. "Whatever these memories are, it's like she doesn't *want* to remember. There's a huge barricade around part of Skaelka's brain. And I need someone to slingshot me *over* that barricade."

Kimmy looks up at Quint. "Quint, increase the power—but remember, the flow of energy between Skaelka and me must *still* remain balanced. Do you understand?"

Quint does understand—but that doesn't mean he can *do it*. "Yes," he finally manages. His palms are sweaty, and he tucks the cane under his arm for a moment to dry them on his pants.

Then he adjusts two dials and lifts the cane again. "I will maintain the balance."

"The brain-poking now resumes," Kimmy says. Her eyes cloud over as she goes into a half trance, probing for the correct path into Skaelka's past.

"Ninety-seven megawatts of energy now passing through the cane," Quint announces.

"It's working," Kimmy says. "Keep it up."

And then it happens . . .

The moment when Kimmy makes it over the barricade is clear: a shimmering sphere of imagery suddenly erupts into existence and Skaelka's mindscape is projected into the air.

"Whoa . . ." Dirk whispers.

A dazzling, tumbling avalanche of thoughts and memories are on display. But they are bound together, incomprehensible—until Kimmy begins to detangle them. It's like a mental Rubik's Cube, and the colored blocks are beginning to line up.

The first clear image hits Quint so hard he nearly loses control of the cane. He's looking at Jack, Skaelka, and Rover—the day before they left on their post-apocalyptic road trip.

Rover . . . Dirk thinks. *We need to find out what happened to Rover.* But Dirk doesn't speak—he doesn't want to distract Quint.

Instead, Dirk watches in stunned silence as bits and pieces of Skaelka's journey—the parallel adventure she took while he, Quint, June, and Jack were road tripping and campaigning—plays out before him . . .

The next projected memory shakes Dirk to his core: Rover, leading Skaelka toward a huge building. A building Dirk recognizes . . .

"The museum! Where I got my sword!" Dirk exclaims, pointing at the summoned image. "Drooler, I was there. It's where we lost Big Mama."

Drooler *meeps* softly and nuzzles into Dirk.

And then Skaelka's memories begin to unfold at a blinding, breakneck pace—like watching a movie on the fastest of all fast-forwards . . .

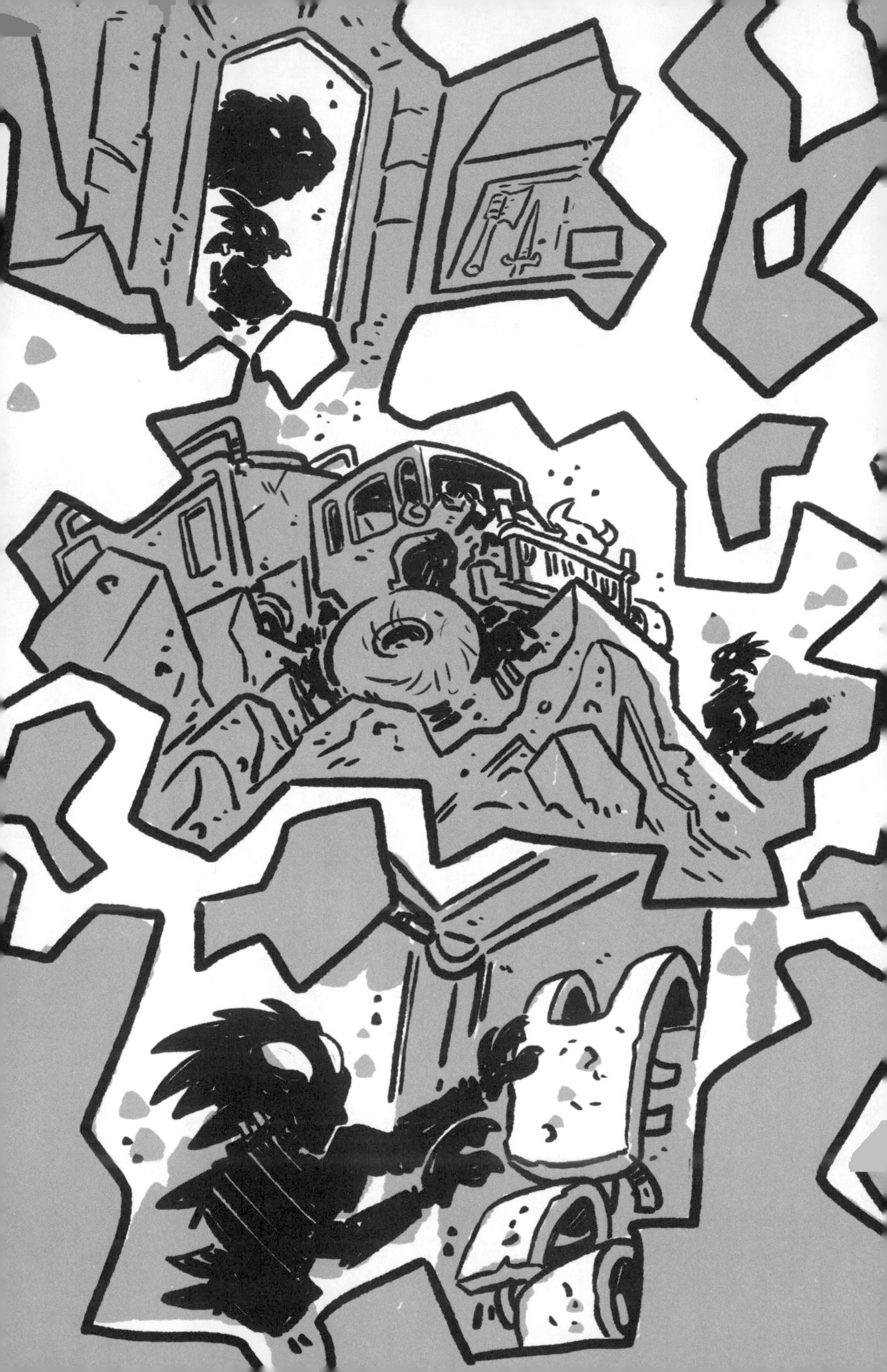

"The monsters didn't get Rover!" Dirk shouts
happily. He pulls Drooler close and whispers,
"That's Jack's monster dog. You'll meet him
someday. You guys'll get along like spokes on a
wagon wheel."

Quint's cane glows red-hot, and the image
changes, a new scene snapping into place.

Kimmy gasps, nearly breaking the mind meld.
"That's the same place I saw in the Drakkor's
mind! Where it was like some monster king!"

The projected image sends Dirk staggering back. Instantly, his relief at finding out Rover was safe has evaporated—

Dirk sees more than he saw earlier, when Kimmy revealed the Drakkor's memory. And what he sees now turns his knees weak and causes his flesh to crawl.

It is a colossal structure.

A fortress.

But this fortress—it's like nothing he's ever seen before. It radiates colors and hues that—and he knows this makes no sense, but he's certain of it— do not occur in nature. The structure glows from the inside, like some ancient creature from the deepest depths of the sea.

The shape, the angles—they shouldn't be possible. *That place*, he thinks. *That place should not exist.*

Finally, Dirk manages to look away—and his eyes find Quint.

Beads of sweat appear on Quint's face as his fingers race across the cane, adjusting dials and flipping switches, trying desperately to maintain Kimmy and Skaelka's connection.

"That fortress . . ." Dirk starts, voice cracking. He turns his face away, doing everything he can to avoid looking at it head-on. "Please, Kimmy, push past that memory. Get to the part where

Skaelka navigated the maze. Quickly."

"No," Kimmy says. "We need to see. So Skaelka knows what happened to her."

Kimmy's ears twist and her clouded eyes go ablaze as she struggles to force her way further into the memory. Details of the fortress come into focus, but they don't come easy: Kimmy and Skaelka are trembling and twitching, and the flowing energy between them surges.

Quint's cane grows shaky in his hands. "I can't hold it steady much longer," he says.

"Getting . . . very . . . close . . ." Kimmy manages. Her words comes in ragged growls.

Galamelon frowns. "How many more memories do we gotta watch?" he asks impatiently, glancing at a clearly broken pocket watch. "I gotta hit the can and the sign says I can't use the cornfield. And I thought we were trying to find a way to *walk out of this maze*—instead, the only walking I'm seeing is a stroll down memory lane!"

"Shut it . . ." Dirk snarls.

Kimmy's projection suddenly shifts! She's done it! And what she's done causes everyone to recoil in horror.

A shadowy figure materializes—and a blood-curdling SCREAM escapes Skaelka's lungs.

chapter sixteen

> NO! NO, NO, NO!

Skaelka's scream is a high-pitched, horrifying howl of agony! She throws up her arms, hiding her face, like she's physically shielding herself from the figure in the projection.

"Who is that?" Dirk asks, shivering. The idea that there's a monster out there that could instill this sort of fear in Skaelka, the greatest warrior he's ever known, turns his blood to ice.

Suddenly, the cane wobbles and sways in Quint's hands—toward Skaelka, then back toward Kimmy, like a pendulum. The fear and terror flooding through Skaelka is destabilizing the fragile balance of energy.

"Kimmy!" he shouts. "I can't maintain the connection any longer!"

Skaelka's jaw clamps shut and her mind seems to burst open! Projected memories are hurtled forth in a frenzied stream of indecipherable images.

When the brain-poking began, Dirk was nervous. Now he's fully petrified. "It's gonna be OK, Drooler. I think . . ." Dirk whispers, turning, putting his body between Drooler and the telepathic action unfolding before them.

Quint's fingers are a blur as he desperately tries to steady the energy flow. But too much is happening too quickly—he doesn't know where to direct his attention. Dials begin to spin on their own and the cane emits a piercing, pentrating wail that builds and builds until—

"No!" Quint gasps, as the cane is violently wrenched free of his grasp. The projection of Skaelka's mind erupts, ballooning outward, one final image flashing before them . . .

And then the image evaporates in a cloud of nothing. Gone. Like a TV that's been snapped off by someone's angry dad after lights-out.

The air is thick and damp. Almost smoky.

"What happened?" Dirk whispers softly.

Kimmy's eyes return to normal. "The connection was severed."

"I'm sorry!" Quint says, scrambling to retrieve his cane. "I couldn't hold it . . . I'm not ready for—"

"Galamelon!" Dirk roars, turning. "Why didn't you try to help? Try to do *something*?"

"Say what now?" Galamelon says, sitting up, rubbing his eyes. "Dozed off for a second there. Did I miss anything important at the end?"

Dirk looks away from Galamelon—it takes every ounce of restraint he has not to scream. He's angry—angrier than he has been in a long, long time. His mind races—

This isn't right! We're demanding too much of Quint. No one could do what we're asking him to do—what we've been asking him to do from the start of this. He's a kid, like me. A kid who's good with science. He's not a sorcerer or a wizard, and he can't do the impossible!

"Meepity!" Drooler squeaks—and that cools Dirk off, brings him back to the moment. But the moment is only getting worse . . .

A teeth-rattling, earthquake-strength tremor rips through the maze.

"Uh, guys," Dirk says, realizing giant-size trouble is approaching. "Feels like a tank battalion is barrelin' toward us . . ."

"The Squanchers must have heard Skaelka's scream," Kimmy says. "And now they're coming."

The whole maze feels like it's moving now. The cornstalks sway wildly as the earth roils.

It's at that moment that Skaelka's eyes snap open. She raps her knuckles hard against her head, like she's knocking loose old brain dust.

She grabs her axe, jams it into the quaking ground, and springs to her feet. "Quint, I thank you," she says. "You did what any ally-in-arms would do: you tried to help."

"I tried," Quint says, shaking his head. "And I failed."

"NO. You succeeded, *friend*," Skaelka says, and her ever-present scowl turns to a smile.

Quint gasps as he realizes—

Suddenly, the earth begins to split. Everyone
huddles, eyes up for incoming Squanchers.

"Dispense with any fear, fellow war dogs!"
Skaelka says. "Many of Skaelka's memories are
restored, including the correct path through this
maze. I will lead us out!"

"I knew you had this, Quint!" Dirk says,
slapping his friend on the back. "No sweat!"

Quint grins slightly. "Quite a bit of sweat, in
fact," he says, wiping his brow.

"My mentoring lifts all!" Galamelon says.

And in that moment—despite the roar of approaching monsters—Quint thinks, *They're right. With Galamelon's help, I **can** become the conjurer I need to be. The conjurer who can slay the Drakkor. The conjurer who will help turn the tide when we battle Thrull again.*

"The route is fresh in my mind. This way!" Skaelka shouts, as she sprints ahead.

"Skaelka, it's *great* havin' you back!" Dirk shouts, racing after her. They all follow Skaelka, speeding down one long pathway, turning corner after corner.

But one problem remains—

Skaelka's memory is working, their route is correct—but the path isn't free of danger.

Squanchers are barreling in from the left and right while still more close in from behind. And ahead of the heroes looms a thick, impassable maze wall.

There's no way forward.

As the monsters near, one suddenly reels back, pulling up! Its body yawns open, revealing row after row of razor-sharp fangs and a surprising oddity clinging to the Squancher's uvula . . .

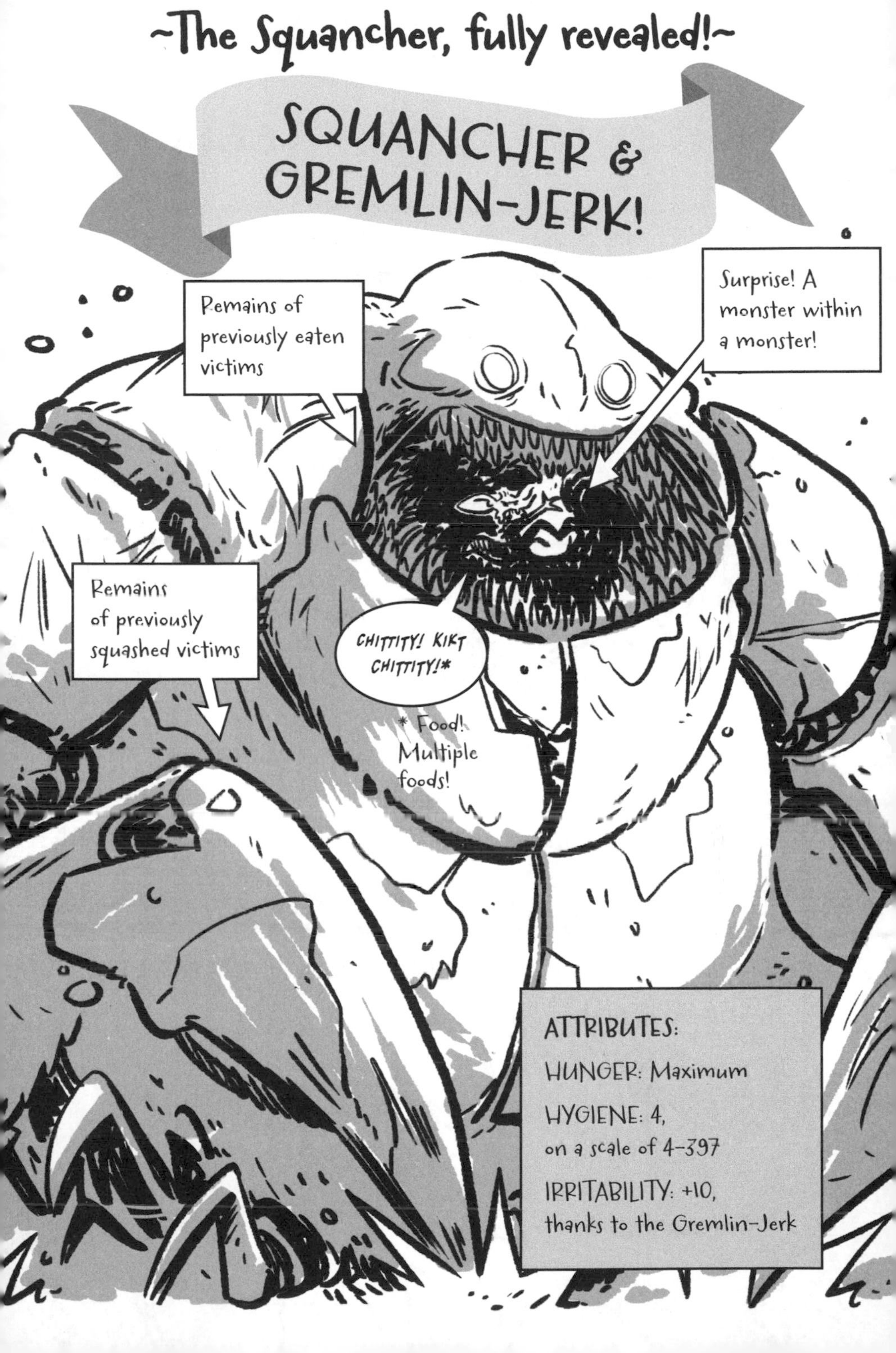
~The Squancher, fully revealed!~
SQUANCHER & GREMLIN-JERK!
Remains of previously eaten victims
Surprise! A monster within a monster!
Remains of previously squashed victims
CHITTITY! KIKT CHITTITY!*
* Food! Multiple foods!
ATTRIBUTES:
HUNGER: Maximum
HYGIENE: 4, on a scale of 4–397
IRRITABILITY: +10, thanks to the Gremlin-Jerk

chapter seventeen

"Lookit!" Dirk says. "There's a little Gremlin-Jerk hanging out in the Squancher's throat!"

"Two monsters for the price of one," Galamelon says. "That's a bargain."

The Gremlin-Jerk shouts *"Chittity! Kikt chittity!"* again, but before the Squancher can roll forward to crush and eat—

"Yeah, Carol, chomp that tooth!" Kimmy cheers, as Carol clamps down on one of the Squancher's massive fangs, wrenching it forward.

"That puppy is some puppy," Dirk says in awe.

Carol is like a mad, movie-villain dentist, ripping the Squancher's fang fully out of its mouth as she drops to the ground.

The Squancher howls in agony while the Gremlin-Jerk cries out in annoyance.

Carol gives a little shake, then watches as the Squancher, overcome by pain, reels back, opening up like some dreadful, other-dimensional snap bracelet. The dazed Squancher totters back and forth—then begins to topple forward.

The Gremlin-Jerk unleashes a series of rapid, high-pitched exclamations—but is quickly silenced as the Squancher belly flops forward. There's a cataclysmic *crunch* as it smashes onto the maze hedge, flattening the cornstalk wall beneath its massive body.

"Aww, look at that! It made a bridge for us!" Kimmy exclaims. "What a sweetie!"

"A new path is revealed!" Skaelka bellows, charging up the Squancher's shell. "Follow me!"

They descend into another row of the maze, leaving the Squancher behind. "We are nearing the point of exit!" Skaelka calls.

"Sounds like you guys pretty much have this under control," Galamelon says, hopping aboard the Wrangler and doing a full recline in the seat.

"Pete!" Kimmy shouts to the cricket-looking monster. "If he gets too comfortable, feel free to give him a flick."

"Right! Left! Oh-ho, this is a tricky one!"

Skaelka barks as they zoom through the maze. "These scheming maze-makers believe they can outwit us with a loop-around, but they underestimate the mind of Skaelka!"

And then, at long last, the path widens. The endless labyrinth turns into a straightaway, lined with snack stands and souvenir T-shirt booths.

"OMG," says Kimmy. "OH. EM. GEE. This is . . ."

"The exit!" Dirk exclaims. "Finally!"

A sign arches over the pathway ahead, strung between two towering Frankie Ferret statues. A wind-beaten banner reads, CONGRATULATIONS! KING POSSUM APPLAUDS YOUR SUCCESSFUL COMPLETION OF THE CORN LABYRINTH OF PERIL! READY TO DO IT AGAIN? ONLY $59. CASH ONLY.

That'll be a nope, Dirk thinks.

Galamelon cheers from his perch atop the Jeep. "I knew entering the maze was the wise choice! I would never lead you astray, for I am—"

GRAWWRGH!

The heroes are passing beneath the exit sign, close—*oh so close*—to freedom, when the wounded Squancher appears behind them. The monster's shell-body uncoils. Inside, the dazed—and slightly squashed—Gremlin-Jerk jabs a finger . . .

*Don't let them escape! We haven't eaten in so very long! And the tall one looks particularly tasty!

Apparently, Squanchers don't appreciate having their fangs yanked out by carapace puppies. And Gremlin-Jerks don't enjoy being crushed. And neither takes kindly to being used as a bridge.

The Gremlin-Jerk flashes a goodbye sneer as the Squancher rolls closed, balling up and barreling forward.

"Carol!" Kimmy shouts. "Watch out behind—"

SLAM!

The Squancher slams into Carol like a living, breathing wrecking ball! Carol goes airborne, rolling end over end, tumbling into a final 360-degree flip. Then a piercing *KRAK* rings out as she crashes through the exit sign.

A thunderous smash booms behind Quint, Dirk, Kimmy, and Skaelka as the loosened exit sign falls from its hinges. It crashes down behind them, bringing the towering ferrets with it, creating a massive wall of wreckage.

The Squancher slams into the wall, then opens up as it ricochets back like a pinball. The monster is now trapped on the other side. The Gremlin-Jerk waves its tiny fist, cursing the escaped heroes.

"We made it," Dirk says, looking around in disbelief. "And we're OK!"

Quint, bent over trying to catch his breath, lifts his head. Between gulps of air, he manages, "Not all of us . . ."

Dirk follows his gaze. Carol is slowly clambering to her feet.

But Galamelon doesn't stand.

He was thrown from the Wrangler during the crash, and now lies sprawled out on the grass beyond the maze.

Not moving, lying still, in a slowly spreading pool of blood . . .

chapter eighteen

"Galamelon!" Quint cries, racing to his side. "Are you all right?"

"Quint . . ." Galamelon rasps, reaching out to clutch his hand. "My mentee. You are the legacy I leave behind in this world once I'm gone." He closes his eyes. "And I'm feeling pretty close to being gone."

"No!" Quint gasps. "I need you!"

Quint looks at his friends. His eyes are wide and wet.

"Carry on my legacy, guy . . ." Galamelon says, eyes fluttering closed. "Use the conjurations I have taught you . . . And tell the world . . . the story of Galamelon the Great . . ."

Thunder rumbles in the distance as Kimmy walks in a slow circle around Galamelon.

"UNBELIEVABLE!" Kimmy exclaims suddenly. "Even now! Quint, forget about him. Like I've been trying to tell you from the beginning—Galamelon is the *pits*, OK."

"Hey . . ." Dirk says. "Now's not the time. Little respect, huh?"

"Um, nope," Kimmy says. "Ever since the day he sauntered into Fleeghaven, this fraudster has been one giant brainache."

Galamelon suddenly lifts his head. "Kimmy, no. C'mon. Let me have this . . ."

"NOPE," Kimmy says. "You want folks to know the story of Galamelon? Well, I'll tell 'em that tale. Right now . . ."

The Tale of Galamelon the Totally Full of It

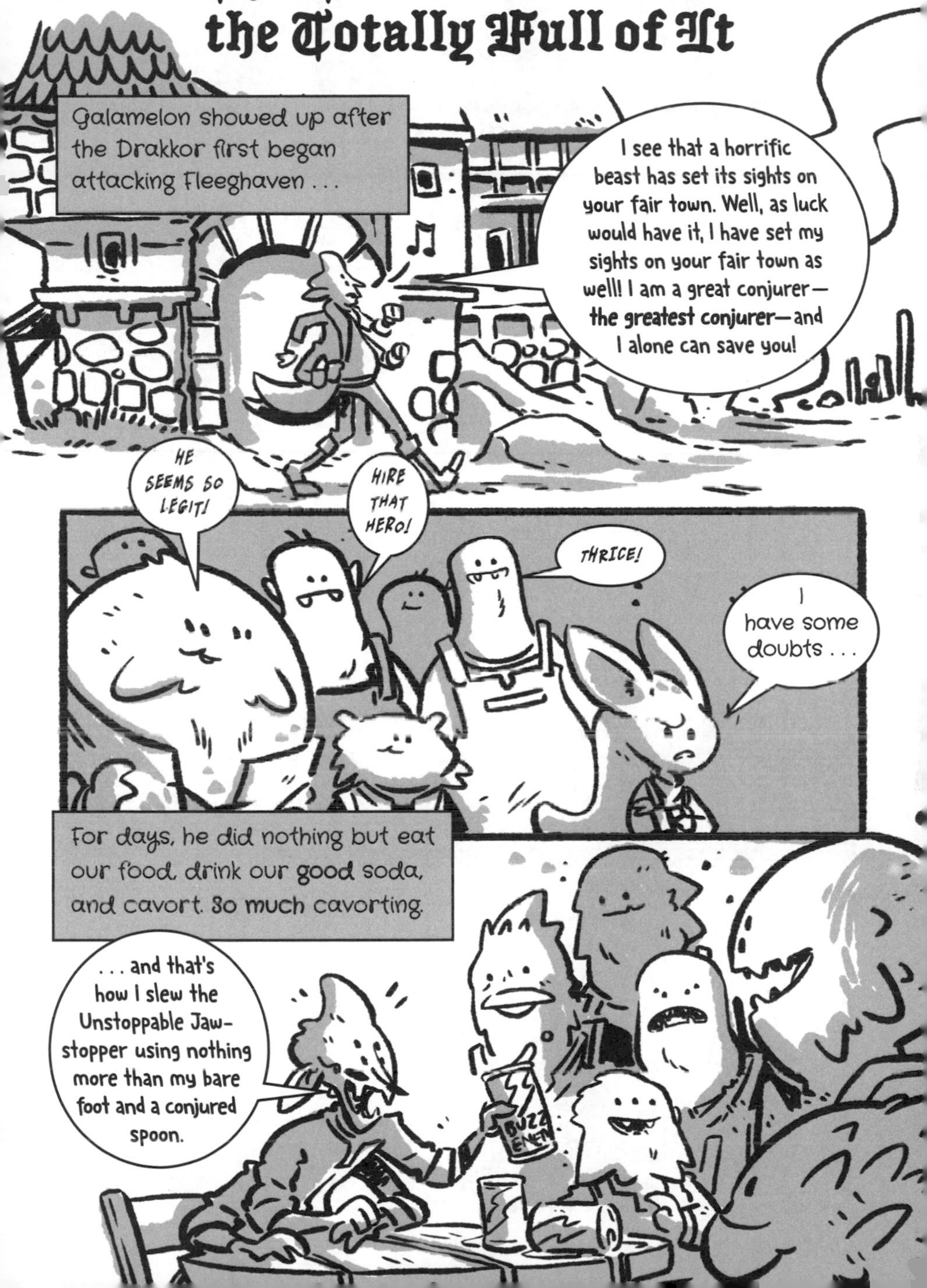
Galamelon showed up after the Drakkor first began attacking Fleeghaven . . .
I see that a horrific beast has set its sights on your fair town. Well, as luck would have it, I have set my sights on your fair town as well! I am a great conjurer—the greatest conjurer—and I alone can save you!
HE SEEMS SO LEGIT!
HIRE THAT HERO!
THRICE!
I have some doubts . . .
For days, he did nothing but eat our food, drink our good soda, and cavort. So much cavorting.
. . . and that's how I slew the Unstoppable Jaw-stopper using nothing more than my bare foot and a conjured spoon.
BUZZ

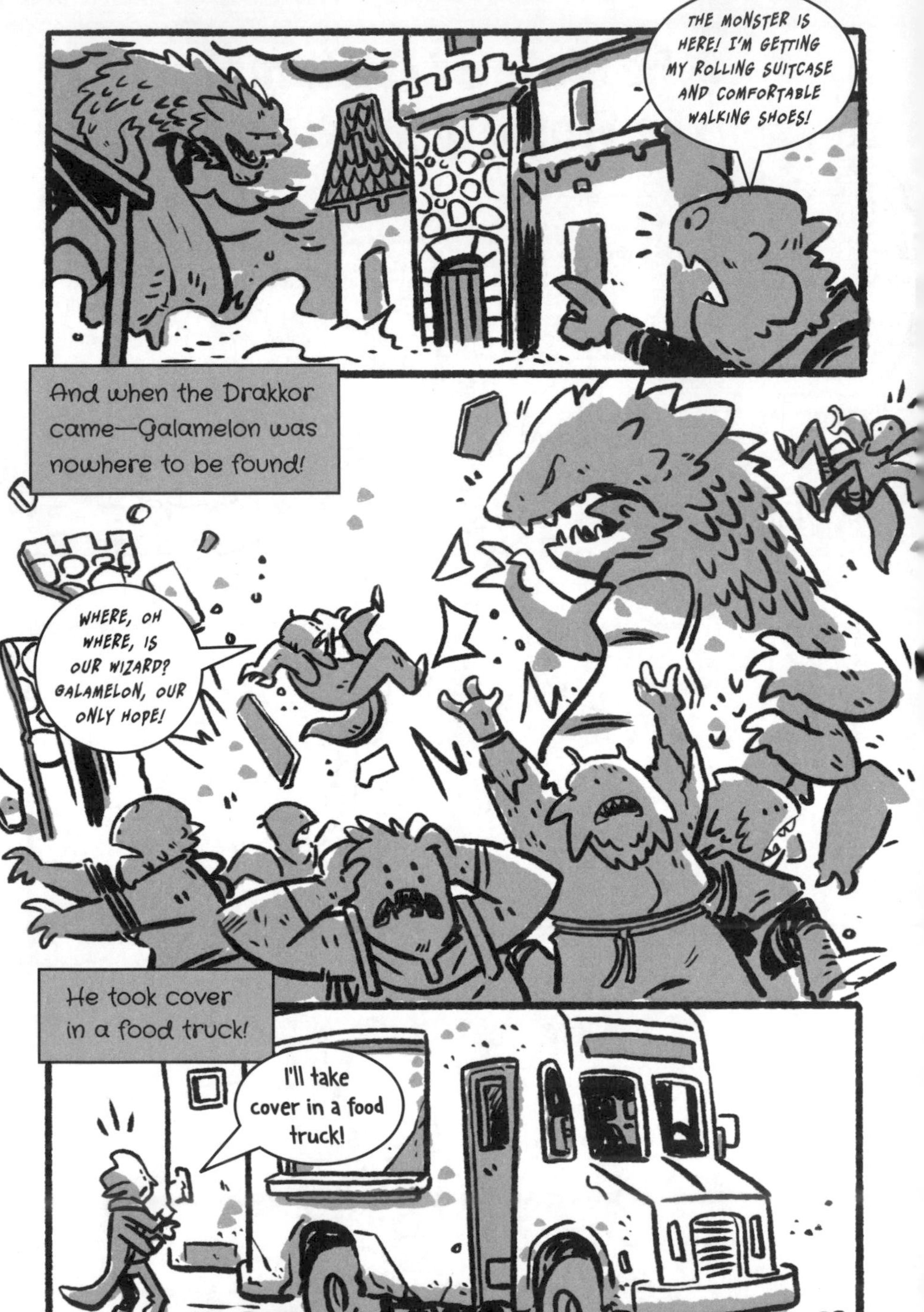
THE MONSTER IS HERE! I'M GETTING MY ROLLING SUITCASE AND COMFORTABLE WALKING SHOES!
And when the Drakkor came—Galamelon was nowhere to be found!
WHERE, OH WHERE, IS OUR WIZARD? GALAMELON, OUR ONLY HOPE!
He took cover in a food truck!
I'll take cover in a food truck!

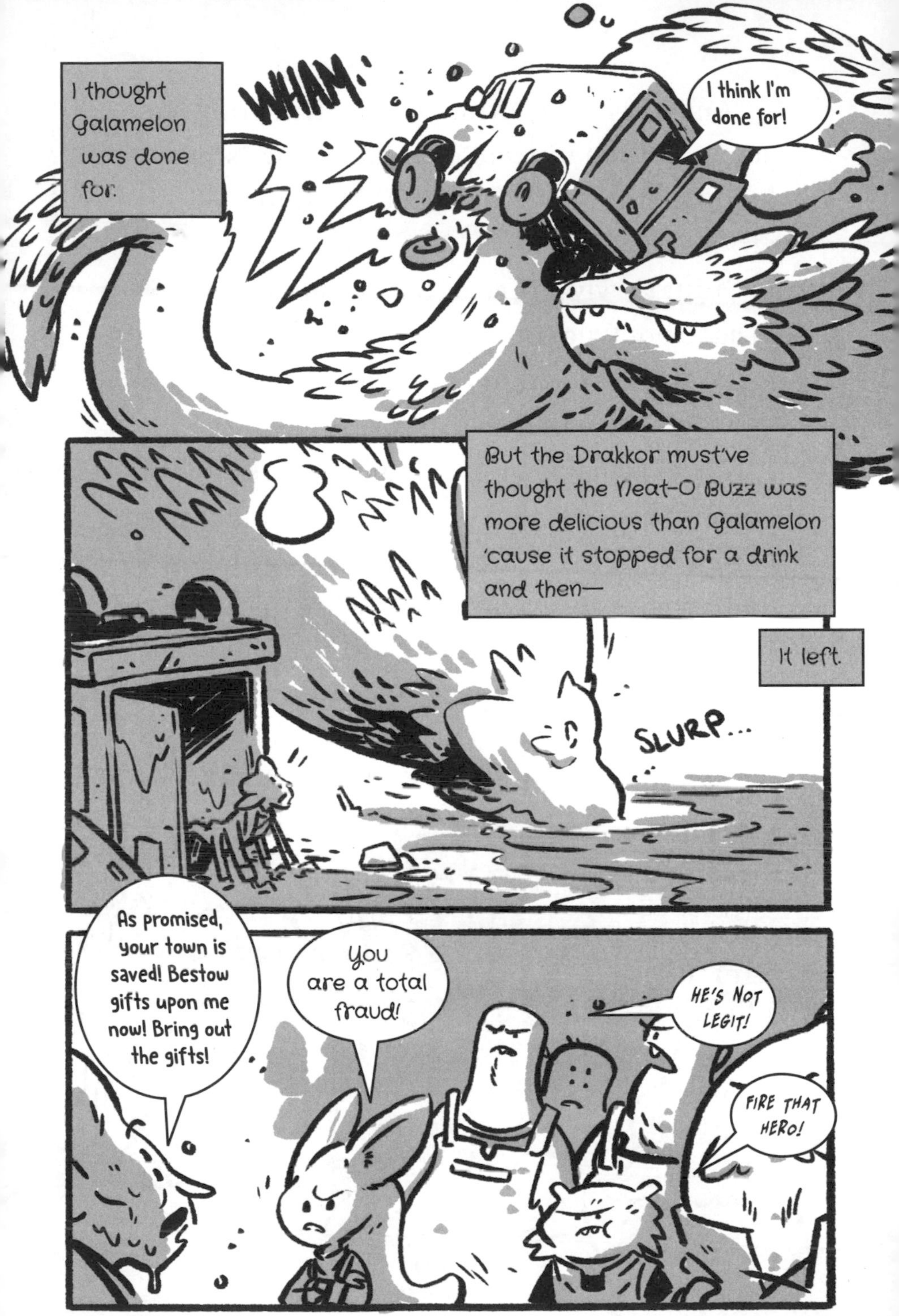
I thought Galamelon was done for.
WHAM
I think I'm done for!
But the Drakkor must've thought the Neat-O Buzz was more delicious than Galamelon 'cause it stopped for a drink and then—
It left.
SLURP...
As promised, your town is saved! Bestow gifts upon me now! Bring out the gifts!
You are a total fraud!
HE'S NOT LEGIT!
FIRE THAT HERO!

"And after that," Kimmy says, finishing her story, "we ran him out of town. But we should have run him even farther. Like, into the ground."

Quint slowly lets go of Galamelon's hand. "That's not true, is it?"

Galamelon looks at Quint for a long, long moment—then his head drops.

"I'm afraid it is . . ." Galamelon says, sighing deeply. "You see, in my dimension, I was a used carapace salesman. I was full of confidence. I had swagger to spare! Oh yes, once upon a time, I was the very best . . ."

"When I fell into *this* dimension, I needed to survive. But I only had one thing going for me: that swagger. So I put it to use: I taught myself a few simple tricks, and rebranded myself as the world's greatest conjurer."

Quint takes a few shaky steps back. "But . . . No, that can't be," he says. "I've *seen* you perform conjurations—real ones! You freed the Queen in Armor with a conjuration so powerful it shook the Possum Palace to its very foundation. We all felt it. Right, guys?"

Dirk and Kimmy both frown, confused. "When the place shook super hard?" Kimmy asks. "That was just 'cause the stage started spinning and the Drakkor fell through the roof."

"What? I . . . But . . . " Quint's face falls. "Oh."

A bolt of lightning suddenly cracks. Gathering thunderheads are turning the sky ashy gray.

"Storm's a-comin' . . ." Dirk says. He licks a finger and holds it up. "It'll be headed toward Fleeghaven. And that's finger-lickin' *bad*."

Kimmy stands over Galamelon and looks to Quint and Dirk. "Sorry to burst your bubblegum. But at least you know the truth . . ."

Quint turns his back to Galamelon. "So that's it, then? It's hopeless?"

"Now, Galamelon," Kimmy says. "It's also time *you* knew the truth."

"Huh?" Galamelon grunts.

Kimmy slips her foot beneath him, nudges him over, then flip-kicks a crushed plastic bottle into the air. Snatching it, she exclaims, "YOU'RE NOT DYING, YOU NUMBSKULL! You're not even bleeding—you're lying in a pool of Neat-O Buzz!"

Kimmy waves the bottle. "You had *this* in your pocket—and it burst open when you were knocked off Carol."

Dirk smirks at Kimmy. "You knew all along."

Kimmy shrugs. "Hey, it got him to come clean."

"But of course I am alive!" Galamelon exclaims, leaping to his feet. "I conjured myself back from the brink of death!"

BONK.

Ow! Oh no. I am once again in the throes of death!

Nope, no one's buying that act again.

Quint spins around, flooded with relief—but also anger. Galamelon is alive—and Galamelon is a phony.

But . . . things are *not* hopeless! Quint can feel something nagging at the back of his mind, telling him all is *not* lost. Some thought, saying, *You guys can still do this.*

"Neat-O-Buzz Energy Juice!" Quint suddenly realizes. He's thinking hard and fast now—his brain doing what it does best: figuring things out. He's putting the pieces together.

Quint picks up the smushed bottle. *Galamelon must have swiped this from the Possum Palace. There was Neat-O Buzz for sale outside the maze. And at the motel where we spent the night. Somewhere else, too, before. But where . . .*

Quint suddenly blurts out, "Of course! The movie poster! In Fleeghaven!"

𝔖ponsored by
𝔑eat-𝔒 𝔅uzz 𝔈nergy 𝔍uice!
𝕮oming this summer!

A smile plays at the corners of Quint's mouth. "Kimmy said that every time the Drakkor comes back, it's bigger, evolved, *scarier*—right? Which means . . . Galamelon, you've saved the day!"

"Who saved what now?" Galamelon is busy slurping juice off his stomach.

Quint hurries on. "When Galamelon was in Fleeghaven, the Drakkor left *after* it drank the Neat-O Buzz, right? I don't think that's a coincidence. I believe Neat-O Buzz Energy Juice is the thing that *causes* the Drakkor to level up!"

"I get it!" Kimmy says. "Actually nope I'm lying I don't get it. But I want to! More, please!"

Quint taps the bottle. "The Drakkor didn't leave Fleeghaven because it took pity on Galamelon. It left because it got what it wanted: Neat-O Buzz! And *that's* why the Drakkor chose King Possum's Family Fun Palace as its lair. Because there's tons of Neat-O Buzz there!"

"You are saying the Buzz of Neatness is what the Drakkor desires?" Skaelka asks.

"Precisely! Or, almost precisely—but yeah! The Drakkor needs to consume that stuff so he can continue getting stronger and bigger and *more evil*!" Quint concludes.

"OK . . ." Dirk says. "But then why does it only attack the town when it rains?"

Quint is momentarily stumped, but Kimmy gasps. "Ooh! Ooh! I know this one! Remember I told you that after it finally rained and we knew we'd be able to grow our dough crops, we threw an *epic party*?" she explains. "We celebrated with Neat-O Buzz! And *that* was the first time the Drakkor attacked! So now, the Drakkor must just assume that every time it rains, we break out the Neat-O Buzz."

"Like Chekhov's hog!" Dirk says.

"Pavlov's dog," Quint corrects.

Kimmy continues, "So the Drakkor keeps coming back, looking for more. But it never finds any 'cause we stopped drinking that junk after that night 'cause that junk is *yuck*. Tastes like cherry-flavored stomach lining—but not in a good way."

Quint takes three quick steps toward Kimmy. "Tell me . . . in town . . . *is there any Neat-O Buzz left*?"

"Yup! We shoved it all in the armory, next to the Cine-Bites meal truck."

"Armory?" Dirk wonders, before realizing she means the fake, movie set armory.

In moments, everyone is aboard the Wrangler. Carol is practically prancing, eager to stretch her many legs and *run*.

"You are all very welcome!" Galamelon says as he settles into his seat. "Clearly, had I not swiped that Neat-O Buzz, we would never have figured any of this out. So do I get a reward now?"

Dirk tosses Galamelon a plush possum. "Courtesy of the king. You've earned it."

Galamelon grins and tugs the pull cord on the singing stuffie's back. The critter belts out, "Pizza, pizza, it's good for you!"

And with that, Kimmy gives Carol a gentle tap-tap. They're off . . .

chapter nineteen

Lightning slices through the gathering clouds as the sky turns from gray to black.

Carol gallops at full speed through the darkness, racing to stay ahead of the storm, ahead of the Drakkor . . .

"Is it snack time yet?" Galamelon asks.

"Nopers," Kimmy says.

"Dance party time yet?"

Kimmy cracks a grin. "Yeah, duh. HIT IT, PETE!"

Breakneck race home dance party!

Smushed in the back seat, Quint ignores the oddly timed dance party.

There's still a chance to turn this whole mess into victory, he thinks. *And do it without conjuring.*

He looks down at his cane. It used to hold a world of potential: Incantations and conjurations. An incredible mix of science and other-dimensional energy. But maybe Dirk was right. Maybe it's all simply too dangerous. And after Galamelon's confession, the idea of being a conjurer just seems like a cruel joke.

Exhaustion overtakes Quint, and his eyelids shut as two days of hero questing on just three minutes of sleep finally catch up. Carol's gait along with Pete's strange music is oddly soothing, and soon he's fast asleep . . .

Quint is jolted awake by a sudden rumbling. He gulps, thinking it's thunder crashing, fearing the storm has arrived.

But no. It's . . . cheering?

"Huh?" Quint wipes drool from his cheek and lifts his head, which had been resting on Skaelka's shoulder.

"You are fortunate I now *remember* you," Skaelka tells Quint, flashing a loving—but still disturbing—grin. "Otherwise, I would have been forced to *dismember* you."

"Missed ya, Skaelka," Quint says.

"Aww, so mushy," Kimmy says.

"Time to focus, gang," Dirk says. "We're here."

THE HEROES HAVE RETURNED FROM THEIR QUEST!

THE QUEEN IN ARMOR HAS BEEN FOUND, AS WELL.

"How went the slaying of the Drakkor?" a monster calls out. "Did you make it suffer as it has made us suffer?"

"Not yet," Kimmy says, as Carol slows to a trot. "But fear not, buddies—the Drakkor is on its way!"

A terrified gasp comes from the gathered · monsterfolk.

"*On its way?*" one oafish monster cries.

"*Fear not?*" another shouts.

"Yup!" Kimmy says, all perky, "'Cause—"

"Your prodigal son has returned!" Galamelon interrupts, standing and waving. "Now, can someone point me in the direction of the bathroom?"

The sight of Galamelon turns the monster-folk's fear to fury. "You left to slay the Drakkor, and instead returned with that bozo?"

"Rain will soon come, the Drakkor is not dead, and Galamelon is back! We are doomed!" a monster cries, then hurries off to retrieve a rolling suitcase and comfortable walking shoes.

Kimmy holds up a hand, silencing them. "Galamelon is definitely still lousy—*but* his lousiness actually came in handy-dandy. So, no one kill him . . . yet."

"HEY!" Skaelka shouts, standing in her seat. "Skaelka has also returned. And she will not leave until the Drakkor has been felled."

"Who's Skaelka?" a monster asks.

Skaelka sighs. "*Me,*" she mutters. "The *Queen in Armor.*"

A few monsters mumble their approval.

"You all wanted the heroes of Hero Quest," Dirk says. "Now, you didn't get those *exact* heroes—but you did get a warrior and a conjurer. A warrior and a conjurer who will *not run* when the Drakkor shows up."

"Quint has a plan!" Kimmy says. "A plan that will *work.*"

Quint gulps. He feels like a giant spotlight has suddenly been turned on him. Looking out at the monsterfolk, he sees their fear-stricken faces. A few, who were caught mid-farmaculture, hold monster versions of pitchforks—the prongs trembling.

Quint feels a sudden elbow in his side. "This part's all you," Dirk whispers.

"Ahem," Quint starts. His words are shaky and he expects his voice to crack at any moment. "Well, you see, the plan is like this. First, you will retrieve the Cine-Bites truck and bring it to the center of town . . ."

Quint pauses. The monsterfolk are rapt, hanging on his every word. He sees the same thing he saw when they set out to slay the Drakkor: *hope.* It's clear the monsterfolk are willing to do whatever needs doing. He continues, gaining steam as he talks . . .

Just then, the first drops of rain begin to fall, pitter-pattering off the Wrangler's hood. It's too late to run. Gray clouds move in over the town.

"Now hop to it, neighbors!" Kimmy barks.

And they do.

Only one small monster doesn't move. He stares up at Quint with wide eyes. "What's with the Neat-O Buzz? Are we gonna have a party?"

"We sure are," Quint says with a confident smile. "A party to celebrate the slaying of the Drakkor . . ."

chapter twenty

FLEEGHAVEN READIES FOR A FIGHT!

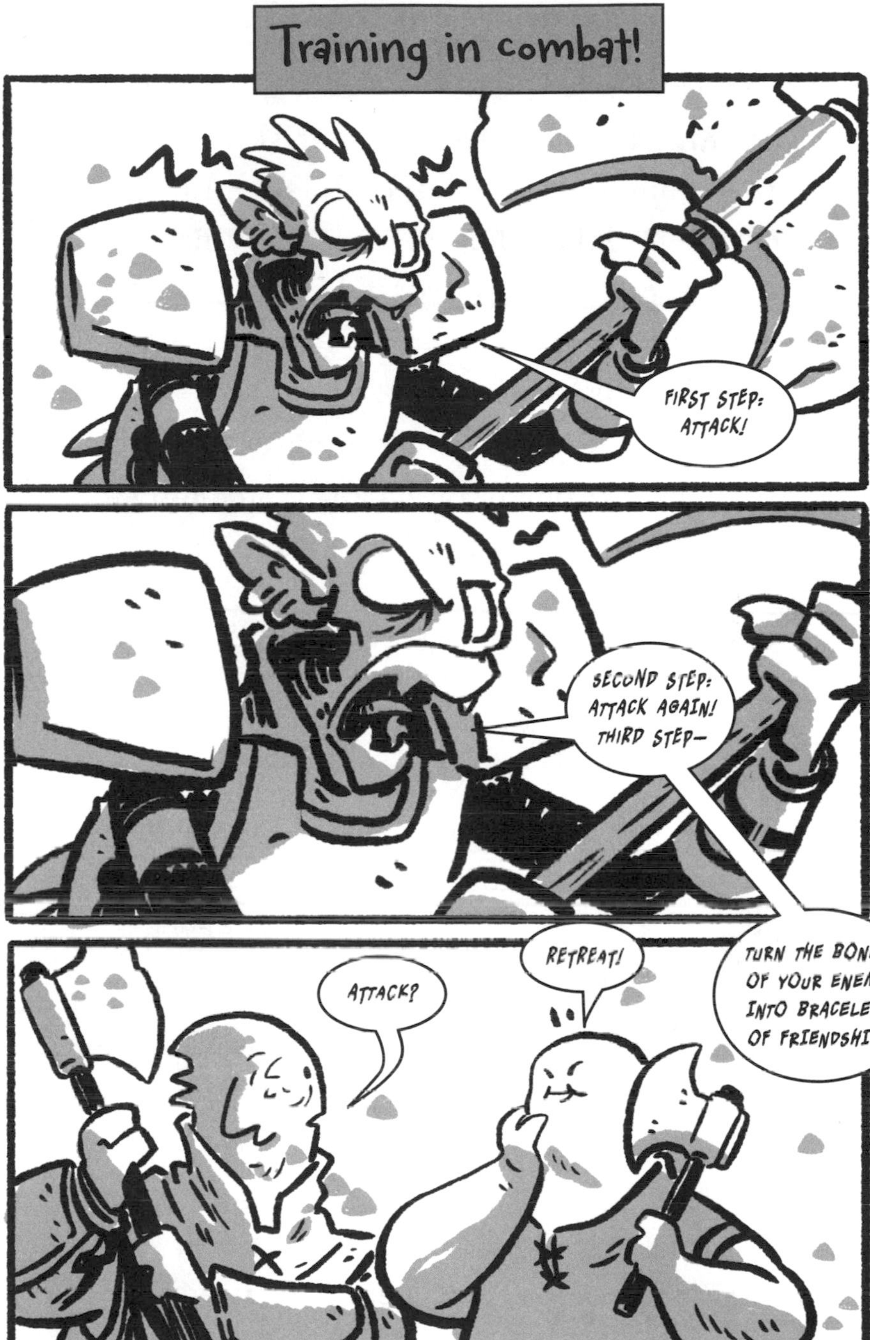
Training in combat!
FIRST STEP: ATTACK!
SECOND STEP: ATTACK AGAIN! THIRD STEP—
TURN THE BONES OF YOUR ENEMY INTO BRACELETS OF FRIENDSHIP!
ATTACK?
RETREAT!

"Love it when a plan comes together," Dirk says.

Dirk and Kimmy are walking briskly through the town, observing the hurried, last-minute preparation. Galamelon follows, carrying four armfuls of poster board, scrawling NEAT-O BUZZ on each one.

The rain falls in buckets.

"It won't be long now . . ." Kimmy says, tugging her ears down for warmth. Suddenly—

WHACK!

"Ow! What hit me?" Dirk says, rubbing the back of his head. Looking down, he spots Quint's conjuring book, lying on the ground.

"Huh," Dirk says, picking up the book.

He glances around—and spots the open door to one of the many Hero Quest production trucks. Dirk thinks for a moment, then says, "I'll catch you two later."

"Hey, bud, whatcha doing in here?" Dirk asks, stepping up into the truck.

Glancing around, he sees tripods, lighting equipment, and spools of heavy-duty cable.

Quint sits at a workbench, quietly building— but he turns at the sound of Dirk's voice.

Quint simply shrugs, then spins back to the workbench. His cane is disassembled. The battery pack has been removed.

And on the floor, Dirk spots a trap-sorta-thing, though how it works isn't clear. But he does spy something that looks like an old-timey prospector's dynamite blaster.

239

"Dude," Dirk says. "You threw away your book. You're taking apart your cane. What's going on?"

"You were right all along," Quint says, as he finishes connecting a long cord to the plunger. "Conjuring is bad news—and that book is, too."

"So . . . what, you're giving up?" Dirk asks.

"No, I'm doing the thing I know how to do best: using old movie equipment to build a trap that will snare the Drakkor so we can slay it."

Dirk raises his eyebrows. "That's the thing you know how to do best?"

"Not *exactly* that, of course. But building gadgets, using science and technology, turning a heap of junk into an evil-monster-slaying device—*that's* a thing I know how to do."

Quint doesn't add "unlike conjuring," but he doesn't have to—Dirk knows that's what he means.

Dirk thinks for a moment, then sighs. "OK, fine, but . . . this book was a gift! You can't get rid of a gift. Even if it's a pair of lousy mittens, you still gotta wait a few weeks to toss 'em. If ya don't, it's just rude."

"If the gift doesn't fit and was clearly given to the wrong person—then you *can* get rid of it," Quint says. "And that's what I'm doing."

Dirk sets the book on the workbench and

pushes it forward until it's touching Quint's hand. "If you wanna quit this, I won't try and stop you. This conjuring stuff is big—probably too big for *anyone*. You know what my dad used to say to me? I told Jack this once—when I was feeling lower than low. My dad used to say, 'Dirk, if you don't try, you can't fail.'"

"Well, *that* is not very good fatherly advice," Quint says.

"Sure ain't," Dirk says. "But I'm saying it now—just so you know—you *did* try, and you did *not* fail. I know you don't see it—but you were making progress."

Quint stares at the book, then lowers his head. "I can't believe I trusted Galamelon," he says softly. "And the worst part—I *knew* he wasn't one hundred percent legit. I didn't know he was a *total* phony, but I could tell he was, y'know, *off.*"

"OK, phew," Dirk says. "'Cause if you couldn't—I woulda been worried."

"Of course I could. But I was just so desperate to fix my gigantic mistake and not make any *more* gigantic mistakes. And as a result—I only made things worse. We wouldn't even *be* here if it wasn't for me."

You're right.

I am?

Yeah, we wouldn't be here. We'd be back at that Possum Palace, in the hallway—**dead**. Dude, when the Drakkor had us cornered, you **saved us**—you even wounded the thing! And that weird séance thing with Kimmy? It worked! Skaelka got her memory back and she got us out of that maze. **You** did that.

Then why do I feel like a failure?

"Because you're learning something new and learning something new ain't easy. You're already good at all this stuff"—Dirk waves at the workbench—"but just 'cause conjuring doesn't come easy doesn't mean you're *bad* at it. You're starting out. And when you're staring out, sometimes it's . . . I dunno. What's the word?"

Quint thumbs through the book, then pushes it aside. What he *wants* to do is hurl it back out the door.

Dirk sighs. "But, dude—conjuring is *still* based in reality! You're *great* at science. And like you keep telling me, *monster dimension* conjuring is like *our dimension* science."

"I'm . . . I'm not sure anymore. It's scarier."

"Scarier than sawing a man in half?" Dirk asks.

A voice suddenly says: "Ooh, I can do that one!"

Quint and Dirk turn to see Galamelon standing in the doorway. "I used to saw slithering warmites in half to prove you could fit two slithering warmites in the trunk of a carapace. Now, to reveal the trick goes against my code—"

"What, the *conjurer's code*?" Quint asks sarcastically. "Give it up."

"No, no! The *used carapace salescreature's* code! And that code is far more secretive and restrictive than any conjurer's code. But . . . I will tell you fellows how it works. You see, unbeknownst to the audience, there are *two* very bendy creatures inside the box. Thus giving the illusion of a body being sawed in half."

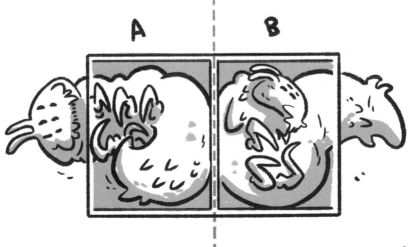

Dirk glares at Galamelon, then finally asks, "That's it? For real?"

Quint nods. "I could've deduced that—had I seen the trick in person, which I didn't on account of Angela Bianucci's lying mom."

Dirk looks at Quint, then at Galamelon, and then back at Quint again—then exclaims, "THAT'S NOT SCARY!"

"But it is *messy*," Galamelon says, "if not done properly. Very messy. I've been banned from eleven carapace dealership grand openings on account of how—"

"Messy!" Dirk says. "That's the word I was looking for. Quint, when you're starting something new, it's *messy*. And you're just not used to messy."

"I should be," Quint says. "After living with Jack and June for so long."

Dirk chuckles softly. "Listen, buddy. If you wanna throw that book away—go for it. Trust me, I don't wanna see you mess up and turn me into a lobster or something. But . . . I dunno— look, I was terrified of magic. Still am. I like stuff I can *see*. I like bad dudes I can *punch*. But here I am, saying you might wanna stick with it and *keep conjuring . . .*"

Quint is silent. Is Dirk just trying to make him feel better? Or is Dirk, maybe . . . right?

Quint looks at the book, and again recalls what Yursl told him: *You now have all you need to do what must be done.*

Maybe she meant everything he needed was already inside him. The book was only an aid.

Suddenly, a voice from outside—with news that causes Quint to forget all about the book and Yursl. "DRAKKOR ON THE HORIZON!"

"Well, I should probably hit the toilet," Galamelon says, clearing his throat. "I'll probably be a while, so—"

"Shaddup," Dirk says, hauling Galamelon to the door.

Stepping outside, Quint sees a flurry of action: Skaelka leading the monsterfolk, directing them to their positions. They carry other-dimensional pitchforks, sharpened shovels and spades, and way-too-realistic bows, spears, and swords taken from the prop truck.

"Skaelka got the monsterfolk ready *fast*," Dirk says, watching them scurry across rooftops and duck into storefronts.

"And there's the Drakkor bait," Quint says, nodding to the Cine-Bites meal truck at the center of town.

"Hero dudes!" Kimmy calls. "Set your trap!"

"MEEP!" Drooler squeaks.

"Meep indeed, Drooler," Quint replies. "Meep indeed."

chapter twenty-one

A few frantic minutes later, Quint and Dirk are peering through the meal truck's serving window, watching and waiting.

The rain pounds the roof above them, sounding like war drums.

Suddenly, the atmosphere changes—the air turns frigid. "I think it's here," Quint whispers, a shiver running down his spine.

The Drakkor has no wings, it can't fly—but it arrives with shocking suddenness.

"There," Dirk says, gulping as he points. "The Welcome to Fleeghaven sign."

At the edge of town, rain pours off the towering, arching sign. The Drakkor looms just beyond it—a shadow, shimmering behind a waterfall.

And then the monster steps forward. Every beam and board in Fleeghaven rattles. The street splits, stone erupts, and the sign falls.

It's a straight shot from the meal truck to the edge of town, giving Quint and Dirk a clear view of the Drakkor. And they're not loving what they're seeing

"It's definitely bigger," Dirk observes.

Quint nods. It's nearly doubled in size since they battled it at the Possum Palace. Its scales are as thick as the Quint-designed armor Skaelka now wears.

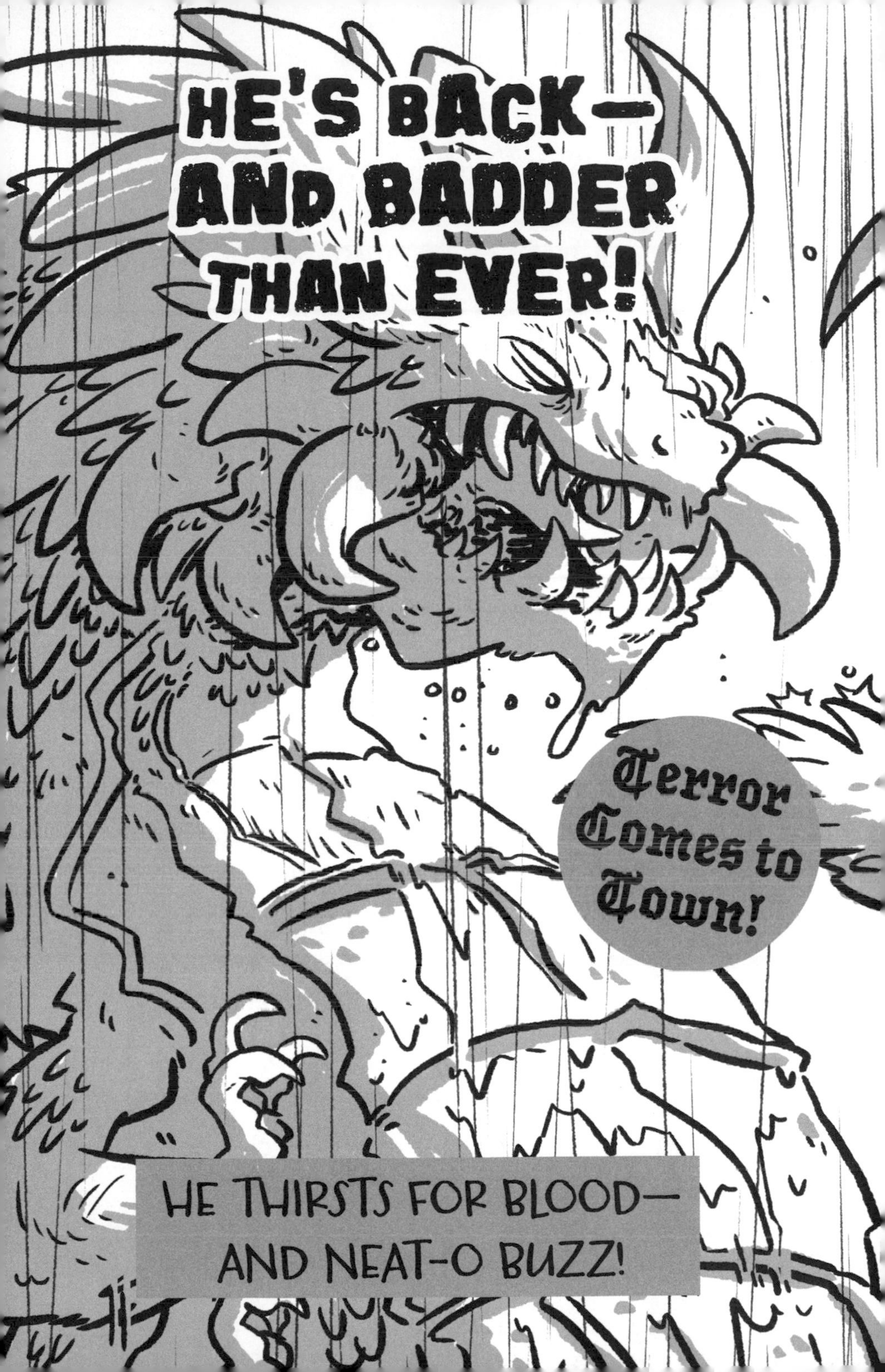
HE'S BACK—AND BADDER THAN EVER!
Terror Comes to Town!
HE THIRSTS FOR BLOOD—AND NEAT-O BUZZ!

The Drakkor displays an eerie, otherworldly intelligence as it scans the town. Rain pounds its scaly head and rolls down over its eyes—but the Drakkor never blinks. It simply searches.

"Unlike previous assaults, there are no fleeing monsterfolk," Quint whispers. "It may suspect the trap . . ."

"Then let's quench its thirst, before it gets a chance to think too hard," Dirk says.

He flicks the taps on the truck's fountain soda machine—and Neat-O Buzz gushes out. Soon, a thick river of syrupy juice is draining through a hole in the truck's floor. Outside, the neon orange liquid mixes with the rainwater, creating a rainbow-colored pool, like radioactive sherbet.

The Drakkor sniffs at the air, head lifting and lowering, and then, suddenly, it snaps straight ahead: eyes locked on the meal truck.

"That got its attention," Dirk says.

The Drakkor could reach the truck with a single ferocious pounce, but instead, it starts a slow, stalking prowl through the town, like a lion on the hunt. Its eyes are constantly looking and searching—scanning every porch, roof, and window for signs of hidden monsterfolk.

It sees nothing.

"Quint, you got enough power?" Dirk asks.

Quint looks down at the dynamite-style plunger at his feet. It looks like something out of an old Road Runner cartoon—and that's not inspiring much confidence: Wile E. Coyote was the one with the dynamite and the detonators . . . and Wile E. Coyote was the one who *lost* at the end of each episode.

Attached to the plunger is a long stretch of electrical wire that leads to the cane's detached battery pack and then snakes out through the rear of the truck.

"Yep," Quint says, eyeing the battery lights. "Enough to power the trap, and then some."

"Good," Dirk says, ducking behind the counter. "Because it's here."

"Huh?" Quint says, then his eyes pop. "Oh!"

At that moment, the Drakkor reaches the meal truck. It sniffs twice, then hisses—a sound that indicates something like amusement.

The town is nothing but eerie quiet as the hidden monsterfolk watch the Drakkor begin to drink, anxiously waiting for what's to come.

"Here goes . . ." Quint whispers. His hand is raised, about to crash down on the plunger, when suddenly—

The Drakkor's head jerks to the side, focusing on the potion shop.

"Freaking Galamelon," Dirk snarls.

The Drakkor's eyes flash, alerted to the ambush. The monster growls and pulls back, just as—

"Now, Quint!" Dirk exclaims. "Take the plunge!"

"Plunge being taken!" Quint cries. His open palm slams down, and the trap is sprung—

SNATCH!

A steel snare snaps tight around the Drakkor!
"GOT 'EM!" Quint cries.

Reeling back, the Drakkor spots the huge Hero Quest camera crane, towering above. The crane's weighted bottom suddenly plummets downward, while the camera shoots up into the air, yanking the snarling Drakkor off the ground—

But Galamelon's ill-timed possum stuffie's song has given the Drakkor warning—warning enough that it has time to lash out with its tail, stabbing toward the meal truck!

"HIT THE DECK!" Dirk cries, yanking Quint to the floor an instant before the Drakkor's barbed tail bursts though the wall! It swipes across the truck's interior in a violent, sweeping arc, then—

YANK!

The see-sawing camera crane carries the monster upward—and the truck with it. Quint and Dirk hang in midair for a second—like astronauts in zero gravity—before being bounced off the walls, floors, and ceiling as the truck flies upward like it's rocket-shot.

"The battery!" Quint cries, lunging, hand swiping but grabbing only air. The pack sails through the window.

"Grab on to something!" Dirk shouts, just before—

THUNK!

The crane's counterweight finishes its long fall, slamming into the ground with earthquake-force! Quint and Dirk's endless hurtling finally stops, and they lay sprawled out on the truck's ceiling—which has now become the floor.

For a moment, the only sound is the creaking of the truck and the rasping of the Drakkor.

And when it appears things can get no worse, Quint and Dirk hear Kimmy shout: "ATTACK NOW!"

They hear the words with perfect clarity, because they hear the words *inside their heads*: a telepathic message sent by Kimmy to every human and monster in town. And the monsterfolk heed her command . . .

TURN THE BOOK SIDEWAYS FOR THIS NEXT PART!

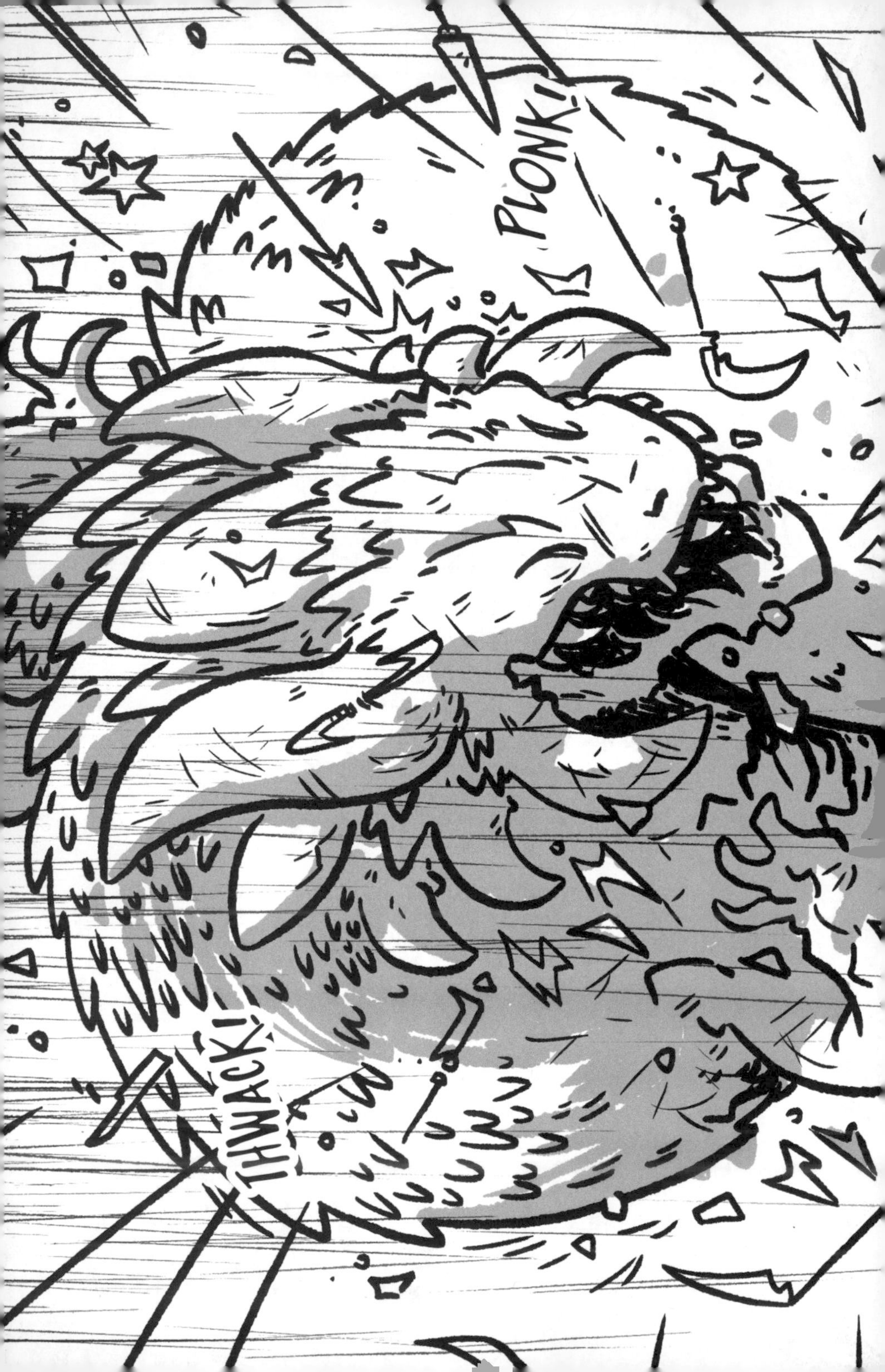
PLONK!
THWACK!

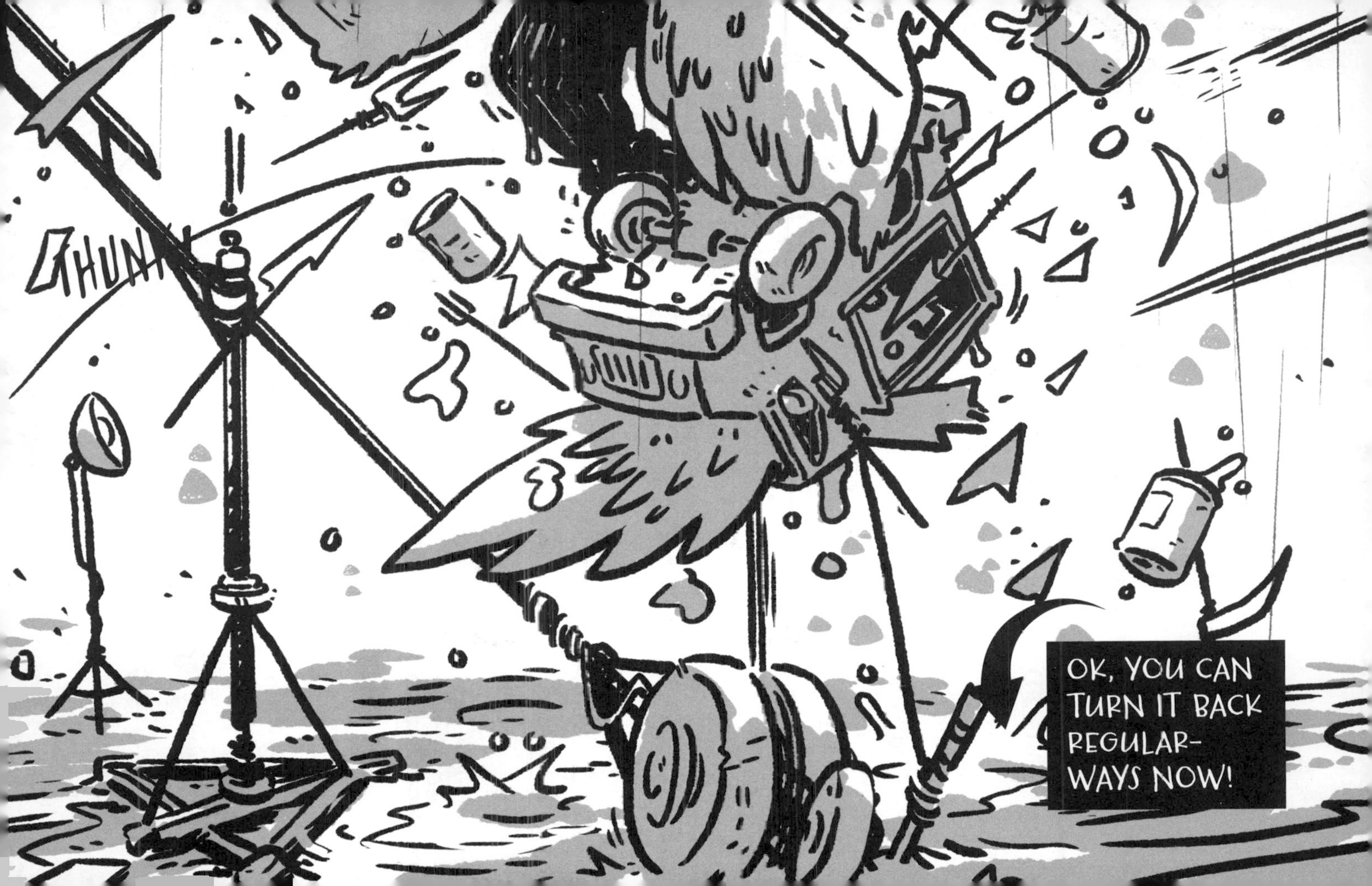
THUNK
OK, YOU CAN TURN IT BACK REGULAR-WAYS NOW!

"STAY DOWN!" Quint cries as the breath-taking barrage of blades, arrows, and well-flung weaponry continues.

"I DON'T KNOW WHAT 'DOWN' MEANS ANYMORE!" Dirk yells.

The Drakkor *shrieks* as projectiles pummel its armored hide—punching, pounding, and finally piercing the monster's rain-slick scales. The monster thrashes, lurching in a sudden, violent swing, whipping the dangling truck side to side.

"Drooler, you gotta wear this!" Dirk says, slamming his helmet onto his buddy's head.

WHUD

KRAK!

That one was quite close.

MEEP?

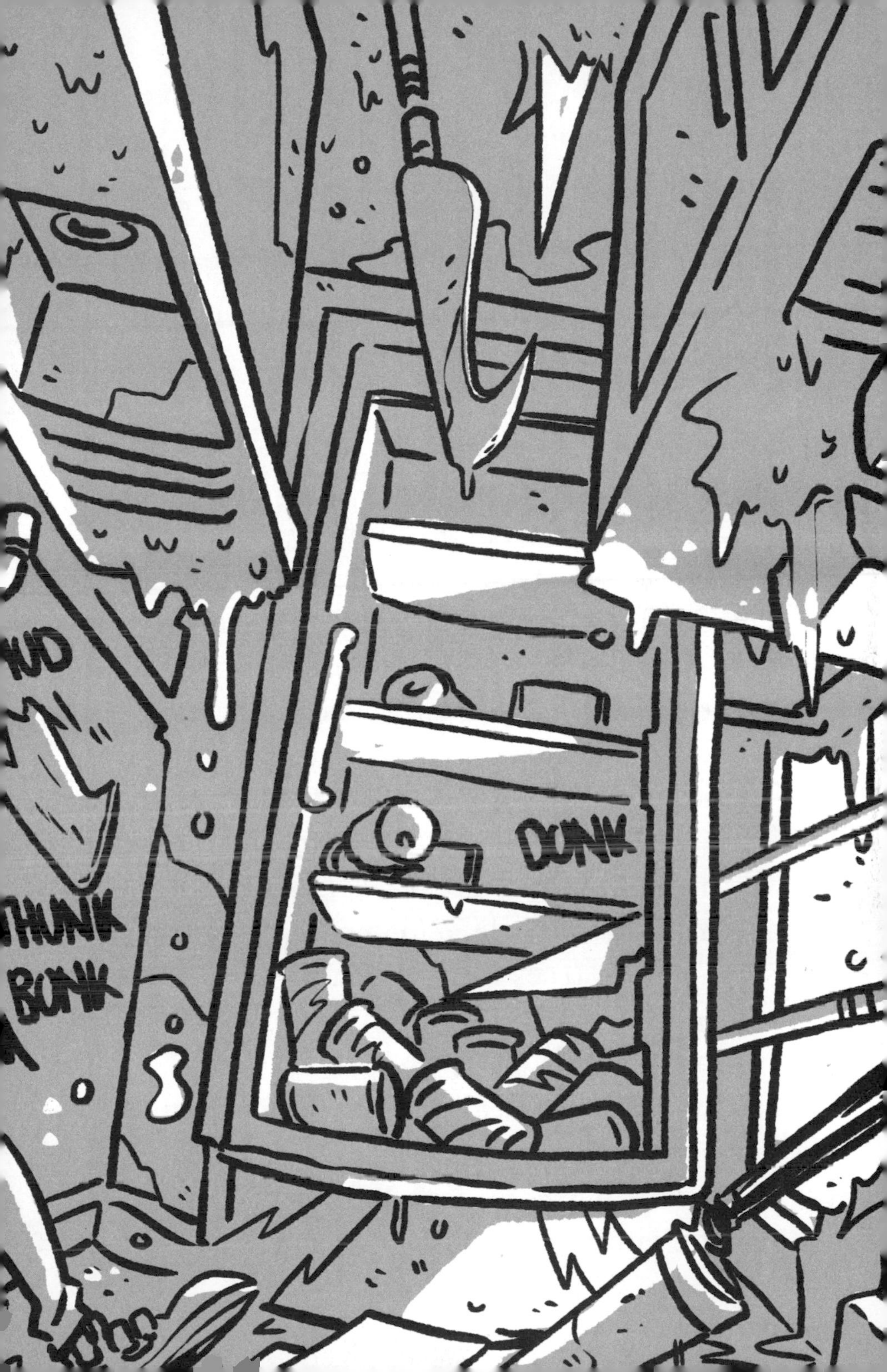
THUNK
BONK
DONK

Suddenly, the Drakkor erupts—a pained cry so loud that Quint half expects his eardrums to explode.

"Someone must have got him good!" Dirk exclaims, scrambling to his feet and shoving his head out the window.

A perfectly thrown pitchfork has slammed into the Drakkor's chest. One armored scale is split in two, revealing glowing purple flesh.

"They hit it right in that wound you exposed, Quint!" Dirk cheers. "Y'know, your sorta misfired conjuration back at King Possum's."

The Drakkor reels, thrashing and jerking. The crane creaks and the metal cable twangs.

"I don't like that sound," Quint says. "I think it's about to—"

SNICKT!

The cable snaps! The Drakkor is released from the crane's hold, plummeting downward, bringing the truck with it, then—

KRAKA-BOOM!

Two tons of truck and immeasurable pounds of monster slam back to earth! The impact is brain-rattling, nerve-frazzling—and nearly bone-shattering.

Quint blinks. Dirk groans. Drooler *meeps*.

"Wow," Dirk says. "We're still alive."

"For now," Quint responds. "You OK?"

"Better than that time I got teleported," Dirk answers. He cradles Drooler in his arms.

"Then let's *go!*" Quint cries, scampering through the overturned truck, Dirk at his heels. They fling themselves through the door, flopping onto the ground, landing mere inches from the rising, roaring Drakkor. Neat-O Buzz gushes from the truck, sloshing across the street.

"The battery!" Quint gasps as he spots it. He scrambles, scooping it up a moment before it's swept away in a river of Neat-O Buzz.

Just then, a shadow passes overhead. Looking up, Quint expects to see, perhaps, the *last* thing he'll ever see: a meaty Drakkor paw.

But no!

"Skaelka!" he gasps.

She stands on the roof of the Stabbin' Hut, a sharpened movie prop axe in her hands. "I PROMISED VENGEANCE!" she bellows. "AND SKAELKA KEEPS HER PROMISES!"

With that, Skaelka leaps—sailing toward the glowing gash at the center of the Drakkor's chest . . .

chapter twenty-two

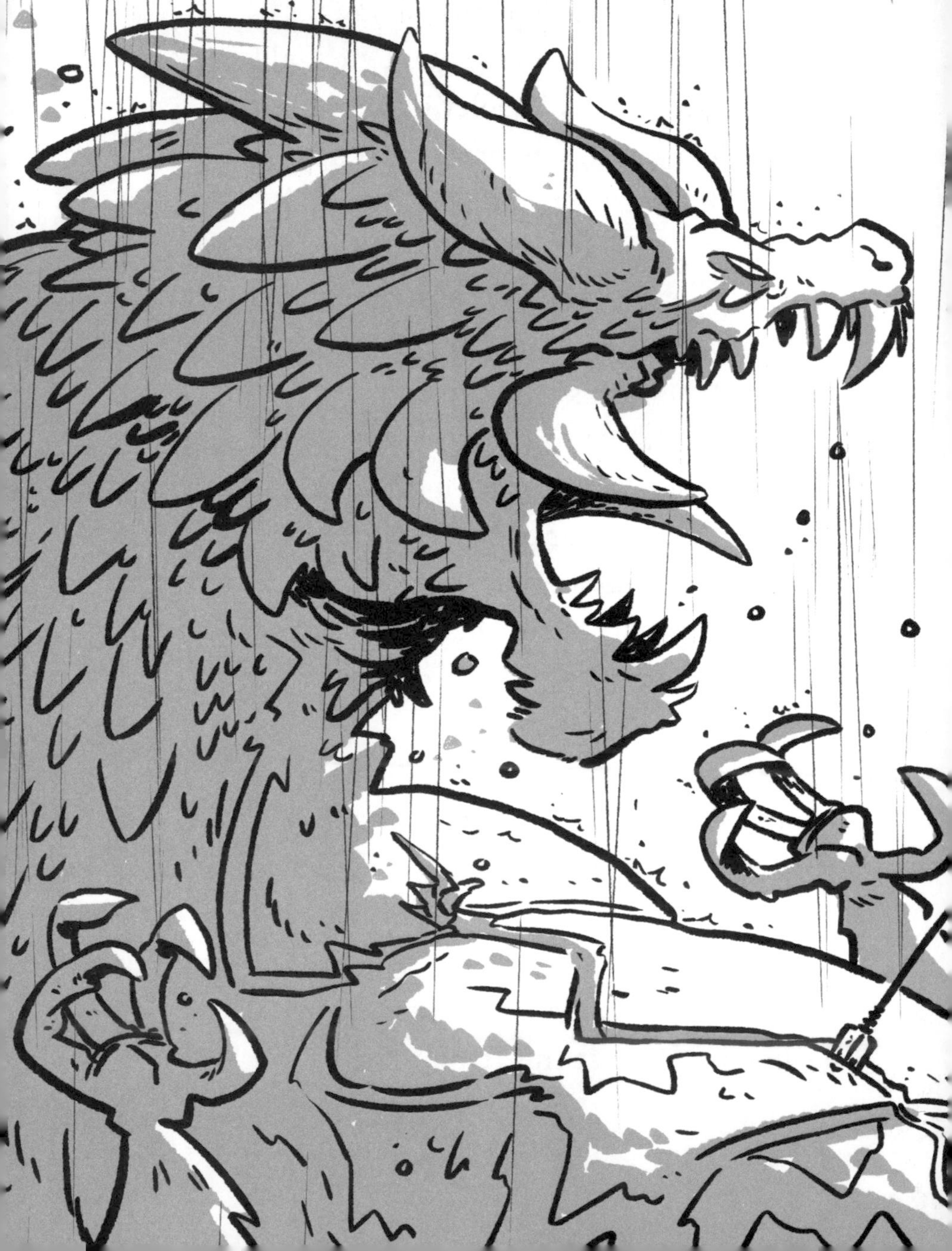

THE MOMENT SHE'S BEEN WAITING FOR!

Skaelka's axe crunches through the Drakkor's cracked scale and slams into the glowing purple wound.

An earsplitting mix of pain, anger, and surprise bursts from the Drakkor.

Frigid cold erupts from the monster's freshly slashed side, turning Skaelka's blade to ice. The Drakkor sways, its collossal legs wobbling, going weak, until, at long last—

SLAM!

263

The Drakkor belly flops onto the ground, showering the gathering monsterfolk with rainwater and Neat-O Buzz. The axe's frozen handle snaps in two, and Skaelka tumbles off the monster, splashing down alongside it.

"Yes . . ." Skaelka says softly, after a deep breath. "She always keeps her promises."

There is a long, quiet moment, and then—

Quint stands, taking in the triumphant scene. *We did it*, he thinks. *And I never even had to do any conjuring.* Although he's not sure if that thought leaves him relieved or disappointed.

"We make quite the team, don't we?" Galamelon says, striding over. "The Wizard, the Warrior, and the Used Carapace Salesman!"

"Uh, friendos?" Kimmy says, her voice cracking. "The Drakkor is, um, *doing stuff.*"

Everyone turns. The Drakkor's tail is thudding against the ground. A layer of skin is shed, causing scales to slip from its body and splash into the pool of Neat-O Buzz.

Quint gasps as he realizes. "The Neat-O Buzz! I think it's . . . healing it. Reviving it. *The Drakkor is changing, again.*"

A sound emanates from the Drakkor—a pained, screeching whine.

"AIIEE!" Kimmy cries out, grabbing her ears and pulling them tight against her head. "The Drakkor's pain . . . It's excruciating . . ."

"Well, yeah," Dirk says. "Skaelka just axed it."

"No . . . not that . . ." she manages. "This is different . . . I don't wanna . . . But I gotta . . ."

Kimmy kneels, peering into the Drakkor's heavy-lidded eyes. Her pupils spin, going vacant, and horror fills her. She realizes she didn't truly comprehend what she saw in the Pizza Theater, frozen in brain-poking mode with the Drakkor.

And she suddenly cries out, images exploding from her brain, projected into the air . . .

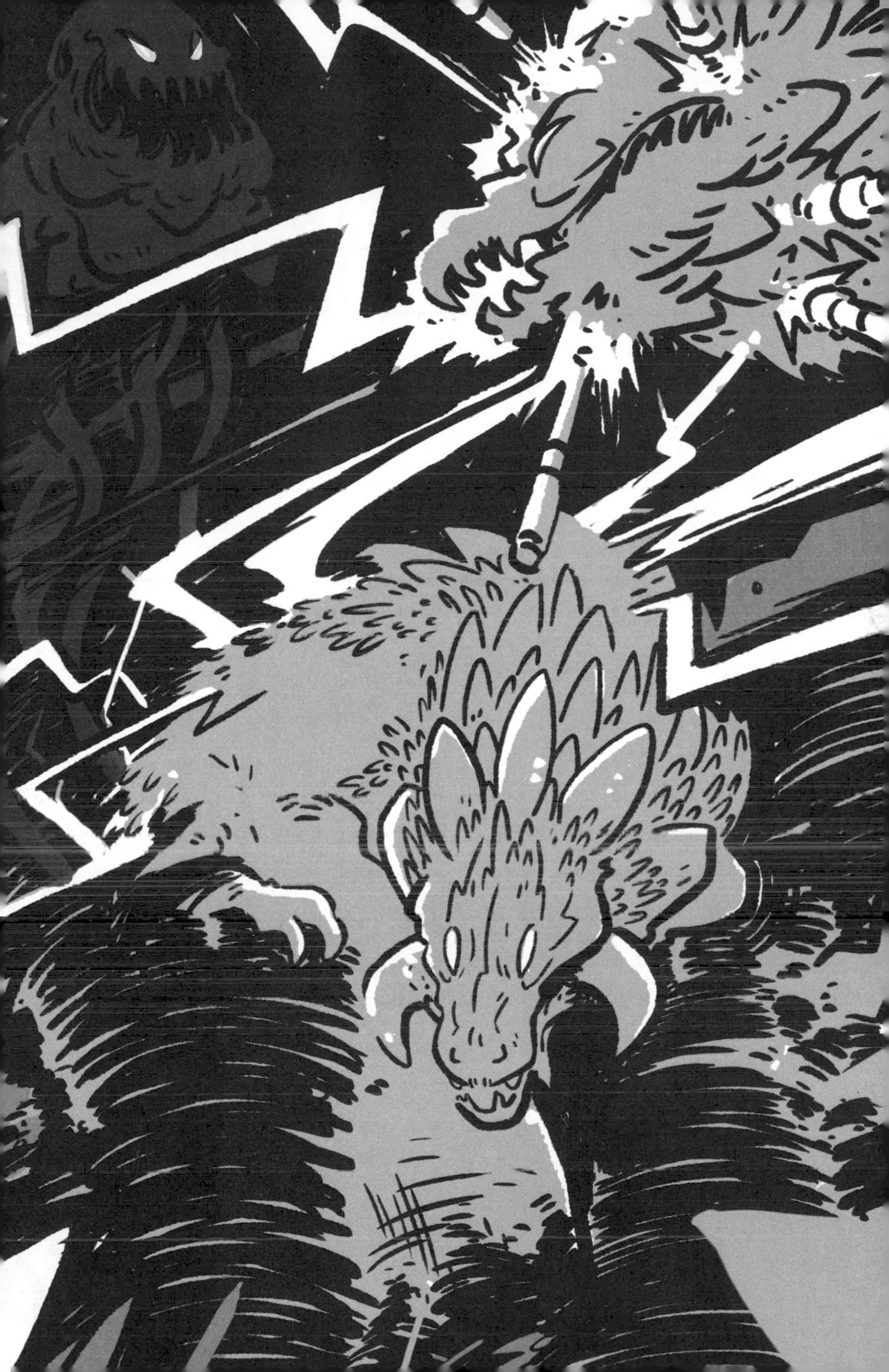

At last, Kimmy pulls out of the monster's mindscape. "The Drakkor . . ." she rasps, gasping for breath. "It wasn't at that strange fortress because it *wanted* to be. Something *hurt it* there. *Tortured it. Experimented on it.*"

Skaelka shifts uncomfortably, tapping the broken axe-handle against her head.

The Drakkor's claws scrape the ground, pawing at the pool of soda.

"Guys . . ." Quint says uneasily. "Did we do the entirely wrong thing, here?"

I thought the Drakkor was using the Neat-O Buzz to get extra evil. But what if that's wrong?

What if the Neat-O Buzz is the one thing that soothes its pain?

Like an ice cube, when you burn your tongue real bad. And **that's** why it kept coming here. It just wanted to, y'know, stop hurting.

Good thing you didn't slay it in its sleep, huh?

I DIDN'T **WANT** TO SLAY IT IN ITS SLEEP!

"Wait, so the Drakkor is nice?" Galamelon asks. "AHA! I always knew it was a good egg. That's why I didn't slay it when you first hired me to. I just couldn't go through with it . . . I'm no monster. Unlike you guys . . . Geez."

Dirk ignores Galamelon. "I don't think the Drakkor's *nice*. There were a lot of *bones* in that Possum Palace. It's no kitten. More like . . . a grizzly or a great white. But it didn't deserve what happened to it at that fortress . . . all that was *done* to it there."

"And all that we did to it," Quint says quietly.

RAWRRR!

Suddenly, the lumbering beast is rising. Bones snap. New scales pop through its skin. It's transforming in front of their very eyes . . .

"It's just scared!" Kimmy shouts. "It's *mad*—but not *mean*. After all that junk it went through, it's gonna lash out at *anything* that hurts it. Like, y'know . . . A GIANT AXE."

"That is Skaelka's bad," Skaelka murmurs.

Galamelon hurries to Quint. "OK, guy. You're the guy. You gotta use all the amazing conjuring I've taught you to—" Galamelon is suddenly silenced as the Drakkor's tail whips through the air, and—

"Dude," Dirk says, grabbing Quint's shoulders. "Can't believe I'm saying this, but Galamelon was right. Your conjuring is our only chance."

"I know, Dirk," Quint replies, his voice steady. "And I will. But I must be careful. It's the Kinetic Crescendo teleportation that got us here, so—"

Quint suddenly stops, glancing down at the battery in his hands. "Wait . . ."

"What?" Dirk asks.

"Never mind," Quint says quickly. "Skaelka, Kimmy—keep the Drakkor busy! Dirk, with me, to the gaffer truck. I'll need your help . . ."

chapter twenty-three

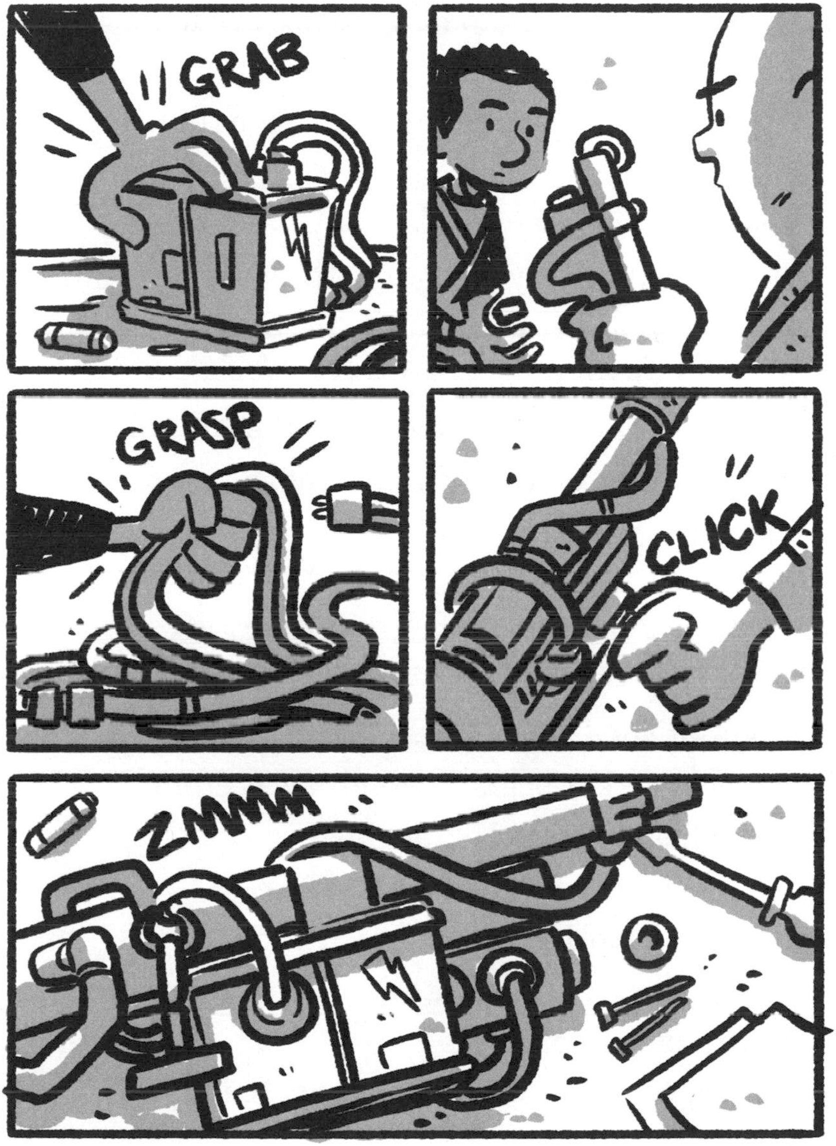
GRAB
GRASP
CLICK
ZMMM

"Hey! WIZARD! WARRIOR!" Kimmy cries, as she dodges a vicious swipe from the rampaging Drakkor. "You dudes almost done doing whatever you're doing?"

"Kimmy appears to be growing tired!" Skaelka calls.

"ALMOST!" Quint calls. He's about to hoist the hastily assembled contraption over his shoulder, when—

"Wait!" Dirk says. "That battery against your side's gonna get *real* hot. You're gonna need some protection . . ."

With a flourish, Dirk reveals the wizard's robe. "I hung on to this. Thought you might change your mind."

"But—"

"No arguing. This is your hero quest—so put it on."

Quint nods. "All right."

The Drakkor is just seconds away from crushing Kimmy and Carol, when—

"HEY!" Galamelon shouts. "There's a conjurer who'd like to chat with you."

The monster turns. Its dark, cold eyes stare down Galamelon.

"Oh, not me," Galamelon says. "Him . . ."

"OK, friend," Quint says to Dirk. "Power me up."

Dirk grabs the detonator plunger dangling from the battery pack and gives it a hard tug, like he's starting up a lawn mower.

GGRRR-VVRROOM!

The Drakkor's killing claws dig into the ground—then it charges.

Quint spins the dial on his cane's shortened blaster. His finger finds the trigger-switch.

He doesn't give himself time to think.

No, this time—he just *acts*.

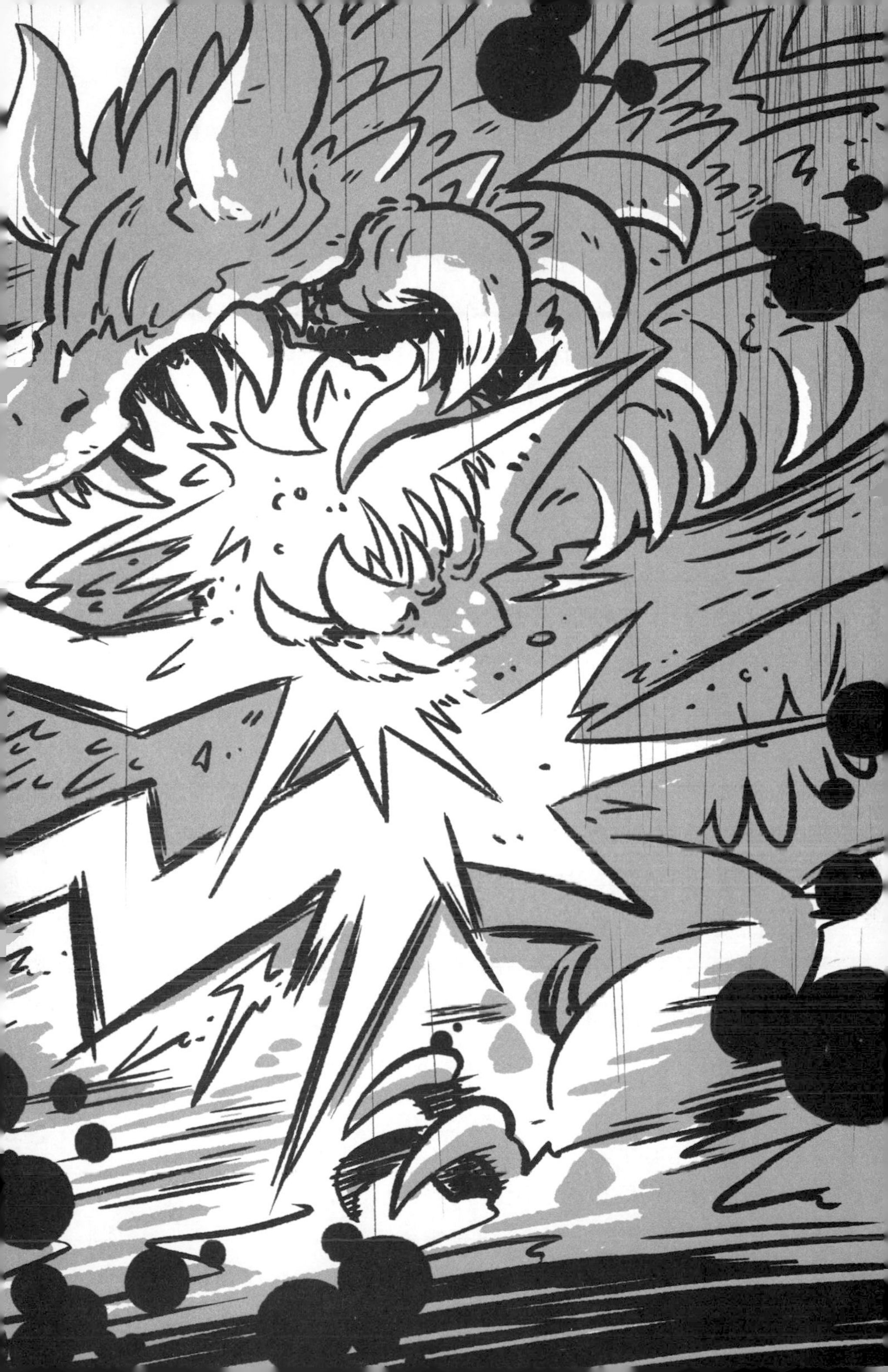

Quint sees the full effect of his conjuration: a swirling globe of heat and light that fully engulfes the creature—then erupts outward as a rapidly swelling sphere of energy.

The sphere expands, filling the town square, pushing toward Quint. He tries to shut his eyes, look away—but a tingling shock wave is coursing through him, and he's stuck, still as a statue.

Then, just inches from Quint's face, the sphere stops—a momentary pause—before it's suddenly yanked back like an atomic yo-yo, drawn into the Drakkor.

There is a small *pop*—like a snap bang, thrown against the sidewalk.

As the energy streams back *into* the Drakkor, a blinding blizzard of purple vapor explodes *outward*. It's like a tidal wave crashing in all directions, nearly taking Quint off his feet.

How long he stands there, immersed in vapor, Quint doesn't know. But he knows when the cloud is finally gone. He knows because he sees his hands on the cannon, and they are steady.

Beneath him is the cobblestone street.

Surrounding him is the town.

And the Drakkor is gone.

"So, uh, where'd it go?" a voice asks.

Quint turns—a sudden, jerking motion that softens into relief as he sees it's Galamelon. And behind Galamelon are Dirk, Drooler, Kimmy, Skaelka, and *all the monsterfolk*—all exactly where they're supposed to be.

And Quint breathes the biggest sigh of relief that ever was sighed. *I didn't mess **that** one up,* he thinks. *Not even a tiny bit.*

"Vaporized?" Kimmy asks.

"Obviously vaporized," Galamelon says. "What you witnessed there was your classic vapori—"

"No," Quint says, his face breaking into a tiny smile. "Not vaporized. *Teleported.*"

"Say what?" Dirk exclaims. "You did teleporting stuff again?!"

Quint grins. "I did. And now the Drakkor has a new home: Sheboygan, Wisconsin. 201 West Avenue, to be precise."

Dirk cocks his head, not understanding. Drooler *meeps*.

Quint gestures to the side of his cannon, where an empty Neat-O Buzz bottle is affixed. "It's their corporate headquarters and main production facility," Quint says with a bashful smile. "The address is on the bottle."

Dirk laughs at that. Grinning with the joy of victory, he gives Drooler a gentle, happy pinch.

"Now the Drakkor can drink all the soothing Neat-O Buzz its heart desires," Quint says. "Hopefully, that gives it a little peace . . ."

The cheers from the monsterfolk grow deafening as they rush into the town square to thank the heroes.

"I feel. . . weird . . ." Quint murmurs, his legs suddenly going rubbery. He sinks to the ground, knees splashing onto the rain-soaked street.

"Hey, hey, hey," Dirk says, kneeling down. "You OK? You with us?"

Quint nods. His voice is a whisper. "That sort of conjuring . . . takes a lot out of a person. I can't do that all the time . . . not even close."

Skaelka and Dirk hoist Quint up.

"Looks like your conjurer's cannon needs a recharge," Dirk says, glancing at the battery. "So even if you *wanted* to, you couldn't."

"Might be a 'special occasion only' sort of thing," Quint says with a little laugh. "Which is . . . fine by me."

"Hey, guys," Kimmy says, reaching into her pocket. "You did what we hired you to do. And a Kimmy deal is a square deal. So without further ado . . . THE MAPPARATUS!"

Quint and Dirk grin, both thinking the same thing: *Hero Quest complete.*

chapter twenty-four

The celebration in Fleeghaven lasts all night—and not a single drop of Neat-O Buzz flows (just to be safe, and also 'cause it's gross).

But Quint, Dirk, and Drooler sleep straight through the fun times, slumbering hard at the Weary Traveler Inn.

They probably would have slept through the next day, too, if not for Kimmy's high-pitched voice erupting inside each of their brains, simultaneously, screaming: "RISE AND SHINE, SLEEPYHEADS! WHAT ARE YOU GONNA DO, SLUMBER THE WHOLE DAY AWAY?"

Dirk whacks the side of his head, trying to hit snooze—before realizing you can't hit snooze on a telepathic wake-up call.

Soon, one by one, the adventurers shamble out of the inn. As they step outside, something stops them in their tracks.

"Would you look at that . . ." Quint says.

"Some fine carving," Dirk says. "Skaelka must have been busy."

"I do," Quint says. His voice is quiet and full of awe. "I really, really do."

"Course they love it!" a voice calls out. "It was my idea!"

Quint and Dirk turn to see Galamelon grinning. He stands at the half-destroyed Cine-Bites meal truck, which he has turned into a rinky-dink souvenir stand.

"The monsterfolk are letting you stay?" Dirk asks, making his way to Galamelon. "They're not gonna ride you out of town on a rail?"

Dirk rolls his eyes. "Well, Galamelon, it's been . . . I dunno. It's been *something.*"

"Ahem. Aren't you forgetting this?" Galamelon asks, and his hand suddenly opens, revealing Dirk's wallet.

"HEY, GIMME THAT!" Dirk exclaims, snatching the wallet from Galamelon's hand and stalking off. "Freaking Galamelon . . ."

Dirk finds Quint with Kimmy, leaning against the Wrangler. Nearby, Skaelka is busy sharpening a new axe.

Quint elbows Kimmy and asks her the same question she asked them, two days earlier. "So . . . you in? You should definitely be in. Say you're in."

"In?" Kimmy asks.

"In for coming with us! To join the fight!"

Dirk sidles up next to them, crossing his arms. "Can't believe I'm saying this, but those brain-poking powers of yours—they'd be good to have around."

Kimmy frowns. "Ugh, I wish. I really do! But . . . this is my home—and I'm staying. Don't start getting all wet in the eye sockets, though, I'll be seeing you soon. Y'know, on account of me having taken, like, nineteen dozen brain-snapshots of you—plus a few real pics, too."

Dirk groans.

"But for real," Kimmy says. "Thank you. Ears crossed that we get to hang again. And when I see you, you guys are gonna be *so pumped*. Especially you, ol' lovable, huggable Skaelka!"

And so, it is nearly time for the heroes to bid goodbye to the town of Fleeghaven. Monsterfolk crowd around them, offering thanks and handing over balls of freshly harvested dough.

"Don't like long goodbyes," Dirk says. He taps the mapparatus, bringing the screen flickering to life. "Time to get a move on."

"Right," Quint says. "Just, um, one second. One last thing I gotta do."

Walking to Galamelon's shop, Quint doesn't know *what* he's going to say. He doesn't even know what he *wants* to say.

"Greetings!" Galamelon exclaims, as Quint approaches. "*You* look like someone in need of conjuring lessons! And I'm just the master conjurer to guide you on your journey!"

Quint frowns. "Dude, it's me."

Galamelon looks away. "I know," he says softly.

After that, neither of them seems to know what to say. They stare at their feet for a long while. And they just might keep staring at their feet, too, if not for Kimmy.

"Ugh, enough with these two . . ." she says, and—for the last time—brain-pokers their thoughts into the air . . .

And with that, it's *really* time for the heroes
to bid goodbye. As they stride eastward, out of
town, the monsterfolk shout their farewells—
along with a few other things . . .

"Please take Galamelon with you!"

"Tell the Blarg Slayer that Kimmy says hello!"

"When is *Hero Quest 6* gonna come out?!"

The heroes trek toward the midday sun. Soon, Fleeghaven is far behind them—and ahead of them, somewhere, are their friends.

"Hey, Skaelka," Dirk says, stopping to offer Drooler a swig of water. "Back in the corn maze . . . Who was that creature that freaked you out so bad?"

Skaelka shivers. "I once knew . . . but I do not know now. Skaelka suspects the answer lies in that fortress. So, we must gather our companions—and go there. I feel additional memories slowly returning. When I lay eyes upon the fortress again, I will know more."

Quint and Dirk nod.

"But that is secondary," Skaelka says. "I must tell Jack I am separated from Rover—and ask his forgiveness."

But Dirk doesn't hear that last part—he's thinking about the fortress—and the horror they saw done to the Drakkor there.

"Quint, we're probably gonna need your conjuring abilities once we get to that fortress," Dirk says. "And I kinda think I'm OK with that."

"Y'know what? I'm OK with that, too," Quint says. And as he adjusts his shoulder pack, he knows that this time, that is 100 percent the truth.

With that, Quint opens his book. "Back to my studies . . ." he says. Drawing his conjurer's cannon, he speaks an incantation, and—*POOF!*

"Ha!" Skaelka snorts. "Dirk is now a crustacean! Wonderful conjuring, Quint."

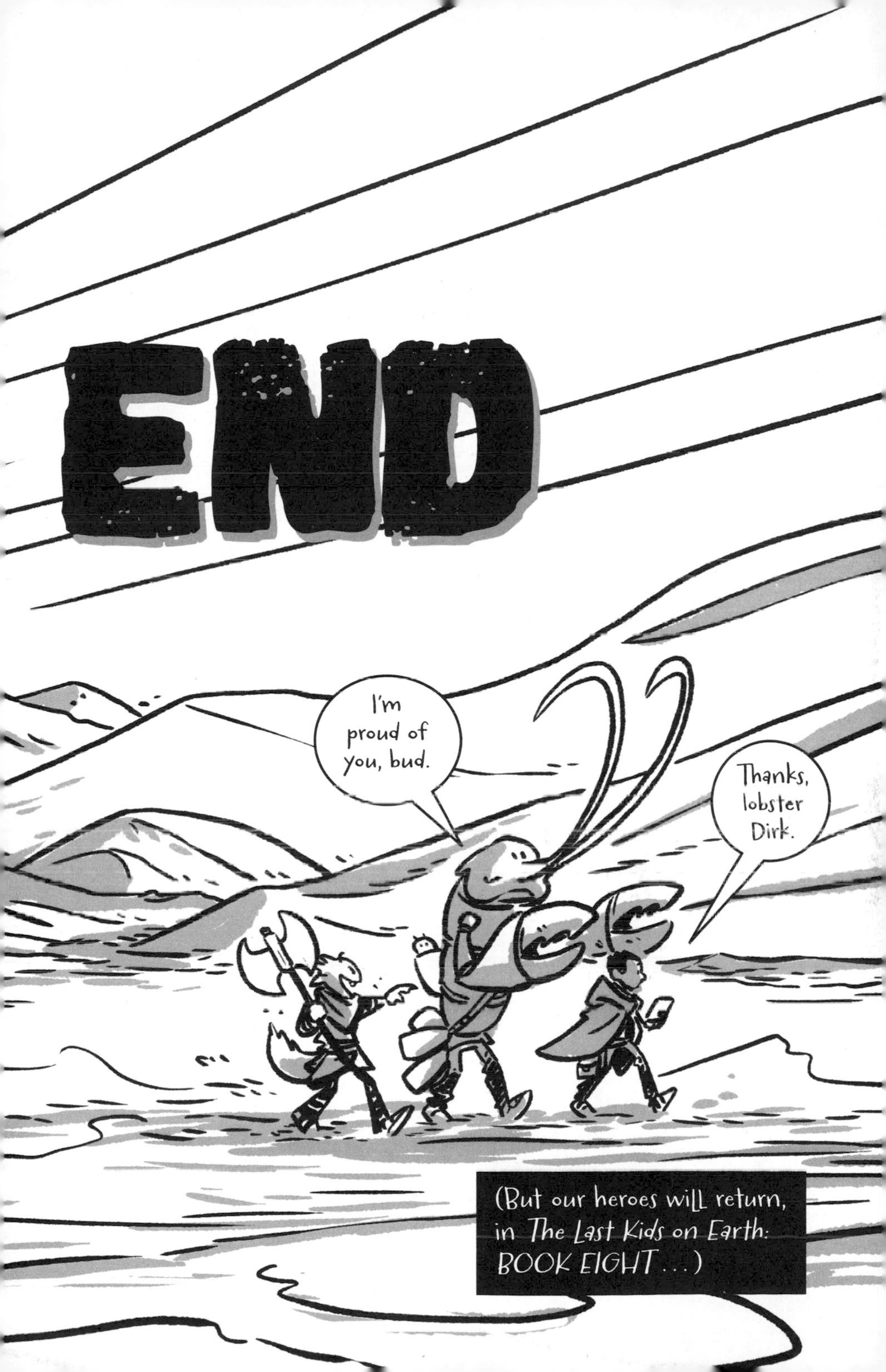
END
I'm proud of you, bud.
Thanks, lobster Dirk.
(But our heroes will return, in *The Last Kids on Earth:* BOOK EIGHT . . .)

Acknowledgments

Thanks to so many people: Douglas Holgate, Dana Leydig, Jim Hoover, Ken Wright, Jennifer Dee, Josh Pruett, Haley Mancini, Felicia Frazier, Debra Polansky, Joe English, Todd Jones, Mary McGrath, Abigail Powers, Krista Ahlberg, Marinda Valenti, Sola Akinlana, Gaby Corzo, Ginny Dominguez, Emily Romero, Elyse Marshall, Carmela Iaria, Christina Colangelo, Felicity Vallence, Sarah Moses, Kara Brammer, Alex Garber, Lauren Festa, Michael Hetrick, Trevor Ingerson, Rachel Wease, Lyana Salcedo, Kim Ryan, Helen Boomer, and everyone in PYR Sales and PYR Audio. And hugely appreciative, as always, of Dan Lazar, Cecilia de la Campa, Alessandra Birch, Torie Doherty-Munro, and everyone at Writers House.

MAX BRALLIER!

is a #1 *New York Times, USA Today,* and *Wall Street Journal* bestselling author. His books and series include The Last Kids on Earth, Eerie Elementary, Mister Shivers, Galactic Hot Dogs, and *Can YOU Survive the Zombie Apocalypse?* He is a writer and executive producer for Netflix's Emmy Award–winning adaptation of The Last Kids on Earth.

DOUGLAS HOLGATE!

is the illustrator of the *New York Times* bestselling series The Last Kids on Earth from Penguin Kids (now also an Emmy-winning Netflix animated series) and the co-creator and illustrator of the graphic novel *Clem Hetherington and The Ironwood Race* for Scholastic Graphix.

He has worked for the last twenty years making books and comics for publishers around the world from his garage in Victoria, Australia. He lives with his family and a large, fat dog that could possibly be part polar bear in the Australian bush on five acres surrounded by eighty-million-year-old volcanic boulders.

You can find his work at douglasbotholgate.com and on Twitter @douglasholgate.

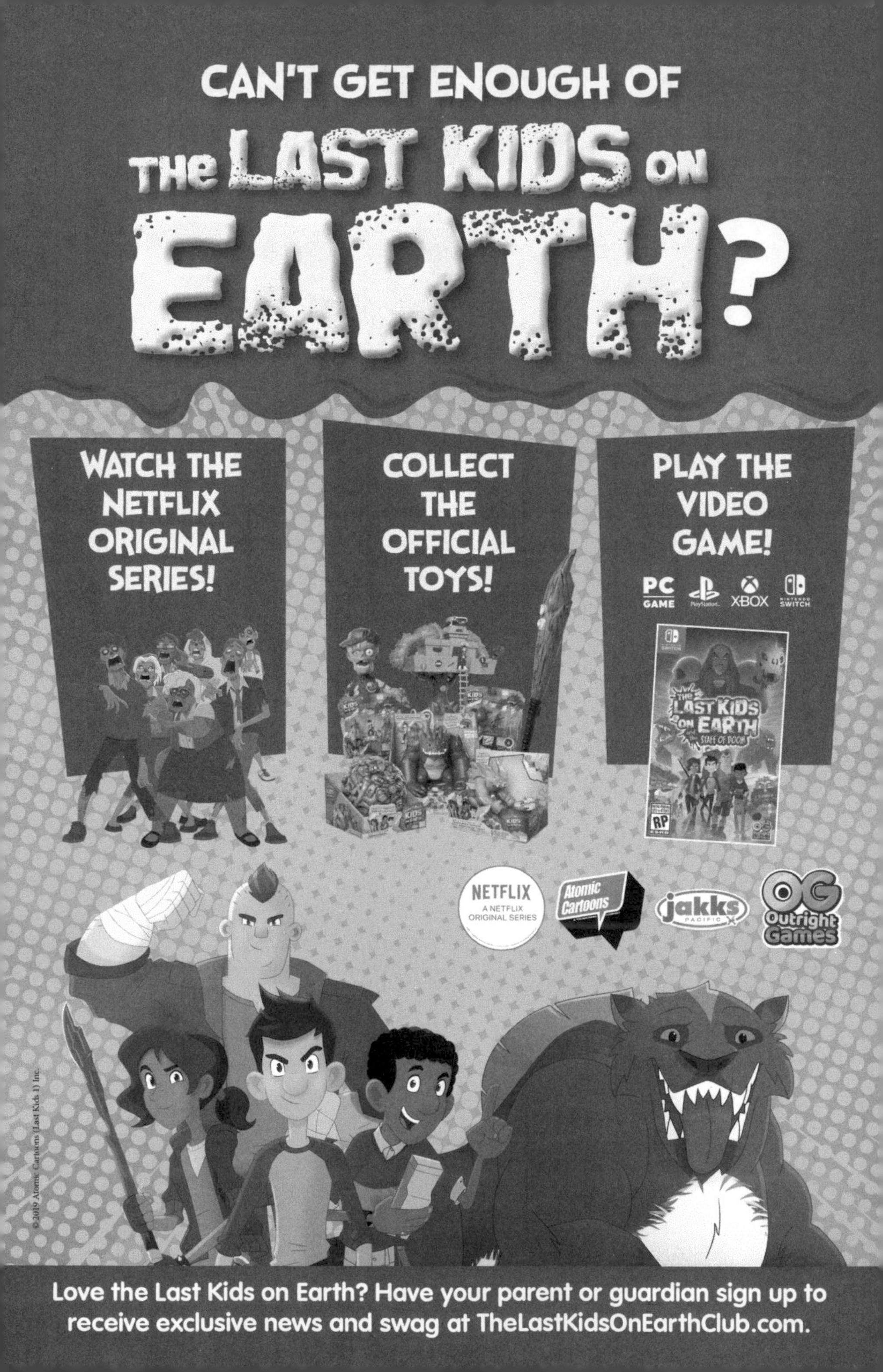
CAN'T GET ENOUGH OF
THE LAST KIDS ON EARTH?
WATCH THE NETFLIX ORIGINAL SERIES!
COLLECT THE OFFICIAL TOYS!
PLAY THE VIDEO GAME!
PC GAME
PlayStation
XBOX
NINTENDO SWITCH
THE LAST KIDS ON EARTH AND THE STAFF OF DOOM
NETFLIX
A NETFLIX ORIGINAL SERIES
Atomic Cartoons
jakks PACIFIC
OG Outright Games
© 2019 Atomic Cartoons (Last Kids 1) Inc.
Love the Last Kids on Earth? Have your parent or guardian sign up to receive exclusive news and swag at TheLastKidsOnEarthClub.com.

THE MONSTER-BATTLING FUN DOESN'T STOP HERE!

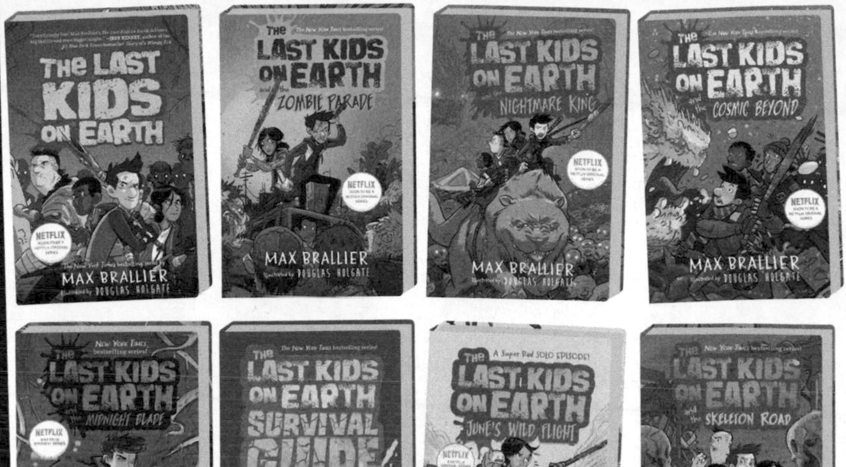
The Last Kids on Earth
MAX BRALLIER
The Last Kids on Earth and the Zombie Parade
MAX BRALLIER
The Last Kids on Earth and the Nightmare King
MAX BRALLIER
The Last Kids on Earth and the Cosmic Beyond
MAX BRALLIER
The Last Kids on Earth and the Midnight Blade
MAX BRALLIER
The Last Kids on Earth Survival Guide
MAX BRALLIER
The Last Kids on Earth June's Wild Flight
MAX BRALLIER
The Last Kids on Earth and the Skeleton Road
MAX BRALLIER
The Last Kids on Earth Thrilling Tales from the Tree House
MAX BRALLIER
The Last Kids on Earth and the Doomsday Race
MAX BRALLIER

TheLastKidsOnEarth.com

Check out more books in the bestselling

THE LAST KIDS ON EARTH SERIES!

JOIN TODAY!

MAX BRALLIER'S
THE LAST KIDS
ON EARTH
FAN CLUB

Have your parent or guardian sign up now
to receive a Fan Club Welcome Kit and swag
mailings with each new book release!
Plus, exclusive Last Kids news, sneak previews,
and behind-the-scenes info!

VISIT TheLastKidsonEarthClub.com
TO LEARN MORE.

SCAN QR CODE

TO VISIT TODAY

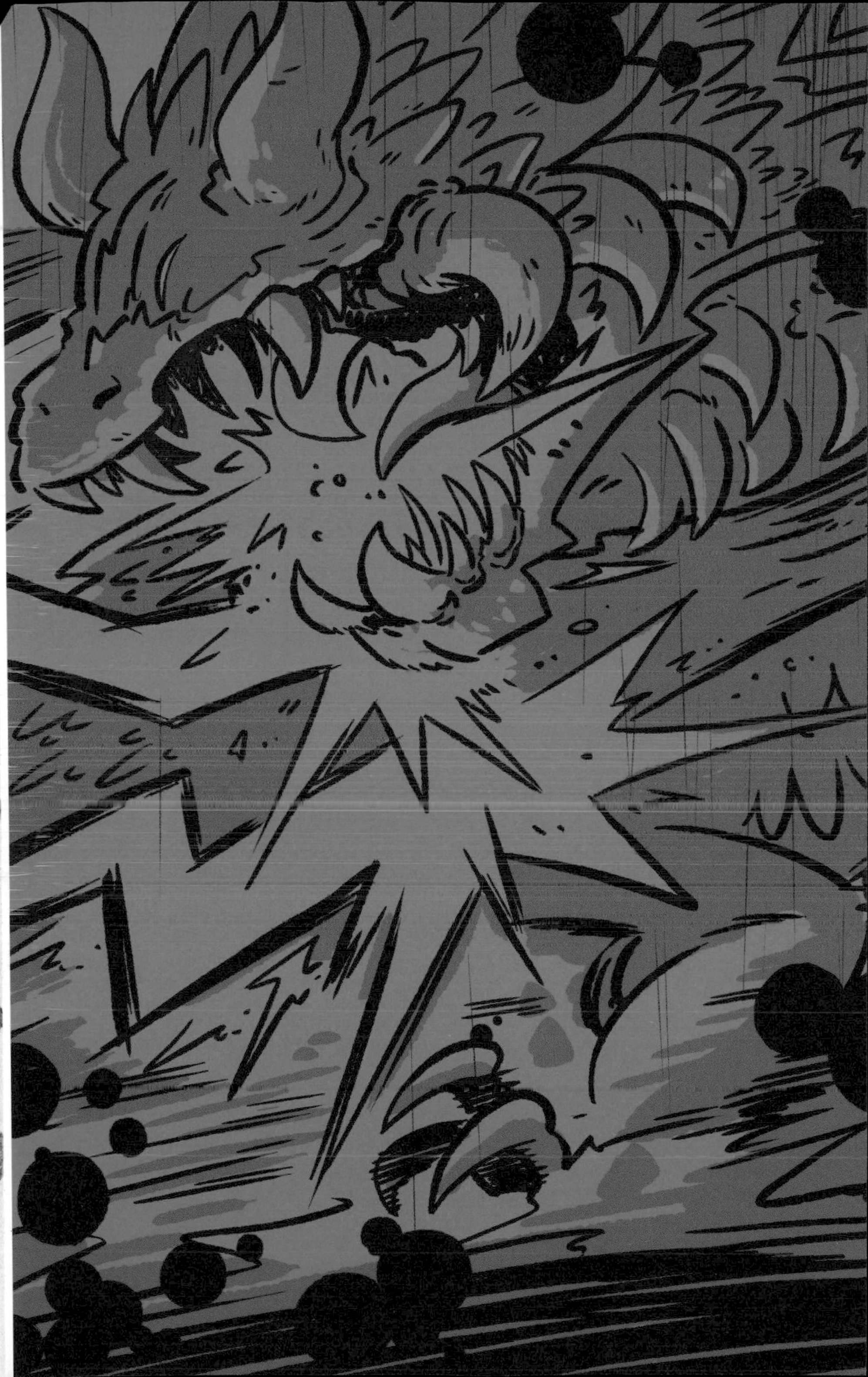

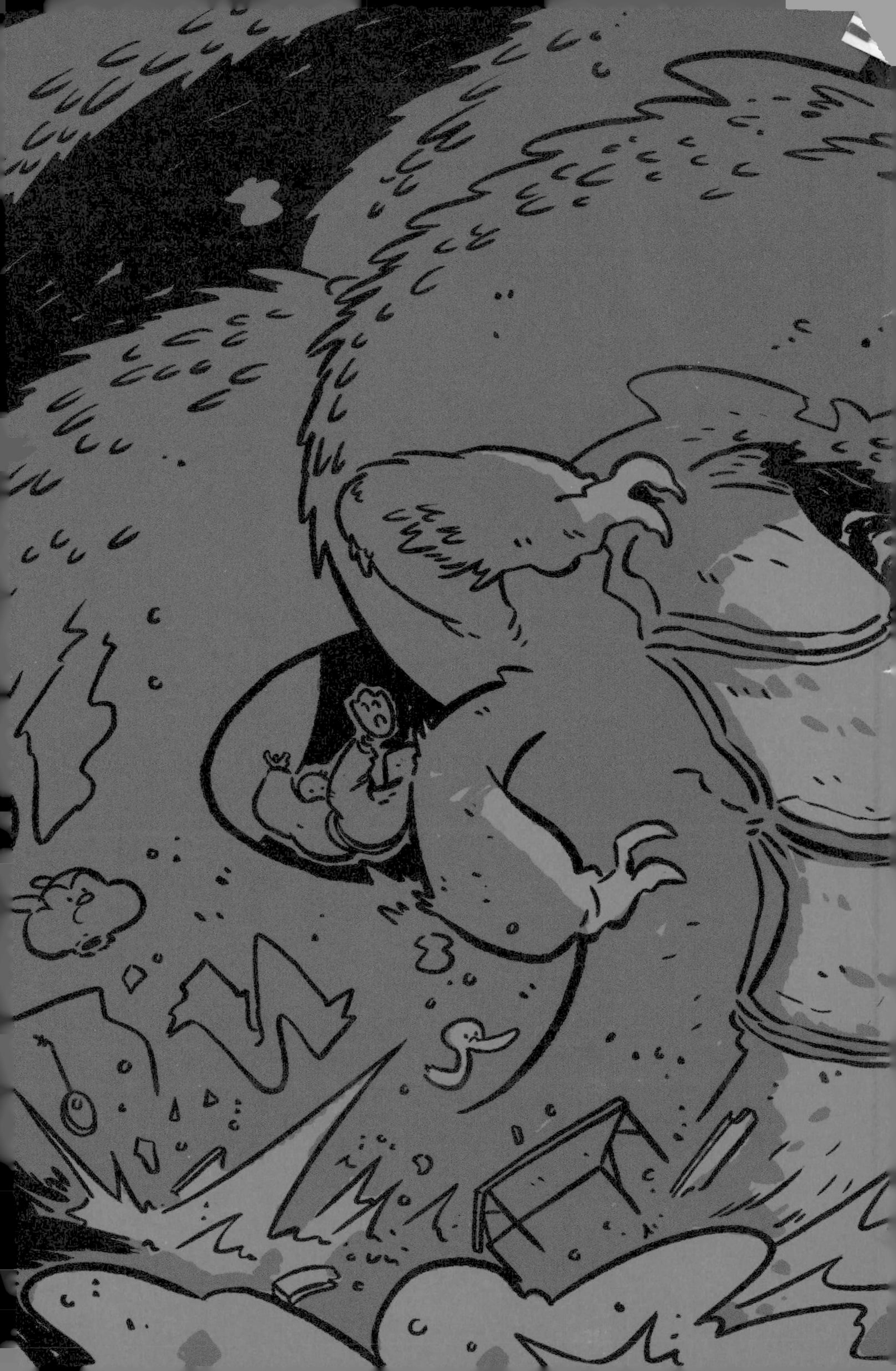